writes rollicking adventure novels filled with subtle
on and made bitter-sweet by an underlying darkness.
ng for grand effects or momentous meetings between
produced one excellent book after another." —*Locus*
gly finished stylist and a master of world building and
on."

—*Booklist*

ites with unusual flair, drawing upon folklore, myth,
for creating ingenious plots."

—*Year's Best Fantasy and Horror*

best writers in the fantasy world today. His writing is
nt and full of energy. His action scenes are breathtaking
ll at characterization is excellent."

—*Writers Write*

prose avoids the excessively florid in its description and
c in its dialogue, opting instead for simpler narration and
rary parlance . . . serves as a refreshing reminder that epic
ed not always be doorstops filled with manly men speak-
erblown rhetoric and grasping their swords."

—*SFF World*

produces excellent work in book after book . . . a great
uilder. His fantasy worlds are not mere medieval societies
gic added but make organic sense."

—*SFReview*

Duncan has long been one of the great unsung figures of
ian fantasy and science fiction, graced with a fertile imagi-
, a prolific output, and keen writerly skills."

—*Quill and Quire*

praise for it

"Enjoyable characters, a de...
ture intertwine in this mult...
and persistent investigator, ...
future adventures."

"An entertaining, fast-paced re...
for mystery and enchantment"

"*Ironfoot* is gritty, magical, at tim...
This is historical fantasy pulled of...
—Greg Key...

"A fantastic murder mystery firmly a...
generous mix of arcane magic."
—Glenda Larke, ...

"I was surprised by how compelling it ...
this."

"An enjoyable easy read . . . hopefully the...
distant future."

"[Duncan has] rich, evocative language ...
skills . . . one of the leading masters of epic ...

"Dave Duncan...
characterizati...
Without striv...
genres, he has...
"An exceedin...
characterizat...

"Duncan wr...
and his gift ...

"One of the...
clear, vibra...
and his ski...

"Duncan's...
the archai...
contempo...
fantasy n...
ing in ov...

"Dunca...
world-b...
with m...

"Dave ...
Canad...
nation...

by dave duncan

the
Enchanter General

trial by Treason

Dave Duncan

Night Shade Books
NEW YORK

Night Shade books may be purchased in bulk at special discounts for sales promotion, corporate gifts, fund-raising, or educational purposes. Special editions can also be created to specifications. For details, contact the Special Sales Department, Night Shade Books, 307 West 36th Street, 11th Floor, New York, NY 10018 or info@skyhorsepublishing.com.

Night Shade Books® is a registered trademark of Skyhorse Publishing, Inc.®, a Delaware corporation.

Visit our website at www.nightshadebooks.com.

10 9 8 7 6 5 4 3 2 1

Library of Congress Cataloging-in-Publication Data is available on-file.

Hardcover ISBN: 978-1-59780-954-2
Paperback ISBN: 978-1-59780-953-5

Cover illustration by Stephen Youll
Cover design by Shawn King

Printed in the United States of America

In the year of Our Lord 1166, being the 12th year of the reign of Henry II, by the Grace of God, King of the English . . .

chapter 1

near the end of summer, in the middle of a day, a cavalcade of horsemen came thundering through the forests and over the landscape in the center of England. Although they wore no armor, sunlight flashed off the sword hilts at their belts and their conical helmets. They rode warhorses, and one of the two men in the lead carried a staff from which flew a colored pennant. The squires at the rear led sumpters encumbered with packs and also barrels that held the knights' chain mail, loaded in sand to keep it burnished and shiny. This caravan frightened the livestock and alarmed the peasants cutting barley in the fields, although I admit their leader was always careful to avoid crops as much as he could. There are no highways near Helmdon, only tracks, and shortcuts will always tempt men in a hurry.

I had expected them to come from the south, but they had failed to find the shortest route and so they entered the village from the north. I am sure that Helmdon did not impress them—a dozen or so cob-and-thatch cottages flanking the road, a public well, a tract of common land, and some majestic elm trees. It even lacked a church, so that the barely-literate Father Osric celebrated mass either inside or outside his own home, depending on the weather. The hamlet's only claim to any importance whatsoever was that it had given its name to an academy that in those days was ranked as one of the finest schools of secular learning in England, if not all Christendom.

Looking back now from my doddering old age, I can appreciate how little the academy must have impressed men fresh from the king's court and the ornate cities of France. In appearance it was merely a somewhat tidier repetition of the village, except that the buildings were slightly larger, for most had two or even three rooms, and so could be glorified as cottages rather than huts; a couple had proper chimneys, which were rare back then. They were grouped around a yard and connected by a boardwalk, shaded by great elm trees. The windows were either fitted with shutters or screens of thinly shaved horn. None were glazed. This had been my home since I was barely old enough to rub down a horse or shovel out a stable.

That warm afternoon, both Ruffian, a stallion, and Bon Appétit, my palfrey, were saddled and tethered in the yard. They heard hooves approaching long before human ears did, and whinnied an alarm. By the time the cavalcade arrived, I was standing on the boardwalk near the entrance, leaning on my stout oaken cane, waiting for the visitors, with Eadig at my side. Other men were emerging from some of the cottages, but we two were obviously the welcoming committee.

There ought not to be any welcoming committee, because the king's men were on a secret mission.

The leading two horsemen rode into the yard, the rest remained outside. By then Ruffian had scented other stallions on his territory and was making enough commotion to raise the Trojan dead, screaming horse insults, and doing his damnedest to pull over a sixty-foot elm.

The young rider in front, the one who carried the pennant, also bore a shield on his back and thus was obviously a squire. I later learned that his name was Piers. The knight he served followed a few paces behind; both men wore swords. The knight's mount was one of the stallions that were so exasperating Ruffian, but it was being kept under admirable control.

The young squire eyed me in the cold way that Normans always eyed Saxons back then, and often still do. In his case, the shiny nose guard between his eyes made his stare even more menacing. "On the king's business, Sir Neil d'Airelle seeks Adept Durwin of Helmdon."

I bowed, although not much. "You may inform Sir Neil that his quest has been crowned with success. This is the Academy of Helmdon, and I am the man he seeks."

Piers glanced around at his knight. Receiving a nod of approval, he then backed his gelding away so that the stallion could take its place. If the squire's stare had been cold, the knight's was positively icy. He was not much older than I, large and dark complexioned, and he sported a thin mustache of the type the king did back then. That was all I could see of his person, although he was obviously well clad and outfitted. In those days heraldry had not achieved the complexity and importance it has reached now, so he displayed no fancy emblems.

What did he see? A twenty-two-year-old male, well built but no giant, clean-shaven, with hair as blond as could be, to match his Saxon name. My tunic was of good linen and well tailored, but on my right foot I wore a boot raised about four inches by an iron platform. The king would not have forgotten to mention my impairment, so Sir Neil should be in no doubt that he had indeed found the man he sought. He eyed me with disapproval, but I could guess that his displeasure was mostly directed at the elbow-length cape I wore over my shirt, for it was dyed green, the insignia of a qualified sage.

I had guessed correctly.

"The king's understanding," he said, "as he explained it to me last week, was that you accepted his silver on condition that you would report to him for employment as soon as you had completed your studies in this . . ." He glanced around with disgust. ". . . *school.*" His accent was not Norman. He might be from Anjou, like the king himself, or perhaps somewhere farther south, like Maine, but certainly not Aquitaine, for there they speak a very different sort of French.

"Sir, that was my understanding also," I said.

"So how long have you been a licensed sage, Durwin?"

I glanced at the shadows of the trees. "About four hours, sir."

"You expect me to believe in such a remarkable coincidence?"

"It wasn't a coincidence, sir."

Neil looked over the tethered horses, saddled and laden with baggage, and then at my companion, young Eadig. Eadig, I must explain, looked all of thirteen, but was in fact four years older than that. His hair was a reddish gold, his complexion peaches and cream peppered with freckles, and at that moment he was gleaming all over with excitement like a silver cup in sunlight. He wore the white cape of an adept.

"Eadig son of Edwin," I explained, "who will accompany us as my cantor."

"And how long has that child been an adept?"

"Three and a half hours, more or less, Sir Neil."

Eadig drew breath sharply to choke off a laugh, but even that was an offensive sound. Back then, Saxons were still very much the underdogs in England. Normans—or other Frenchmen such as Angevins—expected abject respect from them. Other kingdoms had monarchs who could speak to their people and understand what their people said to them, but since William the Bastard had defeated noble King Harold at Hastings, exactly a century ago, England had been ruled by Frenchmen, and mostly absentee Frenchmen at that.

Glaring with fury at our lack of deference, Sir Neil glanced past me to view the audience, for the entire faculty and student body of Helmdon—except for one who was on his deathbed, and another keeping death watch on him—had emerged by then to stand in the background and watch the encounter in progress. I expect that most of them were enjoying the show, for scholars have little love for fighters.

"Who told you we were coming?"

Had I appreciated the danger properly, I might have been able to save the situation even then, but instead I just made matters a whole wagonload worse. Remember that the king's man expected a Saxon lad to grovel, if perhaps not literally in this case, but I was so puffed up with my recent triumph that I felt almost as if I had summoned him there by magic, and he should be kneeling to me.

"No one, Sir Neil. Let me put it this way. I have lived here in Helmdon since I was child. This morning I attained my life's ambition, when the sages voted to make me one of their own. Now one of His Grace's honored confidants has come from France to summon me to my duties in his service. These are great events in my life, Sir Neil."

"What of it? Who else should care?"

"Great events often cast their shadows ahead of them."

The squire in the background crossed himself, but Sir Neil was not to be cowed by hints of magic, and certainly not pleased at my impudence. "You are claiming that you can see the future?"

"Oh, not in general, sir! But sometimes such great turning

points can be sensed in advance. It was for such skills that the king engaged me, sir."

"And so I must put up with you. But then I don't need to tell you where we are going, do I?"

The squire smirked.

And I promptly made an already bad situation a hundred times worse.

"Might that be Lincoln, sir?"

I was gambling, for I wasn't certain of that, and had I been wrong my error might have saved the day. But I was obviously right. The squire crossed himself again and murmured a prayer. The knight's face paled inside his helmet and his hand went to his sword hilt. He was on a supposedly secret mission! Even his horse felt his shock, for it whinnied in alarm and shifted its feet.

"Who else knows about this prophetic vision of yours?"

Seeing my folly at last, I hastily bent the truth to the breaking point. "Adept Eadig assisted me in the enchantment, sir, but we have told no one else the details, only that I, um, had reason to expect a summons from His Grace to . . . I expected a messenger to arrive today . . . I did ask the dean if Eadig could accompany me . . . sir. I know no further details of our . . ." Oh, Lord, that was an even worse error! ". . . your mission, Sir Neil."

Scowl. "So of course you know where we shall spend tonight?"

Almost certainly he would be heading to the king's castle in Northampton, which would provide him with hospitality that he would find much more agreeable than whatever a monastery would offer—probably even a woman—but I had caused too much trouble already. Guessing, even if correct, was not going to help matters now.

"No, Sir Neil. I have told you as much of the future as I can foresee."

He glanced again at my game leg, and then at Ruffian, who was still doing his utmost to rid himself of his saddle and bridle so he could eject the intruders.

"You are right in so far as His Grace sent us to call you to his service. We head now for His Grace's castle in Northampton. Make your own way there. I won't wait for you. And His Grace made no mention of servants, so if you bring that boy—or familiar, or whatever else he is to you—along, then you can pay his board yourself."

With that Sir Neil wheeled his stallion around and rode out of the yard. Eadig ran for our horses and I bobbled after him as fast as I could. Some of the Helmdon squires were already trying to calm Ruffian.

The king's men left in a drum roll of hooves and a haze of dust. They had barely quit the village before we were mounted and racing after them, with me struggling to hold Ruffian back. Eadig was a far better rider than most Saxons ever got the chance to be, but no man could force a palfrey like Bon Appétit to match the stallion when he was in fighting mood, as now.

"They're going to follow the Nene downstream," Eadig shouted over the thumping hooves. "If we cross the headwaters and cut through the forest, we might be able to beat them to Northampton."

"We might indeed," I said, "but we will tag along behind, like good little minions." I could just imagine Sir Neil and his company riding up to the castle gate only to find the two of us already there, patiently waiting. It was a pleasant fancy, but I understood by then that it would be dangerously unwise.

I had totally mishandled my first meeting with Sir Neil d'Airelle, making the man the king had set over me into an enemy instead of a colleague. Had I behaved myself as I should have known to do, I might have persuaded him to give me at least a general idea of what our mission was all about. Then I might have made a better choice of the enchantments to take with me and so might have been able to avert the disaster that followed.

chapter 2

Although I shall not attempt to excuse my foolish pride that day, I must explain what had happened a couple of days earlier to provoke it.

Back then sacred matters were the domain of the monastery schools. Secular academies were much rarer—as they still are—and their mission was to pass on the wisdom of the pagan philosophers: the words of men like Aristotle, Galen, Euclid, and many lesser sages whose names have mostly been forgotten. Nowadays the Church has more or less taken over the academies to educate its priests, and the old wisdom is being suppressed, especially enchantment.

"Ancient song" was what we called enchantment in the academy, but to the priests it was devil worship if it worked and deliberate fraud if it didn't. No one denied that many of the rituals written in the old grimoires did fail in our more enlightened times. The Church claimed that the demons once invoked by those spells had now been driven away by Christ. Most of the sages just assumed that too much of the ancient wisdom had been lost—a regrettable situation, quite insoluble.

I had always disagreed.

Just as the monkish scriveners who copy out the gospels and other holy works of the early church fathers treat them as sacred, never to be modified in any way, so sages worshiped their secular texts. But all mortals are fallible, and when a man spends his life sitting or standing at a desk, copying, copying, copying, then errors must creep in. Minor mistakes in the text do not matter much in a discourse by Cicero or a Pythagorean theorem, but they mattered a lot in the study of enchantment.

With more than fifty grimoires available in Helmdon, we often had more than one copy of a specific spell. When we compared them, it was obvious that the texts could differ in minor ways, for the old scriveners were only human and made mistakes. One text might have *exosso*, which is Latin for "bone," where another had *exosus*, meaning "hateful." To me it seemed obvious that one or other must be an error, and the same would be true for any other differences between the two versions, so we should try to work out a single correct version. The teachers would not accept that, especially when it came from a penniless Saxon stripling. If neither ritual worked, then both texts were corrupted and there was nothing more to be said.

Even as a varlet, I had felt that this attitude was wrong and we should try to correct the spells. Granted, if two versions differed in only five or six details, you could still have a large number of combinations to test, but in practice common sense would usually determine which wording was more likely in each case.

Some disadvantages can be turned to advantages. I was a Saxon in an establishment where almost everyone else was Norman. I paid my tuition by caring for the horses. I slept alone, off in the stable. Most of the students were Norman "squires", and tended to shun me anyway; the few young Saxons, known as "varlets", largely followed their lead, so I had many lonely hours to pursue my private studies. Most of the faculty understood or even spoke the old tongue, but very few of them, and few Saxons even, could read or write it. I could do both, so I more or less had the old pre-Norman incantations to myself. In time my efforts bore fruit.

By correcting some trivial grammatical errors, I managed to cure the incantation *Hwæt segst*, and was scared out of my wits when it prophesied a murder in my future. When that prediction came true, I knew I was on the right track and subsequent events brought me to the attention of the king himself. As it turned out, my fortune was then made.

I eventually realized that most of the "errors" in the texts were in fact deliberate. Most grimoires are the personal recipe books of deceased enchanters, collections made during their training and later, but magic is dangerous. To keep such powers from falling into the wrong hands, the writers had inserted nonsense passages, which I came to think of as trip wires. That custom had been forgotten, but once you knew to look for the interpolations, most were easy to spot. Some were not, of course.

With this insight I began reviving incantations that had been dead for centuries. Sage Guy Delaney, my tutor and mentor, was the first of the Helmdon faculty to accept my work as meaningful, and the others gradually fell into line. With various amounts of condescension, they agreed to let me demonstrate what I was doing. The older men sniffed and lost interest, but soon editing the old texts became a sort of game for the adepts and younger sages. We would each take an enchantment and try to mend it, meeting every Saturday morning to show off our successes, if any, and pass on our failures to someone else to try. We worked in many of the numerous types of Latin: Classical and Church, as well as both the English and French varieties of the language. We also studied in several dialects of French itself, but usually Norman, and in numerous variations of the old English tongue. I don't mean that any one of us was fluent in every one of those, but between us we could always tease out the correct meaning. It was the worst jabbering since Babel.

By that summer of 1166, everyone had come to accept me as one of the best enchanters in the Academy, although I had not yet been granted my green cape. As soon as that happened, I must leave and head over to France to report to the king, because he had sponsored my advanced education. His terms were that I must remain on call in emergency, but report to him when I completed my studies, or by next Christmas at the latest.

My royal sponsorship had brought more than just the pension he paid me. Word that the queen had commissioned me to draw up a horoscope for her son, Lord Richard, spread throughout the county, bringing me innumerable similar requests from the gentry. I had little faith in astrology and found the labor boring, so I charged heavily for my services, but the higher my fees, the more prestigious my work became. I had also gained a reputation in the surrounding countryside as a healer. I treated Saxons for free, but they praised me to the gentry, and them I charged outrageously.

In short, I had risen from impoverished stable boy to one of the most respected enchanters in the academy, and possibly the richest man there. I was happy to continue what I was doing, and had gradually forgotten that the respect I had earned within the academy would not be shared by Norman outsiders. Truly it is written, "Pride goeth before a fall."

On the Saturday before Sir Neil arrived, our repair session gathered as usual, around a table in the largest classroom. That day we comprised two sages, five adepts, and one varlet—namely the baby-faced Eadig son of Edwin. Eadig was in a similar state to me, in that his time at Helmdon was limited. His father was a freehold farmer who had already lost one son to the Church and thus distrusted the monastery schools. He had sent his second boy to Helmdon just to learn to read and write. Illiterate himself, he had neither known how long this would take, nor realized how bright Eadig was. Any day soon Master Edwin was likely to decide that two years was long enough and summon the boy home. Thus, just as the faculty had deliberately put off promoting me to sage, it had delayed promoting Eadig to adept. But he sat in on our trip wire sessions and held his own with the best of us, at least in the old tongue incantations.

Before going on to new triumphs, we always began with the hard cases, meaning enchantments that had baffled at least one of us already and been passed along to someone else to try. And that day the first was *Hwá becuman*, which translates as, "Who is coming?" It is a very long, complex appeal to the ancient goddesses of fate, the Wyrds—exactly the sort of pagan evocation that makes the Church distrustful of secular education in general.

Hwá becuman had already defeated both Adept Maur son of Marc and Sage Laurent—one of the very few senior members of the faculty who spoke the old tongue well—and the previous week it had been dumped on my trencher. So I was up first.

"I have duly decided," I proclaimed, "that our learned colleagues did an excellent job of extracting the bad teeth in this mouthful, and the text is basically correct as it stands." In fact, I thought they had tampered too much. The version I had written out in fair for today's session was closer to the original than theirs had been. "I suspect that we may have encountered another problem altogether."

"He means he didn't get around to it," muttered Sage Marcel del Aunaie, a Norman younger than I, just recently promoted from adept. Unlike all other meetings in Helmdon, trip wire gatherings were very informal.

"Not at all, Your Wisdom," I protested. "I spent many hours on it, but I believe that the problem may be relevancy, or lack of it. Basically the enchanter is asking the Wyrds, or Norns, to tell him who is bringing news to him, the chanter, referred to as, 'your faithful servant.' Skipping over the falsehood of that description, the problem may be that nobody was on the way with news for either of the enchanters, so the venerable ladies chose not to answer their question. The same problem arises with the *Hwæt segst*, which also invokes them: if there is nothing to report, they remain silent."

Another possibility was that the Laurent might have been pronouncing the old tongue so badly that the poor old goddesses—demons according to the Church—had failed to understand what he was chanting. Of course I did not say that.

"It so happens that I have a couple of seriously ailing patients who may send for me at any time. I suggest we give *Hwá becuman* one more chance, which may tell us whether the Wyrds regard medical house calls as sufficiently important to bother with. If nothing happens, we add it to our list of incurable cases."

No one objected, which I suppose was a tribute to my former successes. On our previous attempts with *Hwá becuman*, I had served as cantor for both Maur and Laurent, but this time I would be chanter. I looked hopefully to Eadig, who nodded resignedly, and accepted the two slates I passed over to him. I gave him a pitch, and we began, with me singing the versicles, and he the responses.

In keeping with his babyish appearance, Eadig's voice had barely changed yet, and perhaps never would, so he sang in countertenor range, but he had a pure and tuneful voice, and I enjoyed chanting with him. *Hwá becuman* was long, but well phrased, a pleasure to sing. About halfway through I began to feel the first hints of acceptance. When I glanced across at my cantor, his silvery eyebrows had risen in surprise. The audience wouldn't feel what we did, but they saw our reactions, and soon they could hear changes in the timbre of Eadig's voice. If there was a prophecy coming, it must be recorded; hands reached for slates and wood tablets.

Outsiders might well have supposed that the two of us were putting on an act, but that audience knew better. Medicine, geometry, and astrology were all very interesting, but when you really came down to it, magic was our business.

The singing ended. Eadig sat for a moment with his eyes shut. Then he opened them, stared across at me, pointed a finger, and reeled off something in the croak of a very old woman. It sounded like poetry, but of course it was in the old tongue, and probably a very old version of it. Then he covered his face with his hands and screamed, "Hell's claws! My head!"

Cantors can have serious reactions to major enchantments, and his was a bad one. He writhed and wept, wailing that his brain was on fire, which was very unusual behavior for him. We sang healing chants over him, fetched soothing herbs, and eventually escorted him off to the varlets' dorm to rest.

Only then could we reassemble and try to agree on what the Wyrd had told me. Normans trying to take dictation in the old tongue were at a huge disadvantage, of course, and I was not all sure of what my own scribbles meant, because Eadig's pain had distracted me. What we eventually decided on, after much guessing and translation was this:

Iron wings to iron foot,
Not tide nor tempest trekking tard.
Two red eyes and one looks down,
Pledge to pay to purple pard . . . .
. . . .
Loc Lovise of Lincoln town . . . .

There had been more, but we could not agree on what, and even what we did agree on seemed to make little sense.

Obviously *Ironfoot* was me, the name my seniors had called me to my face when I first arrived at Helmdon and the juniors now used behind my back.

"*Iron wings?*" I said. "Could that be poet-talk for horseshoes?"

"Or *iron* may be armor and *wings* the verb," Sage Laurent suggested, "but either way, the first line means a horseman, possibly armed, is coming to see you."

"*Tide* and *tempest* suggest sea travel," Laurent said.

"And the king is in France!" said several voices. He had gone there in the spring to stamp out rebellion in Brittany. A man who ruled a quarter of Christendom could never rest. It seemed that now he was calling in my debt of service.

"*Tard?*" someone asked.

"Poetic again," I said, growing really excited now. "Short for *retard*, or *tardy*. *Purple* because King Henry's mother is Empress Maud, meaning he was born to the purple." And now he ruled an empire of his own, stretching from Scotland to the Pyrenees. "*Pard* for leopard, the sign of the House of Anjou." I was slightly off-beat there, because the king's arms displayed lions, not leopards, but no one in England could tell the difference, and that certainly included artists.

We fell silent, wrestling with the third line: *Two red eyes and one looks down?* Then Marcel del Aunale shouted, "More poet conceit! Two sunsets and then noon. Expect him on Monday, around midday."

Shouts of agreement swelled into cheers and thumps on the back that felt near to crippling me. My colleagues were paying tribute to what they saw as a magnificent feat of magic, for prediction is the supreme triumph of enchantment. Even yet, I admit I am proud of curing *Hwá becuman*. I have used it only

rarely in the half century since—partly because it is very special-
ized in asking only for news of a messenger, but mostly because
it is very hard on the cantor. But I still remember that first time
with satisfaction. That morning I was so proud of myself that I
thought I would burst.

Others heard the racket and came to investigate and pretty soon
a party developed. Even old Dean Odo le Brys appeared, and
was told what all the excitement was about. His faculties were
failing badly by then, but he accepted a horn of ale to drink to
whatever it might be. The sages were all very concerned about
the dean's health, because the academy stood within a manor
owned by the le Brys family, and there was no guarantee that the
present lord—another Odo le Brys—would allow it to remain
there when his great-uncle died.

Soon after that I excused myself to go and check on Eadig.
He was still in pain, but as groggy with potions as we dared
make him.

I also went to see Guy Delaney, who had been my mentor
and tutor in the academy. Squire Hann was sitting on a stool in
there, keeping death watch. I told him to go and join the party,
then took his place.

Guy was dying and knew it. He had already shed his worldly
cares and possessions; he had received extreme unction. Nothing in our skills could stop the remorseless growth of his tumors,
and now he was so weak that he could barely stand. He had a
wife and children in the village. They came to see him every
day, but he preferred to do his dying on the cot in his sanctum.
None of his old hunting companions among the local gentry had
even sent to inquire after him.

Every time I saw his drawn face and wasted frame I wanted
to weep. I perched on the stool beside him and asked how he felt.

He was conscious, if barely. He didn't bother to answer my question. "Thought it would be you."

"What was me?"

"The cheering in the trip wire meeting. What have you cured now?"

I told him the *Hwá becuman*, the response we had been given, and how we had interpreted it. He whispered praise, generous as always.

"I owe it all to you, master."

He shook his head feebly on the pillow. "I would have been a fool of a sage not to see opportunity when it barked in my face. A boy who had smashed a leg coming off a horse and went right back to riding as soon as it healed? A boy who never stopped asking questions all the way from Pipewell to Helmdon? A boy who rubbed down both my horse and his own before he ate or even quenched his thirst, without ever being told to do so? I knew you'd be something special. You didn't explain the ending. Look something?"

If our magic had just allowed us to combine Guy's wits and the dean's physique, we could have salvaged one operational sage from two tragic losses.

"I can't. There may have been more that we missed. *Loc* is an odd word. It sort of means *look*, but it can also mean something like *no matter*. Thus *loc hwær* means *wherever*, and *loc hwa* is *whoever*, and so on. In this case I think it probably does means *look*, or *look for*, or *look out for*, or perhaps even, *get a load of!*"

"Lovise? Male or female, friend or foe?"

Again I had to admit I didn't know.

"Lovise of Lincoln?" Guy murmured. "Lincoln's in the Danelaw. They speak funny, have a lot of old Danish names there still. Nice town . . . cathedral, big castle . . ."

"I'll tell you all about it when I return—if I am allowed to."

He cringed for a few moments at a spasm. When it passed he murmured, "You won't. Return, I mean."

"I certainly intend to!"

Again the dying man shook his head. We often hear that deathbed pronouncements contain superhuman wisdom, so I didn't want to argue with him, but I owned a fortune in grimoires, which I might have to leave behind at Helmdon if the predicted Iron Wings were in a hurry. I could claim personal ownership of five of the best spell books in the library, and should be very surprised if I were allowed or able to take them with me when the king's messengers came for me. If I wasn't, then I would certainly move mountains to come back and collect them as soon as possible.

"Take Ruffian."

Ruffian was a hunter, and a splendid one, even if he had the temper of an angry boar. Guy had left him to me, which was a sumptuous bequest.

"Of course I will," I said. "He's much in need of exercise. And I'll certainly bring him back."

Guy just smiled. He muttered something about his will and then his eyes wandered and closed. Like Eadig then, he was drugged against the pain, and tended to drift off to sleep at unexpected times. I stayed there, of course, until one of the sages came to relieve me.

That was my next-to-last conversation with the man who had turned a crippled stable boy into one of the king's enchanters.

chapter 3

uy took a turn for the worse the next day, so when I said farewell to him on Monday before noon, we both knew he would not be there when I returned, if I ever did. He confirmed for the fourth time that he wanted me to have Ruffian, claiming I was the only other man who could ride the scoundrel, which was far from true. I already owned a good horse in Bon Appétit, but a sage needs a cantor, and therefore two horses.

Eadig's blazing headache had subsided enough by Sunday that he agreed he would come with me to Lincoln, or wherever it was I was heading. We both knew how much he dreaded his father's summons, and this would be a way of keeping out of his reach for a while. I did suggest that we try the incantation again with him as the enchanter and me as the cantor, to see if there was a message on its way to him.

He said, "Durwin, Your Wisdom, I wouldn't wish this headache on my worst enemy."

That didn't make me feel any better, but I could guess that he preferred not to know his own future. To sin in ignorance is not deliberate disobedience, and he was an honest lad. I included the *Hwá becuman* text in my baggage, just in case.

Shortly before noon on Monday, Ruffian and Bon Appétit began to whinny. I introduced myself to Squire Piers, and then made a fool of myself for Sir Neil.

Our mounts were fresh and without straining them we caught up with the king's men at Burly Copse.

We humbly tagged ourselves on at the end of the line, in the dust cloud behind their packhorses. Sir Neil led a company of four other knights, five squires including Piers, and two men-at-arms, all riding in pairs. All of them were French born except one of the men-at-arms, Fugol, who had been brought along because he knew the way to Helmdon, even if he hadn't found the shortest route from the south.

Sir Neil rode at the front, and I soon noted with approval that he would detour around any standing crops or livestock he might endanger. Not all lords are so considerate, but of course Neil was not a lord, which was something I had overlooked in my folly earlier.

The whole population of Helmdon was out harvesting. The Good Lord had blessed us with fine weather that summer, so the barley was white and the men of the village had long since turned a deep brown color bringing in the hay: scything, tedding, gathering, baling, and finally stacking. Hay was needed to preserve the few livestock kept over the winter, and they sold their surplus to the academy, to feed our horses. The local alewife brewed barley to make ale. This was one of their very few sources of money. Lord Odo's crops had to be harvested first, or course, and then the villagers' own. They looked up as we passed; some recognized Eadig and me and waved.

It is rich country, the middle of England, especially the bottomlands, which are well watered and fecund. Higher ground tends to have heavy clay soil, but that makes for fine forest, where nobles and royalty love to hunt. Iron is mined in places, and timber provides the charcoal to smelt it.

Soon we left the le Brys lands. While we were walking the horses through a shady patch of forest where the footing was tricky, Eadig said, "Shouldn't you be up front with that stuck-up Norman?"

I grinned to hide my own annoyance. "You employ redundant vocabulary. Normans are stuck-up by definition, and Saxons by definition should never say so. Besides, I think he's an Angevin, not a Norman."

"Out of the same slop bowl."

"But the meatier end, these days, since the king is Angevin. So what do we know about Sir Neil d'Airelle?"

"Nothing."

"Not quite nothing. All kings, Eadig, are starved for information. They cannot be everywhere, and King Henry, may God preserve him, rules the biggest realm since Charlemagne's. So all kings have confidants, men they trust, persons they can send out to do something or investigate something and report back. Almost always these *familiares* are noblemen, but King Henry is unusual in that he sometimes trusts commoners with such tasks."

"Ah! Like this Sir Neil!"

"Right. And I should have realized that sooner. Neil d'Airelle is not much older than I am—no more than twice your age." Eadig stuck out his tongue at me, but that was probably how Sir Neil would judge their respective ages. "So it's quite likely that this is his first independent command. How did he catch the king's eye, do you suppose?"

"Killing a lot of men in battle?"

"More likely taking important prisoners who fetched big ransoms. That's certainly possible, but courage isn't the first thing a king looks for in a *familiaris*. Discretion is, I should think . . . Strength and stamina, yes. If this mission is really urgent, then that may be why His Grace has sent a younger man and a slim retinue. They seem to have been traveling very fast."

"Or it may not be urgent at all," Eadig said scornfully. "His Nibs may be somebody's grandson, some old codger who's been pestering the king to promote the boy."

Although I had met King Harry only once at that time, and knew little about him, I doubted that he would put up with pestering from anyone. I did know that he was fanatically fond of the chase, so Neil d'Airelle might be a hunting buddy. He had shown considerable equestrian skill in the way he had controlled his stallion in the academy yard.

"It's a fair guess, though," I said, "that this is Neil's first independent mission, so he's determined to prove himself." That was what I should have seen sooner. An older man, a nobleman who had demonstrated his worth in the king's service, might not have been quite so quick to take offense at my impertinence. On the other hand he might just as easily have ordered his men to bend me over a wall and give me a memorable thrashing.

I thought it over for a furlong or two.

"So Sir Neil's task is either urgent, or he is determined to treat it so," I said.

"But why did the king order him to detour around by Helmdon to pick up an enchanter?"

A penetrating question! And a green, untried Saxon enchanter at that? Henry had many others in his service. He might just be trying out a couple of promising recruits, Neil and me both. I wasn't going to suggest that, even to Eadig.

When I didn't answer, Eadig said, "Could it be he's being sent to arrest someone who employs a house sage?"

"Possible," I said, although serving a royal warrant was a duty of the county sheriff. Men who could afford in-house enchanters usually maintained retinues of knights or men-at-arms also, so resistance would represent armed rebellion. Sir Neil and his gallant little band seemed far too few to counter that.

"Neil's scared of magic." Eadig waited for comment, but I didn't offer one, so he pushed on. "At least he's not familiar with it, because your talk of prophecy scared him." He thought for a long moment. "And he expects you to be his servant and do what he says, except that he doesn't know what orders to give you?"

"You're exactly right there! And I sassed him. Suppose his mission is very secret—which might explain why the king chose to give it to an obscure courtier, who won't be recognized—and then I start bragging that I knew he was coming, to the point where I already had my horse saddled. There went his secrecy! So I got off on the wrong foot with him, and it was my own stupid fault, and we'll have to be on our best behavior until we can make ourselves useful."

At which Eadig pointed out what I already knew very well: that I wouldn't be able to make myself useful until I knew what we were supposed to be doing.

"So just let's enjoy a fine ride on a wonderful summer's day and thank the Good Lord that we don't have to break our backs like those poor wretches over there." I pointed to where some distant peasants were laboriously harvesting barley—each man stolidly scything his own long strip of field, his wife and often children following him, binding, gleaning, and stacking the sheaves.

We made good time on the dry ground. Long before sunset we came in sight of the castle and churches of Northampton, and that was when Squire Piers moved aside and reined in until we came by. Then he rode alongside me, two stony eyes flanking a steel nose.

"Sir Neil is worried that we are a large party to impose on the constable without prior warning. He orders you to find accommodation for yourself and the boy in one of the local monasteries. You are to be at the castle gate at sunup to continue our journey. You are not to wear your capes in the town, and you must not discuss your mission with anyone."

"Enchanters are rarely welcome in monasteries," I said, "and I would not impose on the holy men under false pretenses. Even if I tried, I might not succeed, for I am known in Northampton, and my iron foot makes me distinctive. I come here sometimes to purchase medical supplies. I have friends who will gladly put us up. They will not pry and we shall not discuss why we are here."

He scowled at this upstart Saxon again being difficult, and rode off to confer with his knight. When he failed to return with more orders from Sir Neil, Eadig and I held our mounts back until we no longer seemed to be associated with the king's company. I wondered why Neil did not want to be seen associating with an enchanter. Was it only a fighting man's distrust for learning? If magic would be needed for his mission, why, why, why had the king enlisted an unknown like me, instead of sending one of his tried and true enchanters?

After we had dropped back far enough to be out of sight of our noble bodyguard, we came to a shallow gully that still had a trickle of water in it. Stepping-stones alongside the road showed how deeply it would flow in winter, and I knew that fording it could be tricky at such times. I reined in and suggested that we let the horses drink. Then I dismounted, so Eadig did the same, looking at me quizzically.

"Last night," I said, "I tried an enchantment I have never attempted before, *Battre le tambour*. It's a single-voice chant, not a derelict that we have been trying to cure of trip wires. I found it in one of the grimoires I brought back from Barton two years ago. Commentaries added by users suggest that it works well and is long-lasting, but is not suitable for warriors. I felt a strong acceptance, and so far I have encountered no ill-effects, except I did have a nightmare just before dawn this morning. If you'd like to try it also, this might be good place to do so."

"'Beat the drum'?" Eadig said cautiously. "What's that mean? What drum? What's it supposed to do?"

"You know that creepy feeling you get once in a while, a sense of being threatened? The text is an appeal to guardian angels to warn you of approaching danger. That's why warriors shouldn't use it—they must spurn danger lest their comrades think they're scared. If you're not armed and armored, being paid to risk your life, then running for cover may not be too stupid. The reason I have never chanted it before is that I have never felt the need to. There're no lions lurking around Helmdon, not even a thirsty footpad willing to kill innocent passersby for a copper groat. Having made the acquaintance of Sir Neil d'Airelle this afternoon, I suspect that my life is about to take a turn into harm's way, where the odd nightmare may seem a cheap price to pay for some advance warning of real danger. It's entirely up to you."

Eadig said, "Yes, please!" and held out a hand.

I untied the laces on one of my saddlebags and found the scroll I wanted right away, because I had tied it with a fancy bow. Eadig studied the text for a few minutes. I scanned the road in both directions, seeing no one approaching. Then he began to chant. He managed it all the way through without a stumble. He had the potential to be a great enchanter, and I hated the thought that he might be dragged away to waste his talents as a farmer's bookkeeper.

"Feels good," he remarked offhandedly, and rolled the parchment up tight again. "Thank you, master."

Northampton streets were a maze, narrow and winding, and summer heat had made them even more noisome than usual. They needed a week's steady downpour to clean out the ordure, but they were unlikely to get that for a month or two yet. A steady crush of homeward-bound laborers and servants slowed our progress, and Eadig's continuous grumble about the stink did nothing to make us popular. I feared that someone would scoop up a handful of grunge and throw it at him, for if one did, a dozen others would join in.

We came at last to the academy, which had been jury-rigged by connecting three houses into a labyrinth of tiny rooms and passages. The main door was closed, indicating that no more patients would be seen that day, but I went around to the side entrance, where we were admitted as friends and colleagues. A couple of squires took charge of our horses. I introduced Adept Eadig, who had never been there before, and did not mention my promotion.

I had not been entirely honest with squire Piers. My friends in Northampton were the students and faculty of the academy, which was somewhat larger than Helmdon's, but less renowned. They tended to be a little jealous of our reputation, inclined to consider us as poachers in their home waters. Nevertheless, they were always friendly enough on a personal level, and Dean Gilbert made us welcome.

My usual reason for calling was to trade herbs that we had collected near Helmdon for some that Northampton had obtained by trade, the town being located on the king's highway. They obviously wondered why I had brought no wares this time and why I wanted to stay overnight. If Eadig and I were heading out on a long journey, why hadn't we started early, to make more miles that day? They were too polite to ask outright. Dean Gilbert evicted a couple of varlets so we could share a small but comfortable room under the rafters, with two thickly padded pallets.

Despite what Sir Neil feared, enchanters are mostly a close-mouthed lot, for they engage in confidential activities for their clients—sickness and horoscopes and so on. I trusted our hosts completely, except in one respect. Although I could claim personal ownership of five of the grimoires in the Helmdon library, I would have needed a special packhorse to carry them around with me, for parchment is heavy. For the last two years I had been copying out the incantations I thought would be most useful for me in my career. To keep the skins from buckling up, as they tend to do in the damp, I had been tying them in tight rolls, rather than pressing them into the usual books with heavy wooden covers held in place by rope or brass clamps.

I had brought a satchel packed full of these scrolls, the equivalent of a thick grimoire. I had to leave it in our room when we went downstairs to eat, but I put a strong warding spell on it, so that any nosey parker who touched it would receive a nasty surprise. Spells are a sage's sword and shield, and I already felt that I was going into battle half naked.

Supper that evening became a party, which was a normal result of strangers arriving with news. In this case we visitors had none, but the hosts did, thanks to highway traffic and gossip coming from the king's castle. His campaign in Brittany was reported to be meeting with success—doing better than last year's attempt to bring the Welsh to heel, which had been washed out by endless rain. The castles he had built to contain the Welsh were now being besieged by them.

The rumors said he was also going to teach Aquitaine proper obedience, but the people of that vast duchy, which he had gained by marrying its duchess, regarded him as even more of a foreigner than the English did, and would undoubtedly resist his discipline—or, indeed, any man's. King Louis of France, having at last begotten a male heir, was stirring up trouble in the other lands that King Henry held from him, like Normandy and Anjou itself. Even the King of Scots was starting to make rebellious noises, not to mention the Welsh. I was humbled by the thought that a king with so many problems had remembered the lame Saxon boy who had sworn an oath to him at Barton, two years ago.

Queen Eleanor was still in England, somewhere, and rumored to be with child again, which would be her tenth.

But no one around the table mentioned Lincoln or English trouble that might have caught the king's attention. Dean Gilbert served excellent wine, and we ended with some rousing, mostly bawdy, songs.

When we retired to our garret for the night, I quickly sat down cross-legged on my pallet, for there was not much headroom in our attic. I lifted the warding on my spell bag and brought out my set of futhorc tiles, futhorc being the old Anglo-Saxon runes that hadn't been used for a hundred years. Indeed, they had been dying since Augustine brought Lord Jesus and his Roman alphabet to England. I knew that Eadig could chant the *Hwæt segst,* because I had taught him myself.

"Are you up to this?" I asked, for we were both tired and must make an early start in the morning.

He nodded, grinning his boyish grin.

"You need to bone up on the text?" I had brought the manuscript, but he just shook his head and pulled off one of his stockings, which he used to blindfold himself.

29

I spread out the thirty-seven tiles on the floor between us at random: thirty-six rune tiles and one blank. Then I brought the candle close and said, "Ready." He began to chant, but softly, so as not to disturb our hosts.

Hwæt segst—"What sayest thou?"—is another appeal to the Wyrds, who are always reluctant to be invoked, so I did not expect him to find acceptance on the first attempt. He made no mistakes, though, and after a few minutes his grin returned, so he could feel it working. When he had sung the final words, he reached out with his right hand—Eadig was normally left-handed—and pointed at a tile: *cen*, which means torch, and stands for the Latin *C*, or *K*. After a moment he pointed at another: *yr*, or bow, meaning Y. By then I thought I could guess what was coming, and sure enough the next two were *nyd* and *ing*, so together they spelled out *cyning*—"king."

But he did not stop then. The *Hwæt segst* rarely delivers more than a couple of words, and sometimes only one, so I watched intently to see what followed. Only when Eadig's finger had spelled out another five letters did he point to the blank tile that signified the end.

"Am I done?" he asked.

"You are, and very well done, too," I said.

He pulled off the blindfold. "What did they say?"

"*Cyningswice.*"

His face fell. "I don't know what that means!"

"I've never met the word itself," I admitted, "but I know what it means. You know *Hlafordswice*, don't you?"

His eyes grew large in the candlelight. "Treason?"

"Betrayal—a man betraying his lord, or a woman her husband. That's what the Normans call petty treason. So *Cyningswice* is betrayal of your king, which they call high treason."

Eadig stared at me in horror, eyes and mouth wide.

So our mission must be far more important than I had dreamed, and certainly more than King Henry suspected. If he had consulted Enchanter General Aubrey de Fours, or another of his senior sages, surely they would have warned him that there was high treason in the air? In that case he would certainly have sent the regent with an army.

But then I realized that Enchanter de Fours wouldn't know a futhorc from a pitchfork, and no one had made the *Hwæt segst* work for hundreds of years until I managed to remove its trip wires and Guy Delaney had deduced the best way of using it. In foretelling at least, Eadig and I were better enchanters than the enchanter general. The king did not know what we knew, but we knew more than we could handle.

chapter 4

a s ordered, sage and adept reported for duty outside the castle gate at sunup the next morning, with our distinctive capes hidden away in our baggage beside a day's rations kindly provided by the academy.

We did not have to wait long, for Sir Neil and his squire were the first persons to emerge after the portcullis was raised, with the rest of the troop close behind them. Eadig and I fell in behind, as before. The young knight was undoubtedly keen and had his followers well disciplined, but after a while I began to wonder if he was over-zealous. If this was their fourth or fifth day in exactly the same formation, knight paired with knight, squire with squire, and the two men-at-arms together, they must all be longing for a change of company and conversation. We were in friendly territory, after all, with no expectation of attack.

Again I concluded that this was probably Neil's first independent command, and he was not just anxious to succeed, but terrified of getting it wrong.

We rode through mostly forested country, in a northerly direction, along what was clearly an old Roman road. Most of it was in fair condition, for the king insists that his highways be properly maintained, but some stretches were so broken up that the traffic ran alongside it, on the usual strips of dried mud. Lincoln might still be our destination, for it had been a Roman town. I wasn't going to ask, but I was growing increasingly frustrated by my lack of information.

Although the morning was already hot, the trees shaded us from the sun, and I was enjoying the ride, my only problem being to hold Ruffian back. He wanted to kick dust in all the other horses' eyes.

Cyningswice? High treason. It made sense and yet somehow it didn't make sense. Just because the king was in Brittany did not mean that England was without a government. In his absence the justiciar, the earl of Leicester, acted as regent. So if Henry heard rumors of treason in the heart of his kingdom, surely he would just order the justiciar to investigate? Why send one of his *familiares* to look into it, and a youthful commoner at that? A threat such as that should merit a senior nobleman and two hundred knights. Was our mission merely a sham, to humor some courtier that his worries were being looked into, or that his grandson had been given an important mission, as Eadig had suggested?

The Wyrds would not be deceived. If they said I was going to meet treason . . . But they hadn't, of course. It was Eadig whose destiny they had foretold.

Had I known about treason sooner, I would have brought much darker curses with me.

An hour or so into the ride, when the horses were being allowed a restful walking pace, Squire Piers dropped back to tell me to report to Sir Neil. At last!

I rode forward and we greeted each other with a blessing. Piers gnawed his mustache for a moment before he said more.

"His Grace sent me on this expedition, Sage. He has reason to believe that there may be enchantment involved. He told me to enlist you to advise me on that topic. But he definitely intended me to be in command. I am, you understand, one of His Grace's *familiares*."

So was I, although I had more sense than to say so at that point. The king had sworn me in by that title when he received me at Burton Castle, but *familiaris* could have many meanings: royal troubleshooter yes, but also servant, friend, or family member. I had no illusions that I counted as one of his intimates, most of whom would be high-ranking noblemen. I suspected that the exchequer lacked a category of "peasant boys being educated in devil worship at royal expense," so the king had just lumped me in as a miscellaneous pensioner.

"A very great honor, Sir Neil. I have never doubted that this is your mission. I have no ability, ambition, or authority to give orders to belted knights. Consider me just another of your weapons, like your sword or dagger. I can be deadly if necessary, although I prefer not to be."

"Why not?" He seemed genuinely surprised, even disapproving, which confirmed my suspicion that Sir Neil had not been chosen for the originality of his thinking.

"It is our way, sir. To do serious harm to people usually requires darker powers than we are willing to invoke. Also, we prefer not to draw attention to our art."

He glanced at me to see if I was in earnest, and then nodded reluctantly. An ambitious young knight would do everything he could think of to attract attention, pirouetting on the very brink of suicide. "Your friends did well by you last night?"

"Very well, thank you."

"What did you talk about?"

"Herbal matters, mostly—the safe dosage of rhubarb in a

case of extreme constipation, and so on. Gossip about the constable's habit of taking liberties with his servant maids. Sir, they did *not* pry into my business, and I did *not* mention it."

"That is good. This is a very delicate matter. As your dark arts revealed to you, our destination is Lincoln, a sizable town in the east. I understand that it includes one of the king's great castles."

He waited for a comment, so I said, "I have heard of Lincoln, of course, but never been there."

"The constable of the castle is Lord Richard de la Haye."

"And is he the person you have to investigate, sir?"

"That remains to be seen. He inherited the position from his father, but the fact that the king left him in charge of one of the major fortresses in England would indicate that His Grace trusts him implicitly."

Neil was still very reluctant to tell me anything, so I just waited hopefully until he had swallowed a few more doubts.

He continued, "The sheriff of Lincolnshire, Sir Alured de Poiltona, also resides in the castle. The accusation was so vague that it might apply to him."

On the face of it, he would be a more likely suspect, simply because anyone suspecting serious wrongdoing anywhere in the entire county ought to report it to the sheriff himself. Back then sheriffs were the men who administered the laws. A few years after this, King Henry reduced their duties and transferred much of their power to his itinerant judges. But at the time of which I write, a sheriff was a mighty man indeed.

I still did not speak, but I must have nodded.

"You have heard of him?"

"No, sir. Is he also one of His Grace's highly trusted supporters?"

"The rule of law in a major city and county would not be entrusted to anyone whose loyalty was in doubt."

"May I ask a question?"

"Provided it is relevant and does not touch upon confidential matters."

Saints preserve me! "How sure is the king that there is enchantment involved?"

Sir Neil did not shrug, but his tone implied indifference. "It was hinted at. The gist of the letter was that someone of high rank was plotting with some of the king's enemies." He paused. "You keep nodding."

"I have a theory, Sir Neil. No magic, I'm afraid, just guess-work."

"Tell me."

"A very delicate matter, you say, involving one or even two of His Grace's most respected servants. I have been wondering why he would entrust a tyro like me with the task of advising you on magic in such an affair. I am a qualified philosopher, but I have almost no experience. Two years ago, I met Aubrey de Fours, the enchanter general, when he came to Northamptonshire in attendance on the His Grace. I don't know if the king visited Lincoln on that occasion, but he must have been there several times in the twelve years he has reigned so far. It seems likely that most of the important people in this area must have met the enchanter general and his helpers. Could it be that His Grace wanted a sage who will not be recognized? Me, for instance?"

I thought for a moment I was about to see Sir Neil d'Airelle smile, but he didn't. He unbent slightly, though. "It seems you *can* be deadly, Durwin of Helmdon! You worked this out without magic?"

"Um. Almost without magic, sir. Last night my cantor, Adept Eadig, at my direction, performed a minor incantation seeking guidance . . . The warning he received was to beware of high treason."

Neil made the sign of the cross.

"And," I continued, "there had been no discussion of treason before that, so he wasn't playing games—not that he would. So we now have two independent reasons to suspect major wrong-doing in Lincoln."

"And can you suggest why the king sent me, not a man of higher rank?"

For the same reason that he had chosen me—that he was a nonentity. I must be careful how I said so.

"Undoubtedly because he has faith in you, sir. But could it be because you have never visited this part of England before?"

"I have never visited his English domains before," Neil confessed. "And His Grace told me himself that this was why he had chosen me. You were very clever to work that out, Sage."

My word, we were making progress! If he thought my feat of intellectual prowess worthy of admiration, he ought to try analyzing a three-voice pre-Christian enchantment written in futhorc. "Thus you will profess to be arriving in Lincoln on some very minor business so that you do not alarm the plotters, if there are any such plotters?"

Now it was Neil who was nodding, and his manner was definitely thawing. "Exactly what His Grace suggested."

Because if he hadn't been told to do it that way, Neil would have marched into Lincoln with banners flying and trumpets blowing. I already had a lot of respect for the king's wits. I had very little confidence in Sir Neil's. He still might start flaunting his authority. And whose idea had it been to have him lead such a train? Was he planning to take Lincoln by storm? Did he think his army would protect him from enchantment?

"Officially," he explained, "I am recruiting bowmen for the war in France, a trivial task. The king stressed that my real commission was not only very important but must be kept entirely secret. The only men with me who know our true purpose are Piers, my squire, who happens to be my brother, and my deputy, Sir Vernon Cheadle, the one riding the piebald. You will not, therefore, discuss it, nor will you reveal your, um, calling, while we are there. Look out for signs of enchantment and let me know what you find."

If he thought he could dismiss me like that, I would have to put my foot down—the one shod in iron. "With all due respect, Sir Neil, that won't work."

Glare. "Why not?"

"Because, even if the constable is innocent of the charges and as loyal to the king as the king's own right hand, he will certainly employ a house sage, if only to attend to the health of his garrison. You agree?"

Neil nodded grudgingly. "I suppose so."

"Whether or not he is plotting treason, he may employ several enchanters. No matter how carefully I guard my tongue, they will unmask me in a few hours, and there went your cover, Sir Neil. A flunky sent to recruit bowmen does not travel with an enchanter."

He did not like that. We rode in silence for a while, but it was a fine day for a ride, as I have said.

"What would you suggest then?" The question sounded as if it hurt.

"I need more information, sir. If I am to be of any assistance to you at all, you will have to take me into your confidence."

"I have told you everything. On the face of it, Lincoln is a most unlikely place to hatch a treasonous conspiracy. The shire itself is peaceable and far from any unrest; it is bounded by swamps and marshes to north and south, and there is nothing east of it except, eventually, ocean. The Scots and the Welsh can be difficult, but it is mostly His Grace's many French domains that cause him trouble: Normandy, Brittany, Aquitaine, even Anjou itself. Not to mention the king of France."

Better! Then came another long pause.

"But?" I prompted. "King Henry did not send you to inspect the swamps and marshes."

"About ten days ago, His Grace received a warning that the castle had entertained several unlikely visitors this summer. Some notable nobles have called in at Lincoln, for no known reason—even some from France who own no estates in England and therefore have no honest reason to be here. One is known to be a confidant of that perfidious dog, King Louis. Another is certainly an accomplice of the rebellious archbishop, Thomas Beckett, and may even be a papal legate. Any comments so far, Sage?"

"Just that the last place to look for a conspiracy might be the best place to hatch it. And that a simultaneous uprising at half a dozen places in His Grace's empire might well overwhelm even him."

"It might indeed."

Clearly, if I wanted better information I ought to be using a brazier and branding irons. "And who warned His Grace to suspect trouble brewing in Lincoln?"

"An informant known to the king, a doughty knight of advanced years, but barely literate. He was obviously unwilling to entrust such deadly accusations to a scribe. His letter was hardly legible at all, and certainly not as clear as could be wished. He included a cryptic comment that there was magic involved. This is why you were conscripted to assist." He shot me an inquiring look. "What say you to that, sage?"

I could say that it sounded as if the king put very little stock in the old warrior's accusations. He had delegated the matter to a jackanapes knight, backed him up with a whippersnapper enchanter, and gone back to worrying about more important matters, like sieges and rebellions. I would have expected His Grace to put more trust in his sheriff, Sir Alured, than he did in the twaddling of an aged and onetime doughty knight. I didn't say that.

"Magic makes the problem a lot worse than it would be without it."

"Why? What could magic do in such a situation?"

My head spun at hearing such ignorance. "If it were black enough, it could rally legions of demons against us. I need to think about this, Sir Neil. Could we resume this discussion later, please?"

Given leave, I dropped back to the end of the column. Squire Piers spurred his horse forward to resume his proper place at the head; I thought he had been relieved to see me. And Eadig was trying to hide a smirk without much success.

"How went your little chat with the noble squire?" I asked.

"Pissy. He kept asking what we did all day at Helmdon and was it true that Saxon girls would spread their legs for a single mug of ale. Stuff like that. Then he wanted to know what sort of magic I could do." He paused, but I waited, knowing there was more to come. "And then he scoffed and said we was all just fakes."

"And?"

"I said, 'You see that crow up there?' and killed it."

"Oh, did you?" Curses were definitely not included in official varlet training at Helmdon. "And who taught you to do that?"

"Er, rather not say."

I could not help smiling and suddenly we both laughed.

"Normally I would rip your hide off for that, Adept Eadig son of Edwin, and strangle you with it, but under the present circumstances that may have been an excellent move, and very helpful." Undoubtedly the squire was now reporting to Sir Neil that even that baby-faced *pipsqueak* back there could kill things by pointing a finger at them. "What spell did you use?"

"*Mori vermes.*"

I was relieved to hear it, because it was fairly harmless, and I had learned worse when I was an adept. It is what is called a Release spell, meaning that it can be chanted beforehand and then applied just by repeating its name, as fast as loosing an arrow from a drawn bow. The other sort, those that must be chanted anew every time, are more common, usually much more complex, and are known as Repeat spells.

"Unless the branch was quite low, you probably didn't kill it." I said. "And never rely on *Mori vermes* to deal with anything truly dangerous, like a rabid dog. If you must use it on a man, aim for his eyes. It will blind him for a few minutes and hurt like hot vinegar, so you'd better be a mile away before he gets his sight back."

And then, because I was not Sir Neil, I took Eadig into my confidence and told him the whole story of our mission, as I had just learned it. We were, I admitted, facing a very serious problem, and I had not brought enough rolls with me on this mission, so I might have to send him back to Helmdon for better armament.

Indeed, I couldn't recall packing anything much more dangerous than Eadig's *Mori vermes* crow-stunner, which would be as useful against black magic as a quill pen in a sword fight. I had brought it because my years of living in a stable had left me with a strong aversion to rats.

chapter 5

i think that all of us, even the Angevins, were impressed by our first sight of Nottingham Castle, high on its rock. It is much more splendid nowadays, for King Henry has since enlarged it considerably. We spent that night there as guests of Baron Everard, the sheriff, who was apparently an old friend of Sir Neil's father. I never got near him and had no desire to, for he was an elderly, unimpressive man with a permanently sour expression. Despite the lack of warning, though, he supplied an excellent meal and allowed us to bed down on the floor of the hall with his male staff.

As guests, Eadig and I were granted places near a wall, where the rushes were slightly cleaner and the chances of being kicked during the night slightly less, but lights out means nothing in summer. Although about forty men were already there, not one was even trying to sleep. Most were just sitting around talking, and the rest were playing knucklebones. I stretched out on my back to admire the hammerbeam roof and wonder if there was any chance of another conference with Sir Neil.

I had almost persuaded myself by then that we were engaged in nothing more than a training exercise. Neil and I would snoop around Lincoln for a week, find nothing, and head over to France to hunt down the king and tell him so. The only thing causing me any concern was the futhorc reading, *Cyningswice*.

Then Eadig said quietly, "You've been made."

I sat up and saw a man wearing the brown cape of a healer heading straight for me. I scrambled to my feet.

He was elderly, clean-shaven, and pudgy, with a prominent bald spot surrounded by iron-gray curls, but the effect was natural, not a tonsure. His eyes were bright and his mouth wore a welcoming smile. The robe under his cape was finely embroidered.

He offered a hand. "Sage Fulk."

I took it. "Durwin of Pipewell."

He raised a skeptical eyebrow. "What school?"

"Helmdon," I admitted, embarrassed because professional courtesy dictated that I should have made myself known to him when I arrived. "Licensed sage. Who told you?"

Chuckling, he took my arm in a firm grip. "Well met, Brother Durwin. Come and share some wine with me, as sages have done since the days of Plato."

His brown cape did not proclaim him as a sage, only as a healer, but perhaps he felt entitled to the greater title after a lifetime. And I was not in uniform.

"If I'm wanted," I told Eadig, "I'm with the sage."

Fulk led me out of the hall, under the wondering gaze of at least seventy eyes, and to a door marked with a pentacle. He whispered a password before opening it and leading me in. It was small, as castle rooms always are, and was clearly his sanctum, being crowded by an examination couch, shelves full of jars and bottles, documents chests, and astrological charts on the walls. Fresh rushes covered the floor. The two windows were mere arrow slits, angled downward through massive stone walls, but they had shutters to close in winter. They let in little air in the summer heat, although the walls themselves kept the place bearably cool. I guessed that this might serve as his bedroom when necessary, even if he owned a house in the town as well.

He pointed to a cushion on one of the chests and told me to sit. Then he produced a flask and two beakers. He settled on the wooden stool.

"Who told you that I am a sage, sir?"

"Call me Fulk."

"Fulk, then."

"No one. You're not a warrior, and you're not tonsured like a cleric. Your face is neither as weather-beaten as a peasant's nor as pale as a clerk's. Your hand is smooth, and you travel with a youth to act as your cantor."

"Ah, sagacity but not black magic!"

He chuckled. "Besides, the last time Guy Delaney came through here, he was bragging to me that he'd found a young Saxon cripple who was going to be the finest enchanter in England. Or did he say Europe? *Wæs hæl!*"

I gave the standard response of, *"Drinc hæl!"* and we drank. I had no more than a fruit fly's knowledge of wine in those days, but I could tell that his vintage was subtle on the tongue. I complemented him on it.

"Angevin," he said. "The best. How is my old friend?"

I broke the news of Guy's illness. Fulk was clearly distressed to hear it, and we spoke awhile of my mentor and benefactor. The next topic ought to be my journey, destination, and mission, and I had been forbidden to discuss them.

"How long have you been sage here?" I asked.

"As long as I have worn my cape. Take your age, double it, and then add some. Being a house sage is a noble profession though." That was a hint for me to tell him whom I served, but the pause was tactfully brief. "Except when there is sickness, of

44

course. We had mumps come through here last year—laid the whole garrison low. Or puffed them up, I should say. Slew a couple of men, despite everything I could do."

"I heard that it was in Northampton also."

"Being a sage is no more secure than any other form of service, though," my host murmured, reaching for the wine flask. "Consider Sage Bjarni of Lincoln, for example. Served the constable all his life, then suddenly shown the door, without a word of thanks."

My scalp prickled. I was being offered advice, or a warning, and I wasn't sure which. My *tambour* enchantment wasn't indicating danger, so I pressed ahead. Fulk obviously knew something I did not and it had led him to guess our destination.

"That is true ingratitude," I said. "Tell me more."

"Yes, it seemed strange, for Lord Richard has always been considered a model knight."

Neil had mentioned Lord Richard de la Haye as constable of Lincoln Castle.

"I expect we will hear the true story some day," my host added.

"I hope so," I countered. "I've never been to Lincoln. The big battle there . . . 1141, was it not? Before I was born. The town stayed loyal to King Stephen, as I recall."

"But the castle changed hands several times."

Was I supposed to hear a warning in that or was it merely pass-the-time conversation? "I hope it isn't likely to do so again in the near future?"

Fulk laughed. "Hardly! Those were terrible times, what they now call the Anarchy. King Henry is a strong king, just what we longed for when men were building castles everywhere you looked. Lord Richard is probably getting too old. It happens to us all. Enjoy your youth and guard your health, Sage."

"What of the sheriff of Lincoln, Sir Alured Someone?"

Fulk shrugged. "He's new. I never met him. I can't tell you anything at all about him."

In that exchange of gossamer hints, Fulk had warned me that something odd had happened in Lincoln, and I had not denied that Lincoln was our destination. This was a breach of my orders, but also an invitation to him to tell me more. He probably did not have more information to share, and at that moment there come a tap on the door.

I said, "That is a summons for me, I expect."

"Else a warning for me that my wife will be taking the meat cleaver to me if I am late going home yet again." Fulk opened the door, and the messenger was indeed a page to tell me that my valorous leader wanted me.

Neil had been granted the honor of the guest room, which was reached by way of a spiral staircase with no handrail. Fortunately it was so steep that I could very nearly reach the steps in front of me without bending, and that gave me a sense of security, in that I could have grabbed one if my iron foot had slipped. I managed the ascent without stooping to such indignity.

I rapped on the door at the top, and was told to enter. I was impressed. The room was practically filled by a four-poster bed, but it had two large windows, one of them closed by a fretwork of lead holding diamond-shaped pieces of glass. I had heard of glazing, but had never seen it before. Most of the glass was too thick or tinted to see through, so it admitted little more light than horn or oiled cloth would, but it might keep out the winter cold better. The other opening just had the usual shutters, which stood wide open that warm evening. There was also a stone fireplace, an oaken chest, and a well-cushioned chair. It was a homely, comfy room.

Sir Neil was reclining on the featherbed, stripped down to his shirt and britches, leaning back against a pile of down pillows, quaffing wine from a flask, and admiring his hairy shins. He did not offer to share his wine with me, but gestured for me to sit on the chest, which was better positioned for conversation than the chair. With a cushion, that would have been quite a comfortable perch. Regrettably from my viewpoint, the lid was engraved with images of saints and martyrs, which impressed me deeply.

"Well, Sage, what do you advise me about magic?"

I clutched my cane in both hands, rested my chin on my wrist, and tried to look wise.

"It will kill you, sir. If treason is really festering in Lincoln, your plan is hopeless."

His eyes narrowed down like the slits on a jousting helm. "You had better justify that remark, Durwin of Helmdon."

"Gladly, Sir Neil. About half an hour ago, the sheriff's house sage, Sage Fulk, accosted me in the hall and invited me to drink wine with him in his sanctum."

Neil glared. "I gave you strict orders—"

"Which I obeyed, sir. He identified me as a sage just by looking at me, and I was not wearing my cape." I saw no reason to mention Fulk's story about Guy Delaney. "I accepted his invitation, of course. We talked. I did not tell him where we are headed, but he guessed. Without prompting by me, he mentioned that Lord Richard de la Haye recently dismissed his long time sage, named Bjarni."

"Why?"

"For no known reason. In other words, sir, Sage Fulk was warning me that there is something odd going on in Lincoln Castle. He has heard rumors, and now the king is sending a troop of men-at-arms there, with an attendant sage."

"You think that Lord Richard may have dismissed his sage for dealing in treasonable matters?" At last, perhaps, Neil d'Airelle was starting to realize that he might be out of his depth.

"In that case Lord Richard should have cut off his head, sir. At the very least, Fulk was warning me—and therefore you— not to trust Constable Richard. We should probably assume then that Sheriff Alured de Poiltona is also in on the treachery, yes? Otherwise the king would simply write to the sheriff and tell him to deal with the matter."

I gave him a moment, then continued. "So . . . assume for a moment that Constable Richard is plotting treason. He has been bought by King Louis or he supports the rebellious Archbishop Becket. His very first concern will be to deal with his own house sage, who will detect his change of loyalty at once. Were I that man, I would either stop him by myself, or at the very least I would report his misconduct to the sheriff, or even the king's regent, the earl of Leicester. Either action would be a betrayal of my lord, of course, but surely petty treason is a lesser crime than high treason? So we must assume that Lord Richard has now hired a new sage, and they are both engaged in some deep, dastardly plot against the king."

Sir Neil nodded glumly.

"Again, if I were that sage and cooperating in my lord's perfidy, then I would make sure I was put in charge of security, and I would inspect every visitor *very* carefully. Even if a guest had been invited to come and join the plot, I would not trust him until I was sure of him. If anyone dropped in unexpectedly, I would be on him like a hungry flea. The longer the conspiracy has been underway, the greater the risk that the authorities have heard of it—as they now have, you say—so the tighter they must set their precautions. You must expect this to be true in Lincoln."

Neil scowled and drank from his bottle. "I told you, most of my men know nothing of my real purpose."

"They know that you rode to the sea as if Satan's own hounds were after you, managed a very fast crossing, and have ridden directly here, more than halfway across England. Your men are even now lounging around downstairs chattering with the baron's men, and no doubt grumbling about how hard they are being treated. They will do the same in Lincoln."

"Good point. I must warn them not to talk about our journey."

I shook my head. "And I, as the nefarious chief of security, am at once suspicious of this unnatural reticence, so I enchant their ale or mead to make them babble their stupid heads off. Or I do it to you. It would be easy: Adept Eadig could fix it for me. Your plan will not work, sir! If you barge in on Constable Richard as you are planning, and there is indeed a conspiracy, you won't see another dawn.

"Or else," I added before he could protest, "the enchanters will boil your brains to make you harmless. You will forget your toilet training and ever after be happy to play with kittens and marbles."

He stared at me in horror. "That is possible?"

"Given enough enchanters cooperating, almost anything is possible. If you think the rack or thumbscrews are painful, I could convince you otherwise—me as a traitor's accomplice, you understand, not me personally. Honest, godfearing enchanters do not meddle in black magic. But honest, godfearing men do not go around murdering people, either, and there are lots of murders."

I was feeling very happy about Eadig's attack on the crow by then. Had it not been for that, I suspect, Sir Neil d'Airelle would have refused to believe me, and I might have had to watch him and his entire escort ride to their deaths in Lincoln. As it was, the results were likely going to be very bad.

After a long, hard stare, he took another draft of wine and

wiped his mouth with his wrist. He was not drunk, but his head was not as clear as it should be. I could see him mounted on a sixteen-hand destrier and armed with a fourteen-foot lance being very good at skewering five-foot peasants, but cloaks and daggers were not his weapons.

"It might not be that bad," I continued. "The villains may simply wipe all suspicion out of your mind, so that you will hurry back to His Grace and assure him that he has no cause to worry."

To Sir Neil the prospect of deceiving the king was worse than anything, as I had known it would be.

"So what do you propose, Sage?"

At last!

"First, leave your train here. Go alone, with just your squire and perhaps one man-at-arms. We shall have to think up a way to explain why you are passing through, because Lincoln isn't handily on a road to anywhere. Could you realistically have been making a social visit on Baron Everard here, and be looking for a boat out? Lincoln is on the Witham River, which is navigable to the sea. You can be hoping to sail to London."

He thought about that, probably wondering how his peers would accept his going in without armed support: was that a laudable act of courage or being dishonorably sneaky? To men of war, reputation is everything. At last he nodded. "Continue."

"The baron here would give you a letter of introduction, no doubt, and you could expect hospitality until a boat was found. Meanwhile you inquire around, as does your squire."

Neil nodded, warming to the idea. "And I could locate Sir Courtney!"

"Who's he?"

"The old campaigner I mentioned, the one who wrote the letter to the king. He has some sort of job in the castle—drilling squires in the care of weaponry or something like that."

"Very good," I said, wondering if Neil could possibly be subtle enough to pull this off.

"I can reasonably take a page with me, too. That boy of yours will do splendidly. He could gossip with the other Saxon brats and the servants in a way Squire Piers and I cannot. If those people don't have an inkling as to what is happening, then nobody does."

Hell's vomit! He was subtler than I had expected. Now it was my turn to wonder about honor—could I decently expose young Eadig to this sort of danger?

"I must think about that, sir. Sending children into harm's way can seen as a breach of trust."

"Which matters more, your duty to the boy or your loyalty to the king?" He smirked as if he had caught me out.

"I cannot imagine them ever coming into conflict, sir. I am sure Eadig would jump at the chance of such an adventure, but dare you trust your own life and your mission to a child's discretion? If he lets slip the slightest hint that he is a spy, then he will drag you and your squire down into the pit with him."

Personally, I would sooner have trusted my life to Eadig than Neil himself in such a situation, but I had scored another point.

Neil scowled. "And you, Sage? What do you do in this—stay safe here in Nottingham and chant spells?"

"Certainly not. My leg limits the roles I can play. I cannot reasonably pretend to be a thatcher, for instance. But Lincoln is a large town. Although it has no academy that I know of, there are certain to be enchanters earning a living there, and they will have opinions about Lord Richard's sage. I can easily claim to be a newly graduated sage looking for employment."

Neil yawned. "I need to think about this. I'll decide in the morning."

I pried myself from the grip of the saints and martyrs, and took my leave.

chapter 6

arly next morning, I was again summoned to the guest room, where I found Sir Neil occupying the chair and Piers shaving him. Viewing the two of them so close together and without their helmets, I could see the fraternal likeness quite easily. Then, just as now, it was common for a knight to take a younger brother or cousin as a squire.

Also present, looming large against the light and wearing a dark expression, stood Sir Vernon Cheadle, Neil's deputy. Vernon was a big man with a big mustache—not a trim garnish like Piers's or the king's, but a massive black hedge across his face. Everything about him was large and heavy except his eyes, which were small and untrusting. He was not a man I should want as an enemy, and probably not as a friend either.

Not being offered, or even wanting, a renewal of my intimate association with the saints and martyrs, I remained standing, leaning my weight on my cane.

Neil raised a hand and Piers moved the razor away so he could speak. "Tell him, Vernon."

"Sir Neil has just explained," the other knight told me, "that he has decided to leave his train here at Nottingham and proceed to reconnoiter Lincoln Castle alone, so as not to arouse suspicion. He will take only his squire, the man Francois, and your boy, er . . ."

"Eadig."

"Yes, Eadig."

"A bold plan from a brave man," I remarked, and saw a flicker of anger in Neil's eyes as he detected my mockery. Neither Vernon nor Piers did, of course.

"You," Vernon continued, "will proceed to Lincoln on your own and see what you can learn by discreet inquiry among enchanters in the town. Today is Wednesday. You will report your success, if any, to Sir Neil at the west door of the cathedral after mass on Friday morning. If he fails to show up for that meeting, you will return at once here, to Nottingham, and put yourself under my orders."

"If we are to travel separately, how soon may I leave?"

Vernon looked to Neil for guidance. Piers took the chance to strop the razor on his shoe.

"As soon as you are ready," Neil said. "I must wait until the baron awakens, to appraise him of my needs."

Which time, I had gathered downstairs, might be several hours yet, for it had been well after midnight before the old souse was carried off to bed.

"If I may offer a suggestion, Sir Neil . . . How old do you think Cantor Eadig is?"

Piers paused just before he pinched his brother's nose. His brother frowned at this irrelevancy. "Fourteen? Fifteen?"

"Only one month short of seventeen, and he is wise beyond his years. If you need guidance on enchantment, sir, he can advise you almost as well as I can." I saw that I was spitting into a gale of prejudice and gave up. "Now, by your leave, sir, I shall give Adept Eadig his instructions and be on my way.

It would be best if we travel well apart, so that no one sees us together."

Going down that spiral staircase was even harder for me than going up, and that time I took it backward, like a ladder. Eadig was waiting for me at the bottom, and we headed off to the stable. I had already warned him that he might be asked to visit Lincoln as a spy, but I wouldn't force this on him. He had puffed out his chest and then bravely insisted that he would be proud to serve the king that way and wasn't sc . . . c . . . cared at all.

I ordered both Ruffian and Bon Appétit saddled and asked for guidance out of town. I was given instructions and a pitying look that said only an utter dolt should need them. In fact all I would need to do was follow the river northeast to Newark—another notable castle—and then continue along Fosse Way, another Roman road, until it joined Ermine Street. By then I would be able to see Lincoln. Ermine Street, of course, runs all the way from London to York, which is also known as Jarvik.

I took Eadig with me, because I planned to demonstrate something for which I certainly did not want an audience. Not far outside the city gate we found a patch of woodland where we would be unobserved. There I rode off the road, reined in, and dismounted. Eadig followed my lead and tethered the horses to a sapling, while I rummaged in my spell bag.

"I want to show you something I dared not try in the castle," I said. "On first glance, I would argue that this expedition is all a wild goose chase. As a trained logician, how would you propound this conjecture, varlet?"

Eadig was grinning. "Easy. An ancient warrior wrote a cryptic letter accusing two highly esteemed officials of high treason, which is ridiculous here in the center of England. The odds are that the old man has lost his wits to old age, or drink, or war wounds—he's delusional. To pay any heed to the charges would grossly insult one or both of the esteemed Sheriff Alured and Constable Lord Richard. But the king cannot just ignore such a threat. So he sends a very junior, expendable knight to scout and report back. If the sheriff or constable gets to hear of it and takes offense, he tosses Sir Neil into the moat and the king denies knowing anything about it."

Eadig had more brains than Sir Neil would know what to do with.

"You state the negative case succinctly, varlet. So how would you contend the opposing case?"

He'd known that I would ask him that. "The letter mentioned enchantment, you said? So the king would have had one of his enchanters evaluate it before he made his decision. It could have tested high for significance, which would justify sending Sir Neil to investigate, but also high for duplicity, which would explain why he told Neil to bring you along. Already we have received the substantiating testimony of the futhorc tiles, and the warning Healer Fulk gave you last night."

I complimented him again, thinking that being a *familiaris* could be a life-threatening profession. Kings' gifts are often double-edged.

"So your mission may be dangerous," I said, "even with someone smarter than Sir Neil. He's not exactly stupid, but he must be aware that the next few days will make or break his career. If he does run up against hostile magic, he'll be unmasked in minutes. I can show you one incantation that may come in handy if things get curdled. Can you construe this for me?" I brought out one of my scrolls, and between us we unrolled it.

He peered at it, turning it to the light. "Think so. *Hic non sum*? 'I am not here'?"

"Correct. It's a solo voice spell. Read out each versicle and tell me what it means."

Because in rehearsals we always read the text backward to prevent any dangerous mistakes, he began with the last phrase, which was the same as the first, *Hic non sum*, and did very well with the translation, needing only two corrections. Of course the text made even less sense that way round than it did forward: "Let no hawk see my shadow on the ground . . . no hound must track my scent . . . dull the ears of the owl . . . my shape is as the shape of the wind . . ." It invoked spirits of air, fire, water, and even the grasses of the forest.

"Very good," I said when he had finished. "It's a Release spell, obviously, and repeatable. I know it persists for at least two weeks, and I chanted it the night before we left Helmdon. So watch me. *Hic non sum*."

Eadig must have had an idea of what would happen, but he gasped. After a moment he reached out and poked a finger at where he had last seen me. I instantly reappeared. We both laughed.

"Invisibility?" he said.

"Not truly. There is no such thing as a real invisibility spell, but this one comes close. Three things can give you away. One is touch, as you discovered. If someone bumps into you, you're back again. Another is making a noise, and the third is movement. If anyone glimpses even a flicker where nothing should be moving, they'll see all of you. You must not attract attention in any way: not visibly breathe, or even blink. The safest place to invoke it is probably standing in a corner, face in. And then don't sneeze! Obviously it has its limits, but it might help you out of a tight spot."

He chanted it through in his fine treble and promptly vanished from my sight. Then he sniggered and was back again. After that I could do no more than give him my blessing, some money, and a warning to get his story straight with Neil, Piers, and Francois. Needless to say, I did not leave the vellum roll with him—if challenged, I could justify owning such a thing, but a page could not. I had no other suitable Release spells with me, and we had no time for him to memorize even one solo-voice spell of the Repeat type.

Together we chanted the *Mín færeld* to bless our respective journeys. Then we parted; he went back to Nottingham and I rode on to Lincoln.

As I watched him go, he looked so absurdly young to be sent into unknown dangers, that I very nearly changed my mind and called him back. Had I done so, it is likely that what later became known as the Boterel Conspiracy would have succeeded. Yet Eadig received very little credit for his part in defeating it, and even I did not fully understand how much he deserved more until I read the Confidential Report.

That report was commissioned by Robert de Beaumont, earl of Leicester and regent, some months later, after the cheers had died and the tears dried. He stressed that no one else was to read it, or hear any of its contents. Easy enough for sages! I sat Eadig down with ink, quills, and a pile of paper, then put him into a full-recall trance. A few days later he did the same for me. The result of our combined efforts was an enormous, overly wordy bore. When I read over what I had written, I was amazed at how many details had already escaped my everyday memory.

Ultimately the king put the report into the safekeeping of the enchanter general, namely me. I have used it to jog my memory several times already in writing this account, and it will enable me to relate Eadig's adventures in as much detail as my own.

Most of his life Ruffian had lacked enough exercise, and I wondered how he felt about that now, on a third straight day of our trek, but I was happy enough. The fine weather continued unbroken, and the traffic was slight.

I saw more harvesters hard at work there, too. I found it a comforting sight, for I had experienced wet summers and stormy falls, when the grain is beaten to the ground or fails to ripen at all. I knew the terror of famine that stalks the countryside then. I could even recall the days of the Anarchy, when King Henry's mother and uncle tore the land apart in their struggle for the crown. He had saved us from that, and I would resist any hint of treason against him until my dying breath.

I duly passed the Newark Castle, still under construction on the banks of the Trent. It meant nothing to me then, but I very nearly lost my head there, ten years later.

It was fortunate that I could not lose my way on that journey, because I would have had trouble understanding the locals' directions. I stopped several times to let Ruffian drink at a water trough and enjoy a brief rest, and every time someone soon arrived to fill a bucket at the well and, incidentally of course, find out who the stranger was. The dialect was very hard for me to follow. As Guy had warned me, this was the old Danelaw, the north-eastern half of England, which the great King Alfred had failed to wrest back from the invading Danes. All the same, it was more than two hundred years since his grandson united the whole land to claim the title of "King of the English," and I had never heard rumors of the Danelaw wanting to break loose again.

The land around Lincoln is flatter than a puddle, but the upper town, which includes the castle and cathedral, stands on a ridge, visible for hours before you reach it. Just short of the town, Ermine Street passes by Brayford Pool and then enters the lower town through the south gate. The sheer size of the castle looming over it impressed me as I approached, for it would be a very hard bone to chew, as long as it was properly garrisoned.

As I had told Sir Neil, I was reluctant to seek hospitality in religious houses, and a city as large as Lincoln was sure to boast at least one inn where Ruffian could have his rubdown and enjoy some well-earned oats. I asked some people where to look and understood little of what they told me, but their fingers spoke more clearly than their words, and all indicated that I should go up the hill. It was logical that visitors who could afford to pay for a bed would likely be those who had business in either the cathedral or the castle.

It was afternoon by then, and both Ruffian and I were weary, so I let him set his own pace as he trudged up the road called the Danesgate, with the cathedral towering above us to my right and the castle on my left. The cathedral I saw on that visit was not the present one, which collapsed in the earthquake of 1185. From what I have seen of the great work now in progress, the new one will be much larger and grander.

I barely noticed when Ruffian, seemingly tired of the long hill, turned off on a side way. I wasn't aware of telling him to do so. The alley was narrow and dark below overhanging eaves and second stories. Nowadays in larger cities it is becoming customary for stores to announce their business by hanging painted signs above their doors, but in those days we mostly relied on our knowledge of where everything was, or else we used our noses. Tanners, butchers, bakers, fishmongers, alehouses, even carpenters were easily discerned by their distinctive odors. Others displayed their wares on open counters at the front— ironware, vegetables, draperies, and such—while some tradesmen worked in their windows or yards, where they could be seen: barbers, cobblers, farriers, for example. Those in need of customers would run out to harass passersby. Failing all those indications, the slops and garbage thrown out on the street were often helpful.

One exception, even back then, was the pentacle that advertised a chantry. Ruffian stopped suddenly. I could not recall reining him in, although I must have done, because we were in front of a door bearing a pentacle, boldly marked with red paint.

"That was clever of you, Horse," I said. "Guy never warned me that you could read."

I didn't really believe that he had halted because he knew I wanted to locate a healer, but odd coincidences do happen around those who dabble in enchantment. I did need to speak with an enchanter or two. Why not now? If fortune smiles at you, why frown back at her? I might even beg a bed for the night. I dismounted—stiffly, and probably much to Ruffian's relief. I had just freed my cane from its sling on my back when the door flew open and a large man burst out and slammed it behind him.

I started to say, "Is the enchanter in?" but he did not give me a chance. He took hold of my horse's cheek strap, urging me by gabble and gestures to follow him. As near as I could make out he was saying, "This way, noble sir, you are most welcome. This way, what a splendid horse! And you have come far, sir. Did you have a good journey?" There was more, which I did not catch.

I now saw that, although he was large, he was not yet a man, but a husky youth of around fifteen, with a grin as wide as the River Nene. Clearly he had mistaken me for someone else, but I would rather explain that to the master of the house than argue with a yard boy, even, as I suddenly realized, was an unusually well-dressed and well-spoken yard boy. More likely he was the master's son.

He turned the corner into a gap between his house and the next, a space only just wide enough to take Ruffian and his saddlebags. Normally the way was barred by a gate, but someone on the other side was in the process of opening it for us. This was the sort of welcome I would be gratified to receive at an inn, and I felt guilty at accepting it under false pretenses.

Ruffian announced his approach with a loud whinny, which was answered from the poky little yard ahead. Trusting his judgment, I made no objection, just hobbled along behind, hearing bolts being shot on the gate behind me. A chestnut gelding was watching our arrival with interest, but did not contest it. The yard barely deserved the name, being merely a space between houses. It was obviously the gelding's normal abode, and was filled to capacity by the privy, a couple of water butts, a thatched rain shelter for the horse, and now two horses. The walls were two stories high, enough to keep thieves out and livestock in.

The boy began unstrapping my bulky saddlebags, as he must do before he could unsaddle Ruffian. I dared not let those out of my sight, for I would be almost useless as an enchanter without the incantations they contained. I was about to take the first bag, when another hand reached for it, and swung it out of my reach.

I turned to take my first look at the person who had let us in.

I blinked and took a second.

She was young, little older than the boy, and almost as large—as tall as I, big-boned, and buxom. She was the sort of woman destined to bear a dozen children and bloat up like a hay wain. Her gown of green and white was crisply clean; a cascade of red-gold hair hung down her back from under her bonnet. She had a round and merry face with blue eyes, a button nose, and a complexion as smooth as an egg, lacking any trace of the smallpox scars of city folk or the weathering that soon tarnishes farm girls. She did have a million or so freckles, enough to outnumber the stars of heaven, but I have always found freckles alluring and failed to understand why many women dislike them. She was certainly no classical beauty like the unlamented

Baroness Kilpeck I had encountered at Barton a couple of years earlier, but she would not lack offers for her hand when she was ready to consider them. Even in that gloomy little yard, she gave the impression of standing in full sunlight.

I carefully noted her unbound hair, which advertised that she was not yet married. When our eyes met, a twinkle in hers told me she had noticed my interest and was returning it. I smiled back, to show that the approval was mutual and she lowered her gaze modesty. Meanwhile she was holding my two heavy packs and bracing the door open with one of them, waiting for me to enter. I accepted the unspoken invitation and hobbled past her, into the house.

The doorway was narrow, and neither of us was small. We did not touch, but our noses were barely a finger width apart as I went by her. Like the boy, she was obviously wearing her best— church clothes, not workaday garb. She carried a fragrance of lilac and had darkened her ice-pale eyelashes.

Now I decided that the enchanter must have foreseen my arrival. I was reacting in exactly the same fashion as Sir Neil had on Monday, when he had found me anticipating his arrival—I was both annoyed and worried. There went secrecy! If any back-alley healer could predict my coming, then there was nothing to stop the sage or sages in the castle from foreseeing Piers's. My companions might be heading straight into a trap.

Furthermore, magic is like the law, in that it does not deal with trivialities. More and more this affair was coming to look important; the stakes must be very high.

The big lass let the door swing closed and followed me into the kitchen. She set down the bags gently, which in itself was unusual. A male porter would have dropped them.

The kitchen was roomier than most, large enough to hold a heavy plank table with room for the eight stools tucked out of the way below it. Like kitchens I had seen in the gentry's houses, it had the usual larder, water tub, chopping block, a work bench, shelves of pottery, hanging pans and nets of victuals, a large fire-place with a spit and a grille to hold pots, although currently the hearth was cold. There were stout bars on the window and clean flagstones on the floor. The owner was prosperous.

"My name is Durwin," I said. "The enchanter is home?"

Her smile faltered, as a summer meadow may darken when a cloud passes overhead. She nodded. "But he is indisposed, Your Wisdom."

"You know me?"

"I can feel the wards on your packs." The smile flashed back, teeth like pearls. She obviously considered that we were fencing and she had scored the first point.

Female enchanters or even cantors were a new and oddly worrisome idea to me. I could not have named a single one, they were so rare—probably because the biblical condemnation of witches was usually interpreted to apply only to women, not to men. Then it all fell into place. I had not been foreseen; I had been summoned. I drew a deep breath.

"So your name must be Lovise."

Her eyes widened. Second point to me.

chapter 7

i must have revealed my resentment, for Lovise shed her saucy attitude and assumed a more respectful manner, hands clasped, gaze on the floor.

"That is my name, Your Wisdom."

"And by what right did you summon me?"

"Our father, sir, Healer Harald Larson—he is urgently in need of aid, so Lars and I chanted the *Hwá wer.*"

That was a simple appeal for help, and I was surprised that its range was great enough to reach me in . . . in where? In Nottingham, or all the way to Helmdon? Surely not! But neither case sounded reasonable. "When did you do this?"

"This morning, Your Wisdom, a little time after Lauds."

The timing was paradoxical, for that would be just after I left Nottingham, so I had already been on my way. But the Wyrds had prophesied four days ago that I would meet with Lovise, and it was almost two weeks since the king had ordered Neil to collect me.

"Surely there are other healers in Lincoln who could help?"

"Could help but would not, Your Wisdom."

"How many?"

"Three others, sir, not counting the castle sage."

"And how many responded to your summons?"

"None, sir."

How long did a spell last if it was not implemented? Had the frustrated summons lingered until I rode within its reach? I could not recall such questions ever being discussed in Helmdon. I would need time to think about them later.

"What is his ailment? Is he here?"

"Upstairs, sir."

"If it is urgent, you had better show me."

Nodding, she led the way to the other door, and held it for me. Beyond lay a tiny hallway, very dimly lit, with the entrance to another room opposite, the street door to my right, and a steep staircase to the left.

Reluctant to demonstrate my mismatched legs for her inspection, I stepped aside and let her lead the way upward. I was rewarded with a good view of two very fine, surprisingly slender, ankles. At the top was a tiny landing, with a door on either side and a ladder up to a garret hatch.

I followed her into what was clearly her father's bedroom. I could have guessed that much even without seeing its occupant. The shutters stood open on that hot afternoon, so it was bright and airy enough, yet it had a shabby air, needing a coat of whitewash to freshen it. It was the abode of someone long settled in their ways, someone who no longer cared for change.

The bed almost filled the room, and the man in the bed lay on his back with his eyes shut, breathing stertorously. He was indeed old, older than I would have expected Lovise's father to be, with wisps of white hair trailing on the pillow and silver stubble on a scraggy face that had sagged over missing teeth. On that scorching day he was covered by a single sheet, and his bare arms lay exposed outside it. Before I could touch him, his eyes opened and struggled to focus on me.

He began to mumble incoherently. "Who's this why strange man youth in my room the hussy en'nertaining strange men measuring me I'll be bound coffin maker sniffing at me thinks I'm rotting worms, worms not a priest . . ." And so on.

I walked around to the window side, where he was, and bent to study him. Listening to him, I had first thought that he must be dead drunk, but I detected no ale or wine on his breath. Lovise stood on the other side of the bed, watching me intently, and I didn't think a woman who could identify an enchantment by touch would have mistaken intoxication for serious disease. I considered a stroke, but his pupils were the same size and his mouth showed no twist. His pulse was steady and beat at much the same rate as my own. He was not feverish. In fact . . . startled, I looked up at Lovise and she nodded.

What my fingers sensed when I felt his forehead was chill— not the chill of a corpse, but the flavor of enchantment, learned by every sage in his training. Lovise had detected it on my warded saddlebags. So Harald Larson had been cursed? Helmdon's standard instruction was skimpy on curses, because we never met them. My treatment for this one would take some planning.

I nodded in the direction of the door and led the way back downstairs, while hearing Larson continuing to mumble to an empty room.

"Please sit, Your Wisdom," she said as she followed me into the kitchen. "You must need refreshment after your journey, and I can talk while I prepare something for you. All cold, I am afraid, because we keep no fire on such a warm day, but we have fresh bread and ham and onions and of course our fine local cheese. And fresh, juicy berries, picked today."

She rinsed her hands, gave me water and a towel for mine. She produced a large pottery beaker and filled it with ale, bustling around efficiently. Housewife as well as enchanter—she was talented for her years. How many years? I wondered. Not yet twenty and perhaps much younger, for her size might be misleading.

"What do you think ails your father, Lovise?"

"He has been cursed, Your Wisdom."

"Please call me Durwin. Your father has been tutoring you in enchantment."

"Me and Lars, too. Just healing enchantments, sir, er Durwin. None of the higher philosophical arts like they teach in academies."

"Which are mostly hocus-pocus to deflect the Church's bigotry. Enchantment is our heart and soul. And do you know who did this to him?"

The boy, Lars, swept in from the yard, saw the bucket in which his sister had deposited our wash water, scooped it up, and swept back out with it. If you own a horse, you always know where to dispose of excess water.

"I can guess," Lovise said grimly, sawing at a crusty loaf that both looked and smelled delicious. "Healing's become a dangerous business in Lincoln of late."

"Then I need to hear the whole story."

Lars returned and flopped down on the bench across from me, still grinning. He grabbed for a slice of bread before his sister could block him. He had not yet lost the juvenile energy that compelled him to do everything as fast as possible.

"My name is Durwin," I told him. "I'm a healer. Your sister's about to tell me what ails your father."

"Sage laid a curse on him." Evidently Lars could chew and talk at the same time, but he should be heard and not seen when doing so.

"What sage?"

"The constable's sage, Quentin of Lepuix."

"You don't know that!" Lovise snapped. "Take our . . . You will stay the night with us, Your Wisdom?"

I glanced at the window to judge the height of the sun. It seemed that I was about to obtain exactly the sort of information I had come to Lincoln to find, so I must not leave before I had heard it. But I had already learned enough to confirm that Sir Neil and his party were heading into danger, so should I go galloping back along the Nottingham road in the hope of intercepting them? I obviously couldn't do both at the same time, evening was drawing in, and I had a patient upstairs in need of treatment. Ruffian and I were both tired. I must concentrate on my own mission and leave my associates in God's hands.

"That's a very kind offer, which I am happy to accept."

"Take our guest's bags upstairs, Lars."

Lars obediently stuffed the rest of the bread in his mouth and disappeared, heavy packs and all. I heard his boots thundering up the stairs. He reminded me of a colt named Pepper, dropped by one of the Pipewell Abbey's mares when I was a child, all legs and frantic haste.

"I wish I had his energy," I sighed.

"But not his wits, sir."

"They did not strike me as lacking."

She smiled apologetically. "No, I misspoke. He is oversudden, is all. There is nowt wrong with Lars that he won't soon grow out of."

"If he grows much more you'll need a bigger house. Now tell me the story."

"Yesternight our father went to a meeting. When he failed to return by sunset, we began to worry. I sent Lars off to bed and waited up. The watch brought him—Father, I mean—home after midnight."

"In his present condition?"

"Worse, for he was reeking of wine. His clothes were soaked with it. If he had not been who he is—if one man in the watch had not recognized him and they had taken him for a common drunk—they would have locked him up in the stocks until morning." She slid a platter across to me and began to load it with ham, onions, bread, and cheese.

I reached eagerly for the knife on my belt. "Why?" I asked. "What reason would the constable's sage have to lay a curse on your father and tip wine over him? Is he a practical joker?"

"Far from it, Your Wisdom." Lovise refilled my beaker, ignoring my protests that I must keep my head clear. "Listen, sir, er, Durwin. For years there were three healers in Lincoln town: Nerian, Peter, and Harald. Plus the castle sage, of course, to look after the health of the garrison. This past spring, when Sir Alured took over as sheriff, he brought his own sage with him, Quentin of Lepuix. Bjarni, the house sage, had served the de la Haye family since before the Battle of Lincoln, more than twenty years ago, but Sir Alured told Lord Richard to dismiss him. Bjarni and his wife moved into the town and he set up shop as a public healer, a fourth. The other three made him welcome, for they had all the work they needed and he was well known and respected in the town. But Bjarni died a couple of weeks later, may he rest in peace."

"Amen." Healer Fulk had told me of Bjarni's dismissal, of course, but had not mentioned his sudden death.

A rockslide out in the hallway announced Lars's return. He flopped down on the bench even before the door slammed shut behind him. Lovise pushed a loaded platter across to him.

"Did Bjarni die of a broken heart?" I asked. "A sudden change in a man's life can do that."

At last Lovise sat down to eat her own portion, notably smaller than the other two. "None know. He just died. He was replaced by Walter, and none know where he came from. Or what good he does, for I hear that nobody consults him. Soon after that, Healer Nerian was bitten by a mad dog and died. He was replaced by another stranger, Tancred. And in July, Peter decided to sell his practice and take employment as house sage to some lord down south, near Wintanceaster."

"And who replaced him?"

"Henri of somewhere."

So three healers of Saxon or Danish lineage—Bjarni, Nerian, and Peter—had been replaced by four with French names: Quentin, Walter, Tancred, Henri. And the last native healer lay upstairs in a coma. My hopes that I might learn something from the local healers' community were being amply rewarded already, but not quite in the way I had expected. "There's a pattern there, certainly. And now Harald . . . ?"

"Now Harald has had a narrow escape from being denounced as a public drunk," his daughter said bitterly. "What would happen to his practice then? Nobody wants to be treated by a sot. Luckily business is slow just now, because so many folk are busy out harvesting. I managed to treat the few patients who came in today, implying to the nosy parkers that Father had been called away to treat a noble lady in the country. Lars helped me."

"I held them down while she stitched them," Lars explained. I assumed that he was just joking, but wasn't certain and didn't ask.

"What happened after the watch brought your father home?"

"I wakened Lars to help me carry him upstairs."

"Warn't enough room for two," Lars said indignantly. "I put him over my shoulder and carried him up by myself."

"You must be a very strong young man," I said. He leered at the compliment and nodded proudly. I tried not to think what could have happened had he overbalanced on that precipitous staircase.

"Lars washed him and put him to bed," Lovise continued. "That was when we realized that he wasn't drunk at all. This morning we hunted through his grimoires to find an antiphon. We found two, but neither worked. So we chanted the *Hwá wer.*"

"Father taught us that one in case we needed help when he wasn't around," her brother explained.

"Did you feel acceptance?"

Lovise said, "Yes," and her brother nodded.

"Faint, though," he said.

The *Hwá wer* is a cry for help. If they had directed it correctly, it should have brought every healer in town. It would not have brought carpenters or thatchers, but healers should all have felt the urge to go and see what was wrong with Harald Larson, their colleague and, hopefully, friend. Even if they didn't feel it consciously, they should have found themselves heading this way when they had intended to go somewhere else, just as I had. The fact that they had been able to resist the call showed that they had armored themselves in advance with a counter spell. The stench of conspiracy was growing stronger.

"Yet no one responded?"

"Only you, Your . . . sir."

"Call me Durwin, both of you. I'm a licensed sage from Helmdon Academy, but if anyone asks, pretend that I'm your mother's sister Mary's son from Pipewell, and a man-at-arms who limps because he was wounded in battle, fighting for the king in Wales last year." I watched their eyes brighten as they realized that I was taking their story seriously. "What was this meeting your father attended yesterday?"

Lovise added more water to her ale. "Back when Sage Bjarni was sage, he entertained the healers to dinner at the castle every month. They would talk business: cases they had seen, so that they were all warned of any serious outbreaks, and could count supplies of potions, in case there might going to be a shortage. They might delegate someone to warn the apothecaries about those." She took a sip of her ale. "Or they might meet with a visiting sage, and so on. Quentin continued the custom. After his dismissal, Bjarni never attended, though."

"Understandably so. I'm sure I would not, in the circumstances."

"So that was where Father went yesterday—to the castle, to dine with the sage and the other healers from the town."

The four with French names. And if they all knew about his curse—had even, perhaps been present when it was chanted—then they would have known to resist the next day's *Hwá wer*. Conspiracy now seemed certain, but what sort of conspiracy? At best it might be no more than a bad case of anti-Saxon prejudice—Sheriff Alured from Normandy or Anjou disliked or distrusted Saxon sages and had replaced them all with his countrymen cronies, but even that theory would seem to have required a murder or two.

At worst this might tie in with the king's high treason suspicions, although I recall that I could not immediately see why it should, which in retrospect was incredibly stupid of me. If Quentin and Sheriff Alured were using black magic in the castle in some way, why did they need to purge the town's existing healers? The replacements, it must be assumed, were trusted to support the treason, but I could not see why the town healers needed know what the two villains were up to behind their great ramparts. I wished that I could discuss this with Guy, or some of the other Helmdon sages.

I had been silent too long. Lars suddenly burst out, "Can you help us, Your Wisdom?"

His sister tut-tutted at his manners, but I nodded.

"I will certainly try. I am sure I have some spells back at Helmdon that would be useful in this case, but I brought nothing like that with me. Let me see the texts you tried last night."

Lars was gone in a blink. *Hic non est.*

I knew all the theory about dealing with curses, but I wished I had some practice at it. I knew how to remove a warding from a door or a strongbox, but dare I try something like that on a person? I knew that my grimoires back in Helmdon included several spells dealing with curses, but I had neither studied them nor brought any with me. I did not even know what would happen to Harald Larson if he were left untreated— would he recover on his own or starve to death, unable to feed himself? Before I could ask Lovise whether her father was accepting nourishment, Lars returned.

He brought with him the largest book I had ever seen, both in page size and thickness. He carried it clutched in both arms, and even our resident strongman clearly found it quite a load. The grimoires I knew were mostly made of the best parchment, such as lambskin, but these larger pages meant thicker, heavier leather, probably from cattle. That might be cheaper, or the sheer size of the volume might be intended to impress the healer's patients.

When Lars dropped this tome on the table, the dishes jumped. Lovise went to help him. Together, brother and sister untied the ropes and raised the front cover. The book was obviously very old, with many of the pages starting to crack. The spells they had tried were marked by ribbons.

I placed a candle closer and bent to read, while my companions waited anxiously for my learned opinion. The first was useless for me, because it was written in runes, and not the futhorc I knew. The language was probably Danish, but it might as well have been Coptic or Farsi for all the good it did me.

The other, *Abi maledictum*, was in Latin—rather bad Latin, although that might not matter—and right away I checked the second and third versicles, for that was where trip wires were most often set. Sure enough, there was one in the first line of the second versicle. I read the whole spell through three times, and everything else seemed to make as much sense as spells ever do.

"Did you feel any acceptance when you chanted either of these?" I asked.

"No, sir," Lovise said.

I asked if they had any chalk or charcoal, and Lars found a fragment of charcoal in the hearth. I scored out the trip wire. Boy and girl both gasped in horror, so I knew that their father had taught them the traditional belief that the given texts were sacred and immutable.

"It will wipe off if I am wrong," I told them. "But I am certain that this word is incorrect. That is why you could not gain acceptance."

Lars exploded. "But how can you know that, Your Wisdom?"

"It is what is taught at Helmdon," I said, not mentioning that I had taught the teachers. If I was wrong, of course, neither Lars nor Lovise would ever trust me again, and I already knew that I would very much like to impress Lovise. I read the whole incantation over once more, but found no more trip wires. "Let's try this again. I am sure that I have solved the problem."

My two companions lit up like festive bonfires.

So, back upstairs we went, with Lars lugging the massive grimoire and Lovise some spare candles, which she proceeded to light in her father's room, already dimming as evening drew in. He began to mumble angrily about waste, flames, hellfire, and soap.

We laid the book on the unoccupied side of the bed, and I realized that Lovise regarded herself as senior to her brother, and so expected to be my cantor. My hosts had not prepared separate song sheets for the parts, so both of us would have to read off the original. I had never chanted with a woman before. We had to stand very close and that was distracting, especially the fascinating scent of lilac.

"Ready?"

"Ready," she said.

"Abi maledictum . . ." I proclaimed before I realized that we had not agreed on a pitch. *Concentrate, dammit!* I carried on to the end of the versicle, and Lovise came in with the first response, an octave higher, but matching my key perfectly. Her voice was as impressive as she was, rich and strong. As we reached the halfway point, I felt the thrill of acceptance coming.

I dared not to turn to look at my assistant, but I could glance across at Lars, and he must have been watching his sister, for he suddenly broke into that enormous grin of his.

We finished. We all stared at the patient.

After a lone moment, just about when hope had died, Larson's eyes flicked open. He frowned, stared around the room and then fixed his gaze on me. "And just who in hell might you be?"

"My name is Durwin, Your Wisdom. How do you feel?"

"I feel in exceeding good health, but I want to know who you are and what you are doing in my chamber practically leaning on my daughter."

"I am a healer, sir. You were in need of my services. We can discuss the situation more fully downstairs, at your convenience."

So there was evil thaumaturgy at work in Lincoln, and I had just struck a first blow against it! That I had walked into a trap did not occur to me until later.

chapter 8

ars remained behind, and I could hear his excited jabber as he told his father all about me. I followed Lovise downstairs and into the kitchen.

She spun around. "That was a miracle! Oh, Your Wisdom, I don't know how to thank you enough."

I was shocked to hear myself say, "A kiss would be ample reward."

Lovise was understandably startled. This was not a royal palace, where lechery is always rampant and tolerated if the perpetrators are of sufficiently high rank. In small-town England back then, public kissing would be regarded as salacious behavior even if the participants were legally married. For a man to suggest such a thing to a woman he had known for less than an hour was gross immorality. She should have screamed for her father and brother to come and defend her honor. Alternatively, she should have grabbed up an iron pan and dented my skull with it.

Instead she smiled nervously. "Just a small one."

It began as a small kiss, lips pursed, and my hands holding her shoulders gently and I swear that this was all I intended, but our embrace grew more urgent by mutual consent. Her arms closed around me, mine embraced her. Soon we were locked as tightly as if breathing didn't matter anymore, and our lips were anything but pursed. It was I who called a halt at last, worried that her father might be already dressed and headed in our direction. She was flushed and breathless, and so was I. Neither of us had expected that to happen.

Other men have admitted to me—on the few occasions when I plucked up the courage to ask—that the first kiss between a man and a woman can be extremely informative, and that one certainly was. Had Harald Larson burst into the room at that moment and shouted that I had shamed his daughter and must marry her to save her reputation, I would have thanked him with all my heart.

And I suspected that Lovise, the gorgeous, stupendously desirable Lovise was of similar mind. Avoiding my eye, she murmured, "Was that more magic, Durwin?"

"Just the magic Eve worked on Adam, Lovise."

"Always the man blames the woman."

"But always he is very grateful."

Yes, this is a tale of love at first sight. The rich are likely to be betrothed as children, for commercial or political advantage; love has nothing to do with it. Wooing is faster among the poor: boy meets girl from next village at harvest time or spring fair—looks nice, talks nice, smells nice, tastes nice, feels nice . . . come and meet the family.

I was no longer poor, but I certainly was not rich. I did have prospects as one of the king's *familiares*. Two days ago Helmdon had granted me my green cape and Sir Neil had confirmed that the king remembered me and wanted me in his service. Suddenly I had become a man of stature in the world and the prospect of marriage was no longer an impossible dream. Even if the king paid me little—and kings are always notoriously short of ready cash—my title would allow me to earn a good living as a healer. Now, suddenly, Lovise! Was I just letting my imagination run away with me? She almost seemed to be waiting for me to seek a second kiss.

But instead she said was, "Would you be gracious enough, *Your Wisdom*, to explain to me how you knew what change to make in that incantation?"

I understood the return to formal address. "Do please sit, Maid Larson." I plopped myself down on a stool. She obeyed, not too close to me. We carefully did not look each other in the eye.

"The key phrase was *Qui nemo illa dixisse*, which doesn't make any sense. What's 'nobody' doing in there? Take him out and you get *Qui illa dixisse*, meaning roughly, 'Whoever spoke those words,' which does make sense, and the person who transcribed that spell put the extra word in there precisely to make sure that the spell *wouldn't* work! Then, anybody who stole his copy would find it worthless. If the master himself needed to use it, he just had to remember to omit *nemo*. Understand?"

She nodded at once. "So you have to look for nonsense words?"

"More or less. Sometimes the trip wires are a little more subtle, but the rhythm usually gives them away. Second or third versicles are favorite hiding spots, because later in the incantation the singers may sense the start of acceptance and notice when it cuts off."

"You're telling me that we could alter old spells to fit special cases?"

She was well ahead of me already. "I imagine that would be possible, within limits. I wouldn't try to change *Abi Maledictum* enough that I could use it to make—" I was about to say, "a beautiful girl fall in love with me," but fortunately stopped myself in time. "'Cure warts,' for instance."

I was saved by the boot-avalanche noise of Lars descending the stairs. Lovise hastily jumped up and pretended to be tidying the table. Her brother burst in—he seemed to see every door as a jousting opponent.

"He's coming . . . What—? What's wrong?"

"Nothing's wrong," his sister snapped. "Go, bring me a bucket of water."

He then looked at me. His eyebrows rose. I tried to assume the Face of Absolute Innocence. Lars grinned understandingly—and approvingly, I was relieved to see, because he could have thrown me out into the street and my horse after me. He spun around and stormed out through the back door, with bucket.

Then Harald entered by the inner doorway. Seen upright and conscious, he was tall and gaunt, almost haggard, so that I wondered about the state of his health. On top of his simple gray robe, he wore a brown healer's cape, and that warned me that I might be going to have trouble. He leaned a hand on the door jamb for a moment as he surveyed me, his expression grim.

Fair enough—he was three times my age, a respected man in his city, while I was an unknown and uninvited rapscallion whom he had discovered weaving spells in his bedroom. His pride had been wounded much more than his physical well-being. I did not care about reward—I had already claimed that, or even gratitude, for I had only been performing a task for which I had been trained, but I did need Harald's help and cooperation in my mission.

I rose and bowed. "Honored to meet you, brother."

"Durwin, you said?"

So we were not to be brothers. "Aye, sir. Durwin of Pipewell." I could have named myself Durwin of Helmdon, but that would have sounded like a putdown worse than his rejection of my offer of friendship. I could guess that Harald Larson was no graduate of any learned college. He was a folk healer, who had garnered his expertise and inherited his grimoire from his father or some other local seer. His home indicated that he prospered in his profession, so he must be skilled in it, but his overall knowledge would be strictly limited to his giant-sized book of spells.

"My son informs me that I owe you thanks for my recovery."

Lovise was watching in silence from the far side of the big table.

"I was merely doing what the ethics of our profession require me to do, sir. I am impressed with the way your son and daughter responded to your misfortune, and am glad that I was able to help them."

He nodded uncertainly. "I am curious to know what brought you by so fortuitously. Let us go into my sanctum and share a glass of wine."

Lars hurled the back door open and entered, dribbling water from a brimful bucket. His gaze flickered around, appraising the body language and emotional temperature.

"With respect, Healer," I said, "I would prefer that both Lars and Lovise be present while I explain the situation."

The old man's chin jerked up as he took offense. "For what reason?"

Stubborn as a mule!

"Reasons of state." I drew out a stool and sat down. "Shut the door, please, Lars."

He did, but no one else moved, and a change in tactics was indicated. I slapped a hand on the table. "Your Wisdom! I know I look young to you, but must I go upstairs and rummage through my pack to find my green cape before you will accept that I am a qualified sage? Surely I have already demonstrated my skills to you? I have come to Lincoln by order of King Henry himself and I demand and require your help in the task he set me."

I have often found since then that the king's name can be as effective as a blow to the head with a spiked morningstar. Three shocked people hastily grabbed stools and sat down. Lars was openmouthed at hearing that he was in the presence of someone who had actually met His Grace. Lovise's expression was more guarded, for beautiful maidens must beware young men who make wild claims about their own importance. Her father seemed even more mistrustful.

But now I could smile. "Thank you."

"And what task is this, *Sage?*"

"To investigate rumors of black magic being performed in his castle of Lincoln. A couple of years ago I was fortunate enough to perform a task that drew me to the Lord King's attention. He rewarded me handsomely and funded the rest of my training at Helmdon. Two days ago, on Monday, one of his trusted housecarls arrived on my doorstep with orders to accompany him here for the purpose I just mentioned. That man has gone to the castle to make direct inquiries there. He asked me to inquire among the enchanter community of the city—and already I have learned from Lovise that all is not well."

No one spoke.

"Your daughter has told me how Sage Bjarni and Healers Peter and Nerian were forced out of their livelihoods, all in a matter of a few weeks. That in itself, I find highly suspicious. That two of them also lost their lives is, frankly, terrifying. Now, sir, will you tell me what transpired yesterday after you went to the castle?"

"I wish I could." Harald rubbed his eyes as if that might clear his memory. "A boy brought a note yesterday morning—"

"Just after Terce," Lars interjected helpfully; he was silenced by a glare from his father.

81

"A note from Sage Quentin, inviting me to dine with him to meet his new cantor. Of course I accepted—how could I not? I walked up there as the cathedral bell rang for vespers and was admitted to the castle through the east gate. I was escorted to a room I had not seen before in a building I had never visited before, and there I met them all, already assembled: Quentin, Walter, Henri, and Tancred. Plus there was a newcomer, a cantor, Corneille Boterel."

Yet another French name, I noted. "A boy? A man?"

"Corneille? Oh, a man, probably about my age. Stocky, almost plump. Black hair and beard. Much older than I would have expected for a cantor. Cantors are usually apprentices, as you know."

"But a house sage must employ fairly complex spells for healing and so on. How did Quentin cope without a helper?"

"Oh he didn't," Harald said. "At least Bjarni, his predecessor, didn't. He would always employ an apprentice and a varlet, too. When the apprentice was ready to strike out on his own, the varlet stepped into his shoes and another lad into his."

"So hiring an older man..." Something was niggling at me, a thought I couldn't quite put my tongue on. Corneille? Corneille? ... "Did you find out anything more about this Corneille man?"

"I do not remember! I know Quentin himself handed me a silver goblet and asked me what I thought of the new wine. And that's all."

"There were no servants present?"

"None. I assumed they would bring the food later."

"Did you ever meet any of Quentin's previous cantors, or any of Bjarni's cantors?"

Harald shook his head. "I knew them. Bjarni would include them in our gatherings and introduce them, but I never recall being invited to a welcoming party for one of them."

I saw Lovise bite her lip, so I invited her into the conversation with a questioning look.

"He's driven out all the other locals," she said angrily. "Now he's brought in this Corneille man to replace Father!"

Harald frowned, but did not openly reproach his daughter for interrupting serious man talk. He said, "They know better than to suggest it. I have already refused two of their offers, explaining that I am the third generation Larson to practice healing at this location and I am training my son to succeed me."

A conspiracy aimed at high treason would not shy at lesser crimes like murder; I wondered if Lars had been fortunate not to be hit by a falling chimney pot and how long his luck would last. "Apparently the potion he gave you was intended to steal your wits," I said. "They must have chanted a spell over you to make you act like a drunk, because you were certainly enchanted when I first saw you. They spilled wine on you to make you smell like a drunk, and then they took you out and dumped you in a gutter somewhere to look like a drunk."

"I was very lucky that you arrived at my house so fortuitously," Harald said coldly.

I saw Lovise go suddenly tense. Her father, I realized, had spoken in a curiously flat tone. Then Lars caught the implication too, and bared his teeth. They were all wondering whether I might be another member of the conspiracy, and I could not blame them.

"Yes, you were, weren't you?" I said. As coincidences go, that one was a whopper, and I needed a moment to work it out.

"I have not lied to you or your children. I am not in league with Sage Quentin! If you want me to swear to that on a Bible or some holy relic, I will be happy to do so. Let me suggest another explanation for your apparent good fortune. Last Monday, when the king's messenger arrived on my doorstep in Helmdon, he found me already packed and ready to go, and my cantor also, with our horses saddled. Not being familiar with arcane powers, he was both furious and deeply suspicious. The explanation was that I had foreseen his arrival. Foresight is not easy for us, but it is possible."

"I have never met it," Harald said, not even trying to hide his distrust.

"You have now, I think. The incantation we were trying did not tell us any details, just that armed men from the king would come for me, with a hint that we would be proceeding to Lincoln. If I could foresee the king's men arriving last Saturday, so could Quentin yesterday! After all, for me they were an opportunity, but they are a danger to him, if he is truly working evil in the castle. He may even have foreseen that I would find you, the only honest enchanter left in the city, so he . . ." Then my thoughts shifted like snow sliding off a roof. Had I blundered already?

Lovise said, "Go on, Dur . . . Your Wisdom."

"As you say, he may have been trying to disgrace your father, to create a job opening for this Corneille man."

She nodded.

"Or," I continued, "he may have been setting a trap for me. By removing the spell on you, Healer, I have revealed the presence of another enchanter come to the town. I do not wish to belittle your own talents and skills, my lady. You and Lars did very well. Your appeal for help would have been felt by the others—Henri and the rest, but they would have known to resist its call and would have had means to resist it. If my suspicions are correct, sir, you may have a messenger from the castle knocking at your door before nightfall to check on your condition and find out if anyone did respond to that appeal. Very shortly, in fact," I added with a glance at the evening shadows gathering outside the window.

"If he can foresee the future, won't he already know the answer?" Lars said.

"Not necessarily. Prophecies are spotty and often obscure. They rarely go into details. I was not forewarned that I would be required to deal with anything so dire as the conspiracy you have revealed to me. If I had been, I would have brought much stronger spells with me."

But if this sinister Sage Quentin truly was conjuring up prophecies, then he had probably foreseen Sir Neil also. Neil was a belted knight, sworn to risk his life for his king. Eadig wasn't. What horrors had I sent the boy into? I must just hope that the *Battre le tambour* would warn him in time for him to escape the trap.

And I could see that I had misjudged the problem. "What sort of person is Sheriff Alured?"

Harald shook his head. "I have not met him. He seems to be honest and fair in his judgments—well-thought-of so far, although most people are reserving judgment."

"And Constable Richard?"

"Ah." He shook his head sadly. "Not the man he was. I have not been consulted, of course, but by all accounts his decline has been so rapid that I fear he must have had a fit this summer, or perhaps more than one."

"His condition has worsened since the new sage arrived?"

They all knew enough about enchantment to understand what I was hinting. Now even Harald seemed convinced.

"You think he could have been cursed also?"

"I misjudged the problem," I said. "I thought the traitor must be either the sheriff or the constable, but now I see that the new Sage Quentin is much more likely. He came with Sheriff Alured?"

Again Harald shook his head. "No, just after. According to

what Bjarni told me, he came alone, a healer looking for employment. Bjarni made him welcome. A week or so later, Lord Richard dismissed Bjarni and replaced him with Quentin."

That was not quite what I had been told by Lovise or Healer Fulk the previous evening, but Harald probably had much more reliable information.

I sat for a moment, tapping my fingers on the table . . . then I realized that I was beating time with a very faint rhythm—a drum? *Da-dum-da-dum* . . . It was soft, and yet it did not seem far away.

"Can you hear something? A drumming?" I asked, looking at Lars and Lovise, whose ears were younger and sharper than Harald's or my own. They both shook their heads.

Came a loud knock on the street door, and the drumming faded away. I had been warned, so it was no longer needed.

We all jumped, even I, who had predicted it. Harald, naturally assuming that my accomplice had arrived on time, gave me the sort of look a genuine enchanter gives a mountebank who uses sleight of hand to work fake magic. He heaved himself to his feet.

"No, please!" I said. "Let Lovise answer it, just as she has been responding all day. If it is a serious malady she can call you. Otherwise, I don't want the enemy to know that you have been helped."

I thought he was about to refuse me and insist on his duty as a healer, et cetera, but his daughter reacted faster. She jumped up, reached the door, and went out to answer the summons, just as the knock was repeated, even louder.

chapter 9

(Eadig's account, faithfully transcribed without censor)

it was almost noon before Sheriff Everard was available to
sign the letter of introduction that Sir Neil d'Airelle needed.
By then the valiant knight was in such a fever of impatience
that he left without waiting for dinner, galloping out the castle
gate with Squire Piers at his side, followed by the man-at-arms
Francois and his new, pretend page, Eadig.

The sun was so hot they could not push the horses hard,
and whenever their pace slackened, hordes of flies rushed in to
pester them. The d'Airelle brothers talked together and rarely
even looked back to see if their followers were following. Eadig
was annoyed to see that the others had all acquired fresh horses,
borrowed from Sheriff Everard, while he was still riding poor
Bon Appétit. Granted that he wasn't much of a load, the gelding
was weary after two very long days' travel. He was neither built
nor trained for such long distance labor.

Francois was a grizzled old warrior of about forty winters,
due to hang up his sword soon. His French was hard to understand and he had trouble with Eadig's, but he was quite good

company. For the first few furlongs they chatted about nothing, like the hills they couldn't see because there weren't any, but eventually they got down to predictable nosiness.

"So you're really a sorcerer?"

"I'm an adept. That's like a squire. I mix ink, clean off writing blocks, sweep out sanctums, gather herbs, grind potions." Eadig tried to make it sound as dull as possible.

"But you'll be a sorcerer when your balls drop?"

"They're already hanging too low for this damned saddle, thank you. And I don't think I'll ever be an enchanter. See, my old man sent me to Helmdon to learn reading and reckoning. He'd sent my brother, Ereonberht, to monastery school to be taught his letters, but they taught him to be a monk instead. Now he's Brother Pious."

"Easier to spell, I expect. And the sorcerers are teaching you to be a sorcerer?"

"They're trying, but I think the old man will haul me back home soon." Annoyed at all the questions, Eadig recalled Durwin telling him that the best method of defense was attack. "How many men've you killed?"

"Three or four. Wasn't no older than you when I started."

"G'wan! Don' believe you."

Thus began a long and entertaining account of Francois's early life, first as a mercenary and later as a king's retainer. Eadig didn't believe all of it, but the most incredible part of it was the campaign of 1147, which Eadig knew to be true, because I had told him the same story. Francois had actually been there, beginning his warrior career by helping the young Henry invade England.

It was back when his mother, Empress Maud, had been forced to abandon her effort to drive King Stephen off his ill-gotten throne. That was when her precocious son, aged all of fourteen, had raised an army of his own, mostly mercenaries, and invaded England. He had met with very little success, trying to besiege castles when he had no proper siege engines and not nearly enough men.

"Pretty soon the lads were drifting over the skyline," Francois said, "on account of them not being paid. No man wants to fight on an empty belly. The prince, as we called him back then, couldn't even afford a ship to take us home again. He wrote to his mum, and his dad, and they both refused to help. So then he wrote to Stephen, his uncle, the man he was trying to depose, and asked him for money. Took some nerve, that did! But Stephen sent it to him, just to be rid of the nuisance."

They both guffawed. "That might've cost less than sending an army after him," Eadig said.

"Never thought of that. Whatever the reason, I was sure glad to get back home."

Eadig made an effort to learn a thing or two about Sir Neil d'Airelle. Turned out that there wasn't much to learn. He traced his lineage back to Julius Caesar and some Gaulish queen, but Caesar was known to have fathered half the inhabitants of France. Neil was admired for his maniacal, suicidal jousting and boar hunting, but that was about all. The king, Francois hinted, had sent him off on a bootless errand to get a rival out of the way while he—Henry, king of the English, count of Anjou, count of Maine, duke of Aquitaine, duke of Normandy, duke of Brittany, et cetera—tupped a certain winsome maiden.

Eadig was pleased to hear this low opinion of Sir Neil, because it implied that the king hadn't put much stock in the story of treason and magic, which would be a very nasty mixture. But the English liked to think better of their liege lord. "He's married! Do kings really do that?"

"All the time, sonny. Even more than other men, 'cos they've got more money. Why do you think he sent Pretty-boy Neil all the way over here?"

"He's supposed to be recruiting archers for the war."

Francois said, "Oui?" making it sound very negative. "His brother's been spreading stories about you being able to kill crows with magic. 'S that true?"

"Naw, I just stun 'em. They taste better that way."

That set Francois off on a long story about a time he'd been in a city being besieged, and how he'd been forced to eat rats—and raw at that.

"I don' think I'd ever get that hungry," Eadig said.

"You try it, sonny. After three days without food, you'll eat cockroaches. So tell me about this boss of yours, the gimpy sorcerer."

"Durwin's dad was a hostler and he helped tend the horses. One day he tried to put one over a fence. They fell and the horse crushed his leg. Didn't stop him riding again as soon as it healed, though, and he's the best enchanter in Helmdon."

"So why'd the king send him along with Sir Neil? Just to identify the archers he's pretending to be recruiting? Or to bewitch them into volunteering?"

"Maybe because he's smart and Neil isn't?"

"That could be," Francois agreed. "Could very well be." But he was mad because he'd guessed that Eadig knew more about Neil's real purpose than he'd been told, and Eadig was holding out on him. The conversation languished after that.

At Newark, which was roughly halfway, they stopped to give the horses a break and grab a very hasty and skimpy dinner of bread and cheese at an inn. There Eadig confronted his leader. "Sir, I never lived in a castle and don't know nothing about being a page."

Sir Neil rolled his eyes at such ignorance. "Then Piers will instruct you."

So, for the first hour or so after the journey resumed, Eadig rode beside the squire and was given a long firsthand account of a page's duties. Basically, he was expected to stick close to his master and see to his needs, so usually he would just obey orders—clean his boots, empty his chamber pot, sleep on the bedroom floor, fetch hot shaving water, et cetera. At table, when they were on public view, he would wait on Neil—load up his platter as he directed, or hold dishes for him to help himself, keep his goblet filled, and so on. And make his sleeve available if Neil wanted to blow his nose. At that point Eadig began to entertain hopes of one day turning Sage Durwin of Helmdon into a toad for putting him into this job.

And then he would make him eat cockroaches.

Piers's less-then-compelling descriptions of Eadig's duties continued. Also, when "Page" Eadig was eating in the kitchen at Lincoln Castle with the other low life, he must keep his eyes and ears open, but he'd better not ask any questions in case he gave away secrets. What good was he supposed to do, then, Eadig wondered, apart from serving as an ambulatory snot rag?

The shadows were growing long when the four horsemen emerged from a long patch of woodland and saw Lincoln ahead of them on its ridge—the twin towers of the cathedral, and the castle's two keeps.

Old Francois had been there before, which was undoubtedly why Neil had brought him, and Francois enjoyed giving Eadig a lesson on castles. Most consisted of a curtain wall, enclosing an open space called the bailey, and an inner keep, usually built on top of a mound. That was the most defensible part, which could hold out even if an enemy broke in through the curtain wall. Lincoln was so big, however, that it had room for two keeps.

Eadig had known all the first part and he could see the second part with his own eyes. He hadn't known that the big, round one was called the Lucy Tower, and the smaller square one was the Sheriff's Tower, so he had learned something.

Neil and Piers had seen many castles, but both admitted to being impressed by the size of Lincoln's. Eadig was quite simply amazed. He had never imagined a building of such immense size, with great stone walls reaching to the clouds. It made even the cathedral look small.

The newcomers reached the castle's east gate—which opened into the heart of the town close to the cathedral—not long before it closed; they were challenged, of course, and Piers had to proclaim his brother's name, station, and mission.

There must be a parade going on inside, because Eadig could hear a faint sound of drums, or perhaps just one drum . . . *Da-dum-da-dum* . . . It surely was monotonous. He surely was hungry.

Just before he died from lack of nourishment, word came to admit them. They others had to turn in their swords, but nobody took a second look at Eadig. That was one advantage of looking like a baby. There weren't any others.

The drumming was louder in there, but still same monotonous *da-dum* . . . Oh, Hell's sewer! It wasn't until he was inside the walls that Eadig realized nobody else was looking around to see where the noise was coming from, and in fact it was my *Battre le tambour* working, warning him of danger! Following the d'Airelle brothers, who were following a herald, Eadig dithered. The drumming was still faint, so perhaps there wasn't very much danger. He could turn and flee, but the guards on the gate would want to know what he was up to and stop him from leaving. He could just imagine himself trying to explain the enchantment to a furious Sir Neil.

That simply wasn't an option. No he couldn't.

Francois was sent off with the hostlers and the horses. The inside of the castle was almost as impressive as the exterior. As well as the two great towers, there was a whole village of lesser buildings in the bailey, plus enough space left over to encamp an army. Horses were grazing there, and there were people everywhere: men-at-arms, laundry maids, half-naked serfs, a few priests and gentlefolk in elegant robes.

Having been ordered to stay close, and having no desire to wander off and become lost in the maze in case he ran into the unknown danger all by himself, Eadig stayed very close as Neil and Piers were led to the Lucy Tower, where they climbed a long wooden staircase up the mound to a postern door. Francois had told him about that stair, and that its purpose was to be set on fire if the enemy was able to break in through the curtain wall.

The drumming grew louder, closer, faster. And then, once he started climbing, it faded away to just barely audible. Like a sulky friend, maybe? *Well if you won't listen to me . . .*

The inside of the tower was very poky and narrow. More stairs inside led eventually to what was obviously a top-floor room, because the ceiling sloped. It was dim and stuffy, with only an arrow-slit in the massive stone wall to let in light and air. Two men had been seated at a small table beneath it, playing chess, but they had risen to honor the newcomers. One was elderly and one younger, and they were so very alike that they must be father and son.

Opposite the window was a door, on which the usher rapped so loudly that he surely hurt his knuckles. Then he gently opened it a crack and listened. He knocked again, and a quavery voice bade him enter.

He bellowed, "Sir Neil d'Airelle to pay his respects to Lord Richard," and stepped aside.

Piers and Eadig followed Neil in, and the door thundered shut behind them. The drumming was still there, very quiet and slow: *Da . . . .dum . . . .da . . . .dum . . . .da . . . .dum . . .* This chamber was obviously the castle solar, for it had large windows overlooking the interior of the shell keep, and the shutters stood wide. It faced south, to the battlements on the far side of the interior yard. Men on watch over there must have a view all the way back to Newark Castle, at least. A drape covering an arched doorway moved gently, suggesting that there must be more windows beyond it.

The furniture was sparse, just two oaken chairs, a couple of stout chests, and a stand-up writing desk, but there were rush mats on the floor and some effort had been made to paint murals on the plaster walls—saints and martyrs, peeling badly.

The spidery, gray bearded man humped on one of the chairs was presumably the constable, Lord Richard de la Haye. He rose stiffly and peered uncertainly at his visitors. Despite the heat, he was wrapped in a heavy woolen robe with a fur collar; that, combined with his stoop and a smell of medicinal herbs, suggested that he was not in the best of health, but his smile seemed genuine enough, and he had retained most of his teeth.

"Welcome, Sir . . . I'm afraid I didn't catch . . . Ah, yes. Have we met before, sir?"

In a very loud voice, Neil admitted that they had not.

Lord Richard nodded. "Thought not. Your face reminds me of someone, though . . . That's why I asked." He flapped a spidery hand to indicate that his guest should take the other chair, while he sank gently down on his own. Piers stepped back against the wall, and Eadig copied him, feeling badly out of place in such company and wishing he could fade all the way into what was left of the mural. He would prefer to be a saint, but would settle for a martyr under the circumstances. He was very hungry. Not cockroach-hungry, but getting there.

The constable was staring at Eadig, though, fixing him with two very bleary eyes. "Boy! The wine!"

Wine? What wine? Oh, one of the chests held a tray with a flagon and two goblets, all of silver. Eadig said, "Pardon, my lord," and rushed over there to pour. Then he handed one goblet to the constable and the second to Neil, who gave him an ominous Look to tell him he had blundered already.

"Idiot!" the constable declared. "Don't they teach you anything down there? Always the guest first! And kneel. Tell the bottler to give you a good thrashing, or I'll see he gets one."

The old goat thought Eadig was one of the castle servants.

"Yes, my lord." Eadig went back to his place against the wall, wishing he dared to whisper, *"Hic non sum,"* so as to disappear altogether. It wouldn't work, though; he was trembling so hard he would just pop back into view. But he was a qualified cantor now, and he had identified two of the scents in the miasma: sage and rosemary. Both were prescribed to improve memory, but neither was likely to do much good for Lord Richard, who was obviously senile.

The two knights drank to each other's health.

"Excellent wine, Lord Richard," Neil said. "I bring this letter from Baron Everard."

"Who?"

"Baron Everard, the sheriff of Nottingham."

"Of course he is. Know that, just didn't hear the name right." The constable took it and held it at arm's length to view the seal. "Quentin? Where is the boy?"

The drape was pushed aside, and a much younger man entered. He was unusually tall and even a scholar's robes did not conceal his leanness. He also wore a sage's green cape and a matching skull cap. His eyes impressed Eadig, for although he had a large, bony nose and a close-trimmed beard, he had the stony gaze of a grass snake like one Ereonberht and he had found and kept as a pet when they were young.

The *da-dum-ing* grew a little faster.

"This," the constable mumbled, ". . . my sage, Quentin of . . . Quentin. He handles my correspondence these days. My eyes are not what they used to be."

Very likely his eyes had never been taught to read.

Quentin broke the seal and opened the letter. He read it out in the same strangely accented French that Francois spoke. The baron begged leave to commend Sir Neil, who had been visiting relatives, and was now hoping to return to France by sea. Undoubtedly Neil had written the letter himself, or had Durwin do it for him. The baron had signed it as requested.

"Better you than me," Lord Richard said. "Can't even smell the sea without getting sick to my stomach. Quentin, see that Sir Um is boarded. Boy, my goblet is empty!"

Eadig retrieved the flagon and went down on one knee to refill the crotchety old bastard's goblet.

"And tell the bottler to send you back to the stables. You still stink of horses."

"Yes, my lord." Eadig thought the stables would be an improvement over this madhouse.

Neil held out his goblet, so Eadig filled that one also. But Neil gave him a hint of a wink that the others wouldn't see, and that was both a surprise and a comfort.

"I will be happy to show you and your squire to your quarters whenever you wish, Sir Neil," Quentin said.

Neil took a sip of wine to show that *then* was not *now*. "That will be most kind of you, Sage. Lord Richard, while I'm here, I'm anxious to meet with old Sir Courtney of Blanche.

He fought beside my father at the battle of Lincoln, back in forty-one."

Drumbeats! This time they went louder, and then slowly faded, to show, perhaps, that the damage was done. Eadig wished that his valorous leader had not led with his chin there, trumpeting out his real reason for coming to Lincoln.

"Ah, yes!" the constable said with some enthusiasm. "A grand warrior in his day. 'Bone-breaker' they used to call him. Getting past it now, of course. He can tell you how we had a wager on how many—"

"Sir Courtney," the sage interposed, "has been called to the Lord. We buried him three weeks ago."

"We did? Oh, if you say so. Slipped my mind." The old man angrily drained his goblet.

Eadig watched Neil exchanging dismayed looks with Piers. There went the witness they had come to meet. Now what?

And Sage Quentin was watching all three of them with his reptilian eyes. He knew by now that Eadig was no page. He must know what Sir Courtney had died of, which likely had not been old age. Had that sad event happened before or after he wrote the letter to the king?

"That is sad news," Neil said. "Also, I suppose I should pay my respects to Sheriff Alured."

"The sheriff is not in residence at the moment," the sage said. "He is currently making his rounds of the shire." His eyes gleamed, more snakelike than ever. The noose was tightening.

Lord Richard uttered a noise halfway between a snort and a snore. The goblet slid from his hand, rolled down his lap, and landed on the rug with a thump. He lifted his head, opened his eyes, then closed them again. His head drooped forward. Eadig went to retrieve the goblet; Sir Neil handed him the other, which was also empty, and he placed them back on the chest. Good little page!

"Corneille?" Sage Quentin called.

Another man pushed aside the curtain and came in. How many of them were in there, eavesdropping? He was older and chubby, with a long black beard, and he seemed too old to be wearing an adept's white cape over his gentleman's robes.

"Lord Richard needs a nap now," the sage said. "Please help him."

Corneille nodded, and went to whisper in the old man's ear. The constable blinked awake, or half-awake, then let himself be helped out of his chair. Supported by the cantor, he shuffled out through the curtained doorway, visitors forgotten.

Quentin shook his head sadly. "Come, Sir Neil. Pray let me show you to your quarters."

Da-dum-da-dum . . .

chapter 10

Lovise did not open the front door—she never would for an unexpected caller at dusk—until she had inspected him by looking through the grille. She spoke through it. We listeners could hear her voice, but not the words, and all I could make out of the response from outside was that the visitor was definitely a man.

I listened for the sound of bolts being drawn, but did not hear them. Lovise returned and took her place at the table again.

"A man I have never seen before, Father. He said he was in pain and needed a healer urgently. When I insisted you were still out of town, but I might be able to help him, he said his complaint was not one he could discuss with a woman, and went away."

"Did he ask where he could find another healer?" I asked.

"No."

Nobody was happy with the news. Even without the signal from the *tambour* spell I would have considered it suspicious, confirmation of my theory that I had given myself away by curing Harald's curse. Harald himself was offended that a genuine patient might have been denied attention. I was pleased that my prediction had been fulfilled, and thus my theories about the conspiracy were holding up so far, but I heartily wished they weren't. I had found that elusive idea I had sensed earlier, and it was terrifying.

"You do not employ a cantor, sir?" I asked Harald. He responded better when I sounded obsequious.

"My work rarely requires a second voice. Healer Nerian and I used to help each other out when necessary, until he met with his accident, and now Lovise is capable of filing in until Lars is a few years older."

It was quite clear to me by then that Harald did not properly appreciate his incredible daughter. Lars, of course, would follow his father's lead. Lovise herself might be so used to being treated as a serf that she didn't even resent it. The idea that she might make a better enchanter than her brother would never enter their heads.

"You never use three-voice spells?"

Harald just shook his head. Those would be beyond his ken, and admittedly even in Helmdon they were rarely practiced. I had never heard of four-voice chants.

"How about five-voice?" I asked.

For a moment he looked outraged, as if I had grievously insulted him, but he was more stubborn than stupid, and he suddenly saw what I had grasped just a few moments ago. And he was equally appalled.

"No! They wouldn't!"

"They can, though!" I said bitterly. "That cantor you met must be a fully fledged sage, so Quentin has found the fifth he needed: Corneille, Tancred, Henri, Walter, and himself. *Five!*"

Lovise and Lars were both lost in the woods, of course.

"You don't know what sort of magic needs five voices?" I asked.

They shook their heads and their father said, "Pentacle magic!"

"The blackest of black," I agreed. "We use the pentacle as the emblem of our craft, but we don't use pentacle magic unless we want to raise major devils, possibly even Satan himself. Helmdon has many more than five sages, but we never dabble in that. The dean does have a couple of grimoires that are kept locked up, and there may be some demonic chants in those. I never asked."

I had decided very early that my chances of defeating any sort of treacherous coven were poor, but if the enemy were wielding pentacle magic, I had arrived too late to have a hope. He had not used anything so dire on Harald, else Lovise and I could not have removed the spell, but his purpose must have been to see if anyone would do that. Yes, I had walked into a trap.

Pleading a long day, I asked for somewhere to sleep. I was shown to the second room upstairs, which was obviously Lars's chamber. Lovise, I assume, slept in the attic. As the older child she ought to have preference, I thought, but I was being irrational. Ninety-nine out of a hundred families would rank even the youngest sons ahead of all the daughters. It's easy to see now that my judgment was being warped by infatuation, but I hadn't admitted that factor yet, even to myself.

Despite my weariness, sleep eluded me for a long time. I couldn't see how I could fight Satanism singlehanded. Ideas flashed through my head like falling stars, and died as fast. I might race back to Helmdon to enlist help—but the thought of a wagonload of geriatric sages advancing on Lincoln was ludicrous. I might approach the bishop, but why should he believe me? So far as he was concerned, I would be very close to a Satanist myself.

Sir Neil probably carried a royal warrant, but I had no such credentials. If I claimed to be a king's *familiaris*, who would believe me? I might ride like the wind to London, to warn the justiciar—but again, why should he believe me? Go to France and King Henry himself? He would give me a hearing, but by the time I found out where he was and fought my way through the court officialdom to reach him, the damage might be done—whatever it was, and I still didn't know that.

That left magic, but what magic? At that point I should probably have climbed out of bed, lighted a candle, and reviewed all the spells I had brought with me in my pack. Instead I tried to do it from memory, which kept me awake for another hour or two. I decided I had nothing that could possibly stand up against the demons Sage Quentin could conjure up with pentacle magic. *Hic non sum*, would let me be invisible, but only if I didn't move. *Oculos deceptus*, which I had once used in a disastrous effort to make one man look like another, only worked, if it worked at all, in very poor lighting. And, of course there was *Mori vermes*, which could stun a crow. I knew by heart *Cambrioleur*, a one-voice spell to open locks, but I couldn't imagine it would work on the gates of the castle. And I could think of nothing else useful.

chapter 11

"I fear that Lord Richard is fading fast," Sage Quentin said as he closed the door. "Everyone tells me what a fine man he was in his day." He turned to the two chess players, who were again on their feet, having started another game since Eadig saw them previously.

"Adept Corneille is putting his lordship to bed, Tom. Go and help him." Both men hurried off into the solar.

"Old Tom and Young Tom," Quentin told the visitors. "They're both Tom son of Tom. Some people have no imagination." His smile never reached his snaky eyes. He paused, looking at Neil and Piers, comparing them. "You must be brothers!"

"We are. I couldn't hope for a better squire than Piers."

And then the cold, cold eyes turned to Eadig. "And who might you be?"

Eadig didn't need the sudden thunder of the *Tambour* drum to warn him. He might not know how to act as a page, but he had a very good idea of what enchanters could do to you if they knew your real name.

"Ereonberht of Nottingham, may it please you, sir." He held

his breath in case one of the D'Airelle brothers corrected him, but neither did.

"It certainly wouldn't please me that my mother had been so thoughtless," the sage said, "but if it doesn't bother you, then I suppose it's all right. Come, your honors, please." He started down the stairs.

Neil followed. Piers shot Eadig quizzical looks. He made violent gestures of cutting his own throat with one hand and pointing after Quentin with the other. Piers nodded. Eadig trailed along behind as the brothers followed the snaky sage.

Darkness was closing in on Lincoln. Back down at the postern door, the sage enlisted a real page to carry a lantern and serve as linkboy. Eadig hung back farther as Neil and Piers proceeded down the long wooden stair to ground level, but he dared not lose sight of them, for the bailey was a maze. Being a long way back from the lantern, and treading in the others' shadow, he found the rutted ground hard going.

Sage Quentin seemed to be doing all the talking.

So! The constable was in his dotage; the man who had written the letter warning the king was dead; the sheriff was away on business. It was all much too convenient. Sage Quentin was now in charge of the castle, or thought he was, and Eadig needed no magic to tell him that he did not trust Sage Quentin.

He wished Durwin were there.

Or maybe it was better that he wasn't?

The drumming in his head seemed to be getting steadily more urgent. The sun had set and the light was fading to dusk. The sage led them across the bailey, zigzagging between buildings, coming at last to a one-story stone cottage near the north wall. The door was open, light showed inside and through the window next it, although two other windows were dark. With any luck there would be food there.

But as Eadig approached the door he heard the drum again, louder this time, almost frantic: DA-DUM-DA-DUM-DA-DUM . . . He slowed down—way down—and yet his stomach kept egging him on. There might be food there, and he was starving—real, eat-your-boots, famine *starving*! That Newark cheese had long since done all the good it would ever do. Francois's cockroaches roasted with cheese sauce?

No, there was no sign of food. There was a squad of men-at-arms, jumping to their feet as the sage and visitors entered. Eadig halted well short of the doorway and watched in horror as the men-at-arms quietly encircled Neil and Piers, who looked around in alarm.

"Just as I thought, Sergeant," Quentin said. "These men are the traitors we were expecting, imposters pretending to be from His Grace the king. Lock them up securely, and don't believe a word they tell you. You can give them water, but no food. Adept Corneille and I will question them later, so leave a light on up here when you leave."

Neil roared and shouted that the sage was lying. Piers reached for his sword, but of course it wasn't there, since he had surrendered it at the gate, and a man behind him kicked his legs out from under him. In seconds the fight was over, Neil being held in an arm lock and his brother pinned on the floor.

Cyningswice! Eadig fled into the night. The drumming faded and slowed, but did not completely stop.

He ran to a store of firewood outside the nearest building and dodged behind it. No one followed him; there was no one else around to notice. He scrambled up on top of the stack, collecting several splinters and ripping his cloak in at least one place. The pile had a thatched roof over it to keep rain off, and there was just enough space for him to squeeze in under it. There he was hidden him from any casual view and could keep watch on the doorway he had left. He made himself as comfortable as he could, which wasn't very, and told his belly to stop rumbling. The drumming was barely audible now, so he was safe—relatively safe—for the moment.

How hard would Quentin hunt for the missing Ereonberht? Not knowing Eadig's real name, he couldn't make him answer a summoning spell. The castle's main gates would certainly be closed by now, although the posterns might still be open. But they would be guarded, and guards were always more suspicious at night. Eadig was trapped there until morning or death by starvation, whichever came first.

The sage departed, following his linkboy. After a while the sergeant led his men away, closing the door, but not locking it, so far as the lurking Eadig could see. He waited what felt like a long time, but there was a still a faint light inside that window alongside the door, and none in the other windows, so obviously there were two or more rooms. His teeth were chattering, but he thought it was hunger more than the temperature that was making him feel so cold. He decided to risk some exploration.

He scrambled down, went back to the building, and walked all around it, staying close to the wall. The windows at the rear matched those at the front, and all of them were barred. There was only the one door. In the darkness, he couldn't see whether it was marked with a pentacle, but that was usually more a warning than a real trap, for it was a point of honor among enchanters not to ward a door so heavily that it would seriously harm an intruder. Would traitor enchanters feel bound by such a custom? He tested the door as he had been taught, passing his hand over it without ever actually touching it; he detected a spell, but a very faint one. Using a trick that Durwin had taught him, he whispered a Paternoster before trying the latch.

That worked. Eadig felt no bad effects when he opened the door. Pushed very slowly, it did not even squeak. There was no one in the first room, the one he had seen before. A lantern on the table held a tallow candle, which gave the only light, however bright it had seemed from the outside. Right beside him was another door, which must lead to the other room or rooms, but no light showed beneath it. When he tested it, the warning chill almost froze his hand off, so he backed away quickly. Whatever that warding did was ferocious! If Neil and Piers were in there, then even Durwin's skills might not suffice to rescue them.

There was also a cellar, as Eadig discovered by very nearly falling headfirst into it, because the trap was open, with the flap lying flat on the floor, conveniently placed to trip people. He was not going to go down there without some light, and there were no handy spare candles lying around—anything at all useful or valuable must be kept behind the warded door. So he would have to take the lantern, and anyone outside watching the window would know the prisoners were not alone.

He decided he had to risk that and he had better move quickly, because the sage had clearly said that he would be coming back with Adept Corneille. The wooden staircase was very steep, almost vertical, and lacked a handrail, so Eadig decided to treat it as a ladder and go down backward. The cellar felt shivery cold after the stuffy cottage above.

He was halfway down when Neil's voice said, "It's Eadig."

"Ereonberht!" That was Piers correcting him. The squire lacked his brother's brawn as yet, but he had more brains. Perhaps Neil preferred to joust without his helm.

Eadig-Ereonberht reached the bottom of the ladder and looked around with horror and disgust. The cellar was much larger than the room he had just left, underlying the entire area of the building, but it was divided it into the same two unequal parts as the upper floor, in this case by a wall of stout iron bars. The ceiling beams were low enough to be uncomfortable for a full-grown man, but not enough to trouble a midget like him. The floor was paved with bare flagstones. As he moved his lantern, spooky shadows crept everywhere.

His side of the barrier was outfitted like a sage's sanctum, crowded by two oaken chests, a huge desk, a couple of stools, a bench, two candelabras, and a row of no less than five lecterns standing tidily along one wall. Why five? Was this where the castle choir practiced?

No, the larger space beyond the bars was a dungeon, completely barren of furniture, but equipped with various iron staples along the three outer walls. Neil and Piers were sitting on the floor at the far end, tethered there by iron collars chained to two of the staples. They had manacles on their wrists and their only comforts were a slop bucket and two water jugs, set between them.

Eadig went over to the barrier and held his lantern high while he viewed the pathetic sight. Neil had a swollen eye. But what sort of sadistic jailer would make his prisoners sit on cold flagstones, without as much as a heap of straw to take the chill off? Summer heat never reached this far below ground. Both men looked frozen.

"Well done, Ereonberht." Sir Neil sounded a lot humbler than usual. To be rescued by a Saxon brat would hurt almost as much as being captured in the first place. "You'd better not stay, though. He promised he'd be back."

"Where are the keys, sir?"

"They took them with them. They might be upstairs, I suppose."

A sage could open locks, but they didn't teach varlets, squires, or even adepts that sort of spell.

"Didn't see them, sir. That other room up there is warded summit horrible. Sage Durwin might be able to clear it, but not me. Let me look here."

He hurried back to the two chests. Neither felt as if it were warded, so he opened them. One held only some writing equipment, spare candles and a tinderbox, while the other contained clothes, all of them black robes of various sizes. They stank horribly, so he shut the lids and went back to the jail wall. "Nothing there."

"You'll have to hide somewhere until morning," Neil said, "then try to get out of the castle. Just walk out with your head up, as if you did it every day."

"But have a story ready," Piers said, "in case they ask, though sentries are usually more worried by people coming in than going out. You didn't steal any of the constable's silver goblets, did you?"

He was brave to be making jokes to cheer up the Saxon kid, but he wasn't mentioning that the traitor sage knew that Eadig was somewhere in the castle, and would warn the guards to look out for him. It was going to be as hard for him to sneak out as it would be for others to sneak in.

Neil said, "Remember to look for Durwin at the west door of the Cathedral after mass on Friday morning. Tell him what's happened, and remind him he is to ride back to Nottingham and report to Sir Vernon."

Great! This was still only Wednesday, and was Eadig going to lope along the road beside him, while Bon Appétit remained locked up in the castle paddock?

But Eadig forget his own problem when his arm grew tired of holding the lantern high, and he lowered it. It was only then that he noticed the floor between him and the prisoners. Clearly marked in white paint on the dark slate, almost filling the whole space, was a pentacle.

He said, "Oh, my God!"

The brothers d'Airelle said, "What?" in unison.

"That's a pentacle!"

"Even we warriors know that," Neil snapped. "Enchanters mark their doors with pentacles."

"But we never put them on the floor! That's a sign of *black* magic, raising demons, Satanism."

Piers said, "Listen! Someone's coming." But Eadig had already heard the drum's urgent clamor.

chapter 12

Cadig raced back across the room to the desk, set the lantern on it, and dived underneath. He scrambled back against the wall, making himself as small as possible, pulling his cloak around him, and tugging his hood up to cover his flaxen hair. Then he whispered, *Hic non sum*, and resisted a temptation to look at his hands to see if he truly was invisible. He was quite well hidden even without the spell, unless anyone deliberately came looking for him. The drumming faded away until it was no louder than the beating of his own heart.

Would the newcomers know that the lantern had been left upstairs and couldn't have come down to the cellar by itself?

The staircase creaked as very heavy footsteps slowly descended and then were followed by more. The first man walked over to the gate in the bars, and waited for it to be unlocked. He was enormous to start with, and carried another man over his shoulder like a sack, so that he had to bend almost double under the low beams. The strain on his back must be horrible.

Then Sage Quentin arrived with a lantern and a bunch of keys. Being tall himself, he had to stoop to avoid the beams, and he was tiny compared to the first man. The gate swung open.

"Dump him in the corner over there," Quentin said.

"That's Francois!" Sir Neil shouted, scrambling to his feet in a clatter of chain. "What have you done to him?"

"He was stupid enough to argue with Odell, here. Never a wise thing to do. He'll have a serious headache when he wakes up. If he doesn't wake up, it won't matter much anyway, not where he's going."

The knight and his squire murmured prayers and crossed themselves in a rattle of chains. The giant Odell went where the sage had pointed and unloaded Francois as if he weighed no more than a feather bolster, but laid him gently on the flagstones, and lowered his head carefully, as if wishing not to hurt him further.

"Now you can go and wait upstairs," Quentin said. "If we need you, we'll call. You did well. I am pleased with you."

The giant uttered a grunt that sounded like pleasure at being praised, and shambled over to the staircase. He was still bent far over, and now dangled arms like twin oak trees. He was the biggest man Eadig had ever seen, seven or eight feet tall maybe, broad and thick, like a tun barrel on legs. The stairs groaned as he went up.

Eadig shivered and hastily repeated his *Hic non sum* incantation in case the shiver had lifted the spell.

Another man came down and placed something on the desk. Then he went over to the dungeon, and so came into Eadig's view, and predictably it was Corneille, the adept with the thick black beard. The one who had put the constable to bed. The sight of him reminded Eadig that his own cape was hidden in his pack. He certainly hoped it still was, because the traitors already knew he had witnessed their attack on Neil and Piers, so they must be eager to catch him. If they had discovered he was more then just a page, they would try even harder.

Corneille said, "So! Sir Neil d'Airelle and his brother, Squire Piers, doughty warriors fresh from the court of King Henry and well suited for our sinister purposes. I have the honor to be your host for this evening's ordeal. Warriors, do not take offense at my humble garb. I assure you that I am a fully qualified Satanist, although in order to better serve our baleful purposes I prefer to dress as a humble adept. We foresaw five of you heading this way, but only four arrived in the castle. I suspect there's another one lurking around the town. Meanwhile, where did Ereonberht go, Neil?"

Both Neil and Piers were on their feet now. The chains from the collars were attached to staples set waist-high in the wall, so they could stand, sit, or lie down, but they weren't going anywhere. There were enough other staples to tether a dozen prisoners, although not all of them were fitted with chains and collars.

"You address me as 'Sir' Neil."

"No, I don't. Answer my question, Neil." Corneille was enjoying himself.

"No. You listen to me. I assume that you have rummaged through my pack and found my warrant with the king's privy seal on it. So now you know that I came here in his name, and you have assaulted my squire and myself and injured one of my men. This is treason. You will hang for that, even if you escape the worse penalties imposed on traitors."

"Shut up. You told the constable that you had been visiting family, so you are no 'perfect gentle knight', just a common liar, sneaking into the castle under false pretenses."

Eadig thought, *Ouch!* Neil did not answer, and he probably found the enchanter's accusation about as welcome as a death sentence. Knights valued their honor above all, even life itself. Of course being caught out in a lie was much worse than the actual lying, but the fairy story had been Durwin's idea, so Neil would consider this humiliation was what he had earned by listening to clerical trash.

Corneille chuckled at the silence. "You came in response to Sir Courtney's letter. We know all about that. He died the very night he sent it, poor old fool. Odell never questions an order. He's as strong as a bull and very useful. If I called him back down and told him to kick you to death right now it, he would do it."

"Your threats don't frighten me, Enchanter."

"And they shouldn't. I have no intention of killing either of you. You will be too useful to us in other ways." He turned to his accomplice. "While we're waiting for the others, let's begin with the summoning."

The enchanters came back to the sanctum area, and Eadig was tempted to whisper his protective spell again, but didn't because he wasn't sure how many repeats it allowed him. The conspirators had no reason to peer under the desk—at least, he couldn't think why they should want to. Unless he sneezed. Oh, why had he thought of that? Now he needed to sneeze . . .

After a tearful struggle, he didn't.

And the conspirators didn't look. Corneille lit a taper from the lantern and returned to the dungeon to light lamps. There were five of those, one hung right above each point of the pentacle, which confirmed Eadig's conclusion that this place was used for the performance of black magic. Corneille carried two of the lecterns in there. The dungeon was now much brighter, which ought to make the sanctum area seem darker, and therefore Eadig even less visible. Maybe.

There was to be no demon raising tonight, though—just two chanters and no black robes. The men took up position under the two lamps closest to the prisoners, each with a grimoire spread open on his lectern.

The first spell was a solo, chanted by Corneille. Eadig recognized it as very similar to the one that was used at Helmdon on herb-gathering expeditions. When the leader—Durwin or one of the sages—was ready to return, he would summon the others to him. It worked, too. The compulsion to obey began gently and rapidly became irresistible. But it didn't work that night, because Corneille was trying to summon Ereonberht of Nottingham. If there was such a person and he was safely home in bed, he ought to be well out of range. Otherwise, he would have a long walk ahead of him. The spell had no effect on Eadig son of Edwin, and certainly would have none on Ereonberht, his brother, who had never been to Nottingham and was now Brother Pious anyway.

Corneille felt the lack of acceptance and turned to frown at the prisoners. Neil was leaning against the wall with his arms folded, and Piers was copying him exactly. Seen like that, they could almost be twins.

"What's his real name?"

"Whose?"

"Ereonberht is not his real name. What is it?"

Neil shrugged and said nothing.

"The boy has an adept's cape in his pack, so the fifth man was a sage. He matters more. So what's his name?"

"You really expect me to tell you that?"

"Yes," Corneille said. "I am certain you will." He nodded to Quentin. *"Tormentum dolorque."*

Eadig shivered, and not just from the temperature. That was not the name of any spell he had ever heard of, but it did *not* sound good. The two enchanters found the correct page in their respective grimoires and turned their lecterns so they were facing the prisoners. Then they began.

It was a long chant. Corneille had a powerful, impressive voice and Quentin's was adequate, especially down there in that cellar, which added excellent reverberation. The Latin was not a variety familiar to Eadig, so he couldn't quite follow the spell on first hearing, but he made out that the victim was *Neilus Airelli Eques*, and he recognized both the names of several nasty spirits and quite a few human body parts. When the incantation ended, the two villains exchanged smiles, so they had sensed acceptance.

"The boy, too?" Quentin said.

"Certainly."

So they sang the whole thing again, but this time directing it at *Puer Petrus Airelli*. While it was going on, the two victims contrived to appear unconcerned, even bored. They could have little or no idea what was in store for them, but by then Eadig did and he wanted to scream.

"Now," Corneille said, closing the grimoire and leaning his forearms on it, "you came to Lincoln with a fifth man. A sage, right?"

Neil said, "Correct."

"And he went to visit Healer Harald Larson, I suppose?"

Neil shrugged. "I never heard that name before. I have no idea where my philosophy advisor is, but I am sure he is obeying my orders. You will find him much harder to deceive than I was."

"Not much of a compliment. What is his name?"

"Go to Hell and eat the devils'—"

Corneille pointed a finger at him and said, "*Viscera!*"

The knight's voice broke off in a gasp of pain.

"Now you understand? His name?"

"Be damned!"

"Probably, but we shall be much happier there than you will be."

Again Corneille pointed and commanded, and again Neil cried out. This time the torment went on longer. He doubled over, clutched his belly, then began to retch, rattling his chains. Piers tried to go to him and was stopped short by his collar. His brother dropped to the floor, screaming and vomiting by turns.

Corneille lowered his arm. "The pain gets worse the longer I point," he remarked casually. "The subjects can never faint, although they may tear off pieces of themselves. Eventually they go insane, laughing and asking for more, but we will be careful not to push you to that point."

Neil struggled to his knees and reached for a water bottle. The collar had bloodied his neck and he had scraped his hands raw on the flagstones.

"Now you know why we didn't feed you," Corneille said. "I did bring a light snack along, for you to enjoy after we're done with this part of the program. Must keep your strength up."

He added, "So the sooner you tell us what we want to know, the sooner you get your reward. Stand up, you blubbering ninny."

Glaring hatred at his tormentor, Neil obeyed, although he almost had to climb up the cellar wall to do so. He had obviously soiled himself in his ordeal, and Eadig was certain that only the iron chains were keeping the brothers from killing their tormentors with their bare hands.

"What is the name of the sage who came to Lincoln with you?" Corneille asked. "And before you answer, I must warn you that from now on it will be your brother who suffers, not you."

"Don't say a word, Neil!" Piers shouted. "I can— *Ugh!*"

"Genitalia!" That word and a mere flick of Corneille's finger was enough to make the squire gasp and stop talking.

"The name, Neil?"

"Go to Hell, shitbag."

"As you wish." The deadly finger pointed again at Piers, who grimaced and writhed, but for a few moments managed to do so in silence; then his gasps became screams. He toppled to the floor and thrashed there, his howls of agony drowning out even the rattling of his chain.

Eadig wondered how long Piers's brother could just stand there and watch. It was several minutes before Neil raised a hand and the enchanter lowered his.

Piers stopped screaming and tried to protest, but he had bitten his tongue and his mouth was full of blood.

"The sage's name is Durwin of Helmdon," Neil said.

"And the boy?"

Eadig waited to hear, "He's right behind you, under that desk."

But he didn't.

"Durwin always addressed him as Ereonberht, but we picked them both up at Helmdon, so the brat was probably lying when he said he was from Nottingham."

"Shall we try summoning this Durwin now?" Quentin asked.

Corneille sighed. "Better not. It's late, he's likely in bed. We don't want him running naked through the streets, or going insane outside the castle gate because he can't get in. We'll collect them both in the morning." He turned to gloat over his prisoners again. "You will have to stay there a while yet, warriors. When my friends arrive, we shall change your minds about a few things. After that it will be safe to strike off your bonds."

Corneille came out of the dungeon and strode straight over toward Eadig, (*"Hic non sum!"*) but the drumming barely changed, for all he wanted was a basket that he had laid on top of the desk when he arrived. This he carried back to his prisoners, sliding it the last few feet across the floor, so that he need not go within their reach.

"That's your reward. I thought you might be stubborn. That was why we didn't give you anything comfortable to lie on. You'll have to wallow in your own filth for a while. Tomorrow I will enjoy watching you scrub the floor for me."

"One day I shall have the great pleasure of cutting out your tripes and making you eat them," Neil said quietly. "That is a promise."

"Not if I get to him first you won't," his squire mumbled, drooling blood.

The enchanter laughed and did not bother to answer. He and Quentin put the lecterns back with the others, and the grimoires back in the chest. Then they blew out the lamps, locked the gate to the dungeon, and departed.

Eadig stayed where he was while he listened to the footsteps overhead, and he thought he could make out Odell's heavy clump going to the door with the others. The light from the trapdoor faded to black and he heard the outer door close. He relaxed in a rush then, as if he were melting.

He felt his way out of his dog kennel and stretched to ease his stiff limbs. He said, "Ain't he a *nithing*!"

"You did very well, Eronberht." That was probably Neil. The brothers' voices normally sounded very much the same, but now Piers's would be muffled by his damaged mouth. "You are a very brave young man."

"Sirs, I am amazed by your courage, both of you."

"Just doing our duty. I am ashamed of my weakness in telling him your master's name. There's food in this basket, but I don't know how to share it with you in the dark."

"Wait a moment." Eadig felt his way cautiously around the walls to the stairway, which he found by banging his right shin on the first step. He climbed up on hands and knees. The trap had been left open, probably for ventilation, and he fumbled around upstairs until he located the lantern. He brought it back down to the cellar before he spoke the *Fiat ignis* to light it.

The brothers crossed themselves at this demonstration of magic, but did not protest. The gate was locked, so Eadig had no way of getting close to them, but Neil threw him a loaf, which hit the bars and fell. He pulled it through to his side. It tasted wonderful.

"Have you a safe place to hide overnight?" the knight asked between mouthfuls. He must be starving, also.

"I think so, sir. But I'm worried that I'll be caught going out the gate in the morning."

"I can't advise you. You are being sorely tested and are doing marvelously well for a boy of your years. Durwin told us you were almost seventeen. Is that right??"

"Yes." *And you don't need to tell me I don't look it.*

"Seventeen going on thirty! I will praise your courage to the king, I promise."

Eadig refrained from saying that he would rather take the cash. After such a day and despite the horrors of the last hour, he suddenly found that his eyes would barely stay open. It was time to head back to the woodpile and sleep.

chapter 13

s one so often does after a restless night, I fell into a deep sleep just before dawn. I managed to ignore the town roosters' wake-up calls, but not the heavy footsteps above me, in the garret. They went downstairs. Then up again, and down again, and by that time I was fully awake. As I dressed, I was annoyed to hear Harald chanting in the sanctum below me, so he was back in business. No doubt he felt a responsibility to his patients, and perhaps resented being indebted to me, but when the enemy learned that he was again operational, they would be certain that someone had taken the curse off him. *Damnatio!*

At some point in my midnight brooding, I had realized that I had let Eadig keep his pack when he went off to masquerade as a page. Of course he had his adept's cape in there, so if the conspirators pried in the visitors' baggage, the cape and the cat would both be out of the bag. Perfidy, connivance, and conspiracy were not included in the Helmdon curriculum!

I went downstairs. A man and two women were waiting in the tiny hallway to consult the enchanter; they looked at me with unconcealed curiosity. I was a stranger, walked with a cane, and of course they had enjoyed a good view of my iron boot as I descended.

Lovise was in the kitchen, looking fresh as midsummer dew and busily preparing dinner. She greeted me with a glorious smile. Her brother was at work in the yard and we exchanged blessings as I went by him on my way to the privy. Back indoors, Lovise offered me an excellent breakfast of beer, fresh bread, butter, and honey.

"So what happens today . . . Durwin?"

I wished I knew. My rendezvous with Sir Neil was set for the following morning, but I strongly suspected that he would not attend, and for me to do so would be to stick my head in a noose. My wisest course of action would be to jump on Ruffian's back and ride back to Nottingham and dump the problem on Sir Vernon Cheadle. That would mean deserting Neil, Piers, and Eadig, which I knew I could never do. I might not have a belted knight's absurdly inflated sense of honor, but that did not mean I had none.

Besides, I suspected that Sir Vernon Cheadle had even less head jelly than Neil d'Airelle.

"This morning, if I may, I would like to read through your father's grimoire to see if it contains any spells that might be useful in the present circumstances."

"A sort of *Drop dead!* type of spell?"

Oh, that smile!

"*Dead* might be hard to justify, but a *Sleep for a week!* one would fit the bill nicely."

There was such a spell in one of my grimoires back in Helmdon. I had not brought it.

"I'll see if Father will agree," she said doubtfully, and whipped off her apron so she would be respectable enough to squeeze through the group of patients waiting outside in the corridor. There were enough of them now to spill out of the front door into the street. I realized that Harald might be doing quite well out of the current upheaval. If all the other healers in Lincoln had been replaced by strangers, it would be only human nature for the citizens to switch their custom to him in protest.

In a few moments Lovise returned, struggling with the massive grimoire. I jumped up to help her. The patients out in the hall would all die of curiosity before her father could treat them.

We cleared one end of the great table, and I settled down to my task. About a third of the spells were in either Norse or Danish, and most of the rest in the old tongue, with very few in Latin. I think there was only one in French. The great majority dealt with healing and were useless for my current needs, although I promised myself I would make copies of a couple that I had not met before.

The back door flew open; Lars arrived; the back door slammed.

"Tha's a great wee beast you got out there, Durwin," he said, grinning as usual. "I had to punch his nose a couple of times, but we're good friends now."

"Then you're a fine horseman. Ruffian is very choosy about people." But no doubt Lars was a very good puncher.

He guessed at once what I was doing—visiting enchanters are always eager to exchange spells. "We have another book upstairs in the attic," he said. "Chants that Father never uses. I don' know if any of them work."

Da-dum-da-dum-da . . . Now what?

"There are ways of making them work. I'd very much like to— *Oh, Lord, preserve me!* I have to go."

I had been summoned. Had it happened a few minutes later or sooner, this tale would probably never have been told. I was already reaching for my cane, but Lovise guessed instantly what was happening.

"Lars, hold him!" She moved to the grimoire and began heaving the leather pages around to find the *Abi maledictum* that had cured her father.

I tried to reach the door and Lars's thick arms wrapped me up like the hoops on a barrel. I struggled of course, not because the urgency was already so great but because I knew how bad it would become if I did not answer the call very soon. "Let me go!"

"Won't, sir."

"Lars, you take the responses," Lovise said.

As he moved us both around to where he could read the spell, I tried to hit him with my cane. His reaction was to squeeze me until I thought my eyes would pop. *Da-dum-da-dum-da-dum* . . .

Lovise sang the versicles, remembering to omit the trip wire word I had scored out. Lars cheerfully sang the responses in a lusty baritone, while effortlessly avoiding my efforts to kick him with my iron-shod boot. I shouted and cursed. The others chanted louder to drown me out. I began to panic as the spell bit. I must go, go, go! Then it stopped and I went limp.

Lars set me down and said, "All right now, Your Wisdom?"

"All right indeed," I said, "and my heartfelt thanks to both of you for a brilliant rescue. That was a very close call."

"Just what is going on in here?" Harald demanded, peering in the door.

"All right now, sir," I said. "I was summoned, that's all, and your children's lightning-fast response has saved me."

He was smart enough to see all the horrible implications, but he said nothing more, just shut the door and went back to tending his patients. Quite likely he was wishing that the summoning had succeeded and taken me out of his life. But I had to face the fact that Sage Quentin or whoever else was behind the treason had learned my name. Had one of the d'Airelle brothers been gullible enough to tell him voluntarily? Eadig certainly would not have done so. The incident proved beyond doubt that Quentin was prepared to use foul means to gain his ends, and he knew about me. The battle was on, and the odds were at least five to one against me.

I sat down wearily and told Lars I would love to see the unused grimoire upstairs. He shot off to look for it.

"Will they try again?" Lovise asked.

"Not right away. They would have felt the acceptance, so now they're waiting for me to arrive. And even if they do try again, you know how often spells refuse to work a second time. But it's possible. Tell me about the bishop."

Of the three men of power in Lincoln, the constable was either senile or cursed, the sheriff was out of town, so the bishop was the only possible ally left, improbable as he might be.

Lovise said, "Robert de Chesney. He's a fine old gentleman, much in the royal favor. He often acts as a judge in the king's courts."

"Did he attend the council in Northampton, two years ago, do you know?"

"Indeed he did. It's said that he tried to persuade Archbishop Becket to compromise, but of course he wouldn't."

Never mind Becket, but the rest of this sounded promising! When the king left Northampton, he had gone to Barton, where he had granted audience to a certain pegleg Saxon adept, and then sworn him in as his own man, much to the annoyance of Enchanter General Aubrey de Fours. If Bishop de Chesney had been present that day, he would certainly remember me. He would grant me a hearing, at least.

Lovise had guessed why I was asking. "He's not in town just

now. The king sent him north on some legal matter. He wasn't in the cathedral last Sunday."

Another road blocked! Quentin had prepared his battlefield well. I could believe that the bishop's absence was genuine, but the sheriff could have been enchanted to take himself out of the way, and the constable had been removed permanently. I was alone, one against five.

The door opened, but it wasn't Lars returning, it was his father, who gave me a cold look and said, "There is a lady here asking for you, Durwin of Helmdon."

chapter 14

morning was proclaimed in the castle by roosters, trumpets, and drums, each worse than the other. The cathedral bell joined in, outdoing them all. Eadig knew he must have slept at times, but it had been a very long night. He was frozen, stiff as the logs he was lying on, also dying of thirst and hunger. Neil and Piers had been horribly tortured and threatened with worse magic to come. Durwin was also in danger and might not know it yet. Francois was wounded, possibly dead by now. And yet one peach-faced cantor had so far eluded the devil worshipers' best efforts to catch him; he felt quite proud of that. Although he had a generally low opinion of Neil d'Airelle's intelligence, he would never doubt his courage, and the knight's praise of Eadig's had been gratifying.

Soon people went chattering by, men and women both. Eadig decided the gates must be open by now, so he might as well try to sneak out now as later. He still had the money Durwin had given him, and there must be somewhere in the town he could buy a roast ox on a stick.

He clambered down to the ground and tried to brush off the bark and twigs he had acquired in the night. Then he stepped out into the roadway, which was only a path between buildings, and had to decide which way to go. To his left was the door with the pentacle on it, so he turned around and saw the cathedral towers over the rooftops. Taking that as an omen, he went that way.

In a few minutes the barbican came into view ahead of him. This was the east gate, opening straight into the town. More people were coming in than going out, but there were guards with pikes there, eyeing the traffic.

He could practically hear Sage Quentin's orders: *Look out for an undersized brat of about fourteen with very blond hair, snub nose, and really gross freckles. Do* not *let him get away!*

A hand grabbed his arm and he jumped, almost pissing himself. A grizzled old man said, "Don't let them see you. Come with me."

Eadig kicked his ankle and tried to pull free.

The old fellow showed a random collection of yellow teeth but did not let go. "I'm trying to help you!"

"Who sent you?" Come to think of it, the *Tambour* drum hadn't warned him of danger.

"Not that Quentin shit-head, bet your soul on it."

"I am sorry I kicked you, sir," Eadig said politely. "Please forgive me." His arm was released.

"I've known worse."

The man didn't look like an angel, but help from anyone at all would be welcome. Sending a silent prayer of thanks winging upward, Eadig let his guide lead him through the maze. It was soon obvious that they were heading back to the Lucy Tower he had visited yesterday. That meant that they had to climb that long staircase, up the side of the mound, and he felt very conspicuous doing that. If the sorcerers were still looking for him, there he was. No one started a hue and cry, though, and the drums did not return. Once inside the keep, he was completely lost, but his guide knew where he was going, and in a moment he stopped and rapped on a door.

It was opened at once by a tall, intimidating woman. She said, "That looks like the lad Tom described. Were you followed, Basile?"

"Don't believe so, mistress."

"Very well. Go and tell the others you found him." She looked at . . . She looked *down* at Eadig. "Your name, lad?"

"Um . . . Eronberht of Nottingham, my lady."

"You sound unsure," she said majestically. "And I'm not a lady, I'm Elvire, her mistress of the robes. Come in."

Eadig was astonished to find himself beckoned into what was obviously a lady's bedroom, furnished with a grand curtained bed, wall tapestries and fancy mats on the floorboards. The lady herself was seated on a stool with her back to him, while a maid was brushing out her hair, which was long, black, and shiny. Her gown was a dazzling red color. And she was watching him in a mirror on the wall in front of her. He hastily bowed to her reflection.

"You can go now, Hilda. I'll do that. *And don't gossip!*" Elvire took the brush and shut the door on the hastily departing chamber maid. As she resumed the hair brushing, she said, "This is Eronberht of Nottingham, my lady."

"He's younger than I expected. Welcome, Eronberht. I am Nicholaa de la Haye, Lord Richard's daughter, acting as constable during his indisposition."

Tongue-tied, Eadig bowed again. She was no older than he was, maybe younger—it was hard to tell with girls of that age, they aged so much younger than men did. She was richly dressed and had the poise of a Norman gentlewoman, so that her inspection dismissed him as somewhere on the wrong side of insignificant. She was no great beauty, but that did not matter if her veins held blood of the right color. He could almost hear her wedding bells.

She continued to address his reflection. "You are the boy who arrived in the castle yesterday with a knight and others?"

"Yes, my lady."

"And do you know where they went?"

"Yes, ma'am. Sir Neil and his brother, Squire Piers, are chained up in the sanctum cellar. I saw the sage and his cantor torturing them! Man-at-arms Francois, is badly injured, possibly dead. The last I saw of him, he was still unconscious."

"*What?*" Nicholaa spun around and both women stared at Eadig in horror. "Are you certain? Visitors injured and tortured in the castle without orders from my father or the sheriff?"

"Don't know about the sheriff, ma'am, but your father certainly didn't give any such orders when he saw us. Francois is hurt, and I heard that he was hit by a big man called Odell."

Nicholaa said, "Well!" emphatically, although she couldn't mean that anything was well, quite the reverse. She turned back to the mirror. "Pull that stool over where I can see you, and explain how you know all this."

"I saw it happen, my lady. Not the attack on Francois, but the Sir Neil and his brother being tortured."

"Sweet mother of Jesus! Then how did you escape?"

"I was hiding. They didn't know I was there. See, when Sir Neil was taken prisoner, I escaped, but later I went into the sanctum—"

"The sanctum door is warded," Lady Nicholaa said with obvious suspicion.

"Not heavily. I could open it. I'm an adept, so I know about these things. My lady, might I have something to drink? Maybe eat, too?" he added hopefully.

From that it wasn't too hard to let slip that he'd eaten almost nothing yesterday, and Elvire was ordered to send for some food for him. Then he confessed that he wasn't Ereonberht at all, and told the whole story while eating half a yard of pork sausage. When he finished both story and sausage, he added, "You want me to show you that I can do magic, ma'am?"

"No thank you! I believe that already." Nicholaa had finished her dressing. She wore her hair unbound, maiden fashion, and she sported an amber necklace that must be worth a fortune. She had turned on her stool to face him again. Her nose was on the long side and her jaw a bit too square, but she was worth looking at and knew it. The tall Elvire was standing with arms folded, watching them both with deep disapproval.

"Adept Eadig," Nicholaa said, "I am horrified by your story. My father is helpless—but you know that, since you saw him yesterday. If Sheriff Alured were here, I would take you right over to him to make your accusation, and also have you open that sanctum door for him. If what you say is true, he would . . . But the sheriff is in the south, investigating escheats and purprestures, and he has taken most of his men with him. Even old Bishop Robert is away; the king sent him north on some sort of assize."

Eadig had no idea what escheats and purprestures were and was very vague about assizes, but none of that mattered.

Nicholaa was obviously frightened, which was not surprising. She bit her lip and then said, "Could an enchanter like Quentin have *arranged* all that? I mean could he have used magic to remove the sheriff and the bishop from the town at the same time?"

"Yes, my lady. I'm sure he could. I don't think Quentin's the leader, though. Corneille was giving the orders last night."

For a moment Lady Nicholaa's expression suggested that she

was planning a very unpleasant execution. "But what is he up to?"

"High treason, my lady," Eadig said. "I think he's trying to murder the king. He knew about Sir Courtney writing to the king, and more or less said he ordered Odell to kill the old man, too. He guessed that the king would send someone to investigate, and he used magic to see that there were five of us on our way here, to Lincoln. Only four of us showed up at the castle, so he knows Sage Durwin is in the town."

"But how does he hope to murder the king?"

Of course a fine lady like her would know nothing about magic. Having had a very long night to think it out, Eadig had no trouble in spelling it out.

"He knew that the king would send someone he trusts to investigate hints of treason, and when Sir Neil returns to France, wherever the king is, the king will want to hear his report in person. And then Neil will kill him, because he's been enchanted to do that by black magic."

Nicholaa looked helplessly to Elvire.

"It sounds very farfetched, my lady," the older woman said, "but if there's any truth at all in it, then you must do something, as quickly as possible."

"You don't believe me?" Eadig said. "Just go to the sanctum and you'll find two men in chains and one dead or badly hurt."

"Eadig, the problem is that I don't know who I can trust. You say they've even got Odell. Odell a killer? He used to carry me on his shoulders when I was a child. 'Gentle giant' they called him. And Father? You think his stroke was really caused by a curse?"

It was very flattering to be consulted by such a lady. And she was clever, because he hadn't thought that Lord Richard might have been cursed. "Did it happen after Quentin got here?"

She nodded miserably. "The new sheriff arrived, and Father approved of him, told me he was going to be a very good sheriff. Then Quentin came. And—"

"Did he arrive with Sheriff Alured?"

"No. He just turned up as a traveling enchanter, so of course Sage Bjarni invited him to stay for a while. Father had his first stroke while he was still here. He got very angry with Bjarni because he couldn't heal him, so he sent Bjarni away and appointed Quentin castle sage in his place. That could have been another enchantment, couldn't it?"

"Oh yes, ma'am. But it would be black magic, an' I don't know much about that."

"And soon he had another stroke and Quentin's done him no more good than Bjarni did."

"Some maladies can't be cured, my lady. But Durwin is a wonderful healer. He'd know what's wrong with your father."

"Black magic, right here in our castle!" Nicholaa said. "I promised Father I'd take care of things until he got better. And now that monster is working black magic? He demanded the old jail as his sanctum because he said the Bjarni's room was too small. I didn't object because we never used that building. I had no idea that he was going to turn it into his personal dungeon and torture chamber."

"Course," Eadig said, "I don' want to bring Durwin into the castle for Quentin and Corneille to enchant, but he ought to be warned, because now they've got his name, they can summon him, or curse him."

"You don't know where he is?"

"No, ma'am. He was going to look for enchanters in the town."

"Most of them are Quentin's men," Elvire said. "Walter, Henri, and Tancred. All the old enchanters either left or died."

"We should have been suspicious about that," Lady Nicholaa said. "A new enchanter every month? Who's the other one, the one who hasn't left?"

"Harald Larson."

"Right. I think we should consult him. He's been here as long as I can remember."

"Maybe Durwin's found him?" Eadig suggested. He wasn't sure what spell would do that, but if there was one, Durwin would know it. And perhaps the *Mín Færeld* blessing they had chanted to bless their journey would have led him to the right person. It hadn't done much for Eadig son of Edwin, though.

Nicholaa turned to him. "And we have to get you out of the castle. You're not safe here."

He wouldn't be safe anywhere if Corneille learned his real name, as he had learned Durwin's. And of course Durwin wasn't safe either, and must be warned of that, if there was still time.

"They'll be looking for me at the gates," he said.

Nicholaa nodded. "Yes, the word went out. There's some men still loyal to me, and I was asked if I approved of those orders. That's why I sent Basile and the others to try and find you first. What do you think, Elvire? Could we smuggle Master Eadig out of the castle?"

Elvire looked appraisingly at Eadig. "Oh, yes, my lady. No problem at all. He isn't going to like it, though."

chapter 15

i could not imagine what lady would be asking after me in Lincoln, but I stood up and said, "Then pray admit her." Lars and Lovise rose also, looking as puzzled as I felt.

At least a dozen patients were waiting to see Harald, but they had naturally given precedence to a woman dressed as a lady, so she was right out there in the hallway, and Harald had only to step aside and in she came, followed by her maid. She was tall, middle-aged, imperious, and not a true noblewoman, for her gown and bonnet indicated either a prosperous merchant's wife or a very senior servant.

I bowed. "Sage Durwin of Helmdon at your service, ma'am."

She curtseyed. "I am Elvire, mistress of robes to Lady Nicholaa, daughter of the lord constable and currently his deputy."

Hallelujah! "Then you are indeed welcome, mistress." I presented the Larson siblings and bade her be seated.

Only then did I glance at her maid, wondering if I should evict her from the coming conference. She could not matter. The only reason for her to be there at all would be that no woman who had aspirations to be regarded as a lady would venture into town without a servant companion. The girl in question was young, blonde, simply dressed, and flushing furiously redder than a setting sun. I felt a second, enormous, breathtaking surge of relief.

"I find your bosom exciting, miss. What are you using to pad it out like that?" My question no doubt horrifying Lovise and Lars, because the "maid" was very convincing.

"Dead rats, mostly," Eadig said, and proceeded to strip off his disguise while I introduced him. I was so glad to see him that I wanted to hug him. He would likely have reacted with violence.

I thought Lars would explode, but he managed to keep his merriment hidden well enough that Eadig could pretend not to notice it. So four of us sat down while Lovise began preparations for dinner. For the next hour or so, Eadig related his news as I have already recorded it, up to the point where he had walked unchallenged out of the castle in attendance on Elvire. For him I outlined my adventures in releasing Harald from a spell and being saved from another by Lars and Lovise.

Then everyone was waiting for me to lead them out of this vale of horrors.

"Right!" I said, although obviously almost nothing was right. "Now we all know where we stand. From what Eadig witnessed, the Satanists' leader is this Corneille, a sage posing as an adept. He was the last to appear on stage, right, Elvire? When was that, do you remember?"

"Three or four weeks ago."

"About the time the late Sir Courtney wrote or did not write the letter that brought us here! Corneille completed the five they need to perform pentacle magic. Tonight he will summon his three town accomplices into the castle to work whatever obscenities he is planning. Black magic should be performed during the hours of darkness, of course, preferably around midnight. Can the town healers get into the castle after curfew, Elvire?"

"Not legally, but I wouldn't count on them being kept out in this case."

"Why, if Lady Nicholaa is currently in charge of the castle, can't she just order a squad of men-at-arms to break into the sanctum and release Sir Neil and Squire Piers?"

Elvire nailed me with a killer glance for doubting her mistress's loyalty or competence.

"Because she does not know who can be trusted. Most of the garrison are no doubt loyal, but if Sage Quentin has enslaved Sergeant-at-arms Odell to obey obviously illegal orders, then anybody could be in his power. I know that some of the garrison are terrified of him."

"Odell," Eadig said, "is a real giant!"

Of course Lady Nicholaa herself must be justifiably frightened by what was going on. If her father had been immobilized by a curse, she could be stricken in the same way if she ever tried to oppose the conspirators.

I had another question. "Tell me about the visitors this summer."

Elvire looked blank. "Which visitors were those, Sage?"

"Sir Courtney's letter—which I have not seen—reportedly included a list of noble persons who had visited the castle this summer but had no known business to come anywhere near it."

"There were no such visitors," she said flatly. "Lord Richard has been indisposed, and Sir Alured has been much too busy with his duties as the new sheriff. Ever since her mother died, Nicholaa has been her father's hostess, so I would certainly know if she had been dressing to meet any guests of quality." Case closed.

Clever, clever! Now I saw the plot more clearly. "Then Sir Courtney's letter was not written by Sir Courtney. It was a carefully designed forgery, indicting a list of men whose loyalty the king might suspect, and it mentioned enchantment. Either accusation on its own might not prompt his direct response, but the two together were doubly potent. He sent a confidant to investigate, one of his *familiares*, instead of just forwarding the letter to the justiciar."

No one argued. I realized then also, although I did not mention it, that the list of accused traitors could have served another purpose. The king would almost certainly have handed the letter to his enchanter general for a credibility test, and de Fours would have discovered that there were both facts and lies in it, although his magic would not have distinguished which was which. Had the false accusations not been included, the letter would have registered as truth, and the king would have sent the justiciar with an army. Whoever had planned this, whether Quentin or Corneille, was devilishly cunning—in this case literally so.

"Eadig, I want you to ride back to Nottingham and tell Sir Vernon Cheadle what has happened. He must sent word to Earl Robert of Leicester, the justiciar. Whatever these Satanists are up to must be stopped, and I don't think you and I can do that by ourselves."

Eadig did not want to ride back to Nottingham and miss all the fun. "Bon Appétit's in the castle paddock. Can't get him." Smirk.

I was equally determined that he was not going back into the castle and the peril of death or torture. "Lars, could he borrow your horse?"

Lars laughed. "Methuselah's older than I am. He might be able to carry Eadig halfway, if Eadig will carry him the rest."

Eadig's grin grew wider.

I considered sending Lars on Ruffian, but Ruffian would not carry a stranger without a tremendous battle, and Vernon would not trust a letter delivered by someone he did not know.

"It looks like you're going to be riding Ruffian."

Eadig grimaced. "Should be a quicker death than Corneille would give me."

"He knows you."

"So does Corneille."

I wiped the smile off his face with one deadly look. "No arguments, Adept. The fate of England may depend on you. I'll write a letter for you to take. Now, mistress Elvire, I suppose it is possible that Lord Richard's indisposition was caused by enchantment. Describe how he was smitten."

She did so, but the symptoms of dementia are so easily imitated by curses that I could reach no conclusion. I thanked her and said, "Then I think my first act should be to visit him and see if I can restore him as I restored Healer Larson. It's a long shot, because if it was a curse, or a series of curses, then it began months ago. Reversing an enchantment after so long will be extremely difficult, probably impossible."

"You'll need a cantor!" Eadig said quickly.

"I can chant!" Lars said.

Big as he was, I was sure that he was younger than Eadig, and I didn't intend to hazard any more children in this war. Harald himself would probably want to attend the constable, but his last visit to the castle had ended in disaster, and he was known there. No other healer in the town was available, because Quentin had substituted his own men for all of them. The man had planned his treason with great cunning.

"I'll come with you," Lovise said.

I opened my mouth to refuse and then realized that she was the logical one to take. A woman entering the castle would attract less suspicion than another man would, and be less likely to be questioned while she was in there.

"If your father agrees, I'd be very grateful for your help," I said.

"Let's not tell him until after we've gone."

"Brilliant!" I said and caught Lars and Eadig exchanging amused looks. Heavens, was I that transparent?

Harald joined us for dinner, and the six of us reviewed the situation over and over while we ate, although the seniors spoke more and the youngsters mostly did the eating. I think it was Mistress Elvire's testimony that persuaded Harald to believe in the extent of the conspiracy, which he called a coven. It had already caused an appalling death toll: likely Francois, probably Bjarni, Sir Courtney, Nerian, and Peter. Two of the king's men had been imprisoned and tortured. Harald himself and probably Constable Richard had been incapacitated.

"But why?" Lovise asked. "What under Heaven can he hope to achieve with all this evil?"

I agreed with Eadig's suggestion that it was all an involved, very sly plot to enslave Neil and his brother to perform some hellish evil. I did not put it into words because it would sound so farfetched, even to me. All the enchanters involved bore French names. That did not prove that they had not been born in England, but they could as easily be natives of France, and King Louis was Henry's sworn enemy, who never missed a chance to do him harm.

"Whatever it is, it will happen tonight, at midnight. He will collect his accomplices to join him on the pentacle and the five of them will summon the denizens of Hell."

Eadig was less reticent. "And Neil and Piers will be the victims."

After a few moments' silence, Harald said, "Enthralled, you think?"

"That seems likely," I agreed. "And deluded into thinking nothing is wrong; freed to go back to feed false reports to the king."

"Or kill the king!" Eadig said.

I shuddered. Why had I not seen that? "Or kill the king," I agreed.

Surprisingly, it was Harald who proposed the logical next step. "I have a *Maledicto* in my grimoire."

"Two voice?" I asked.

"Three, I think. I have never used it."

"Let's take a vote on that, because we'll be treading very close to performing black magic ourselves. We six alone know what is going to happen. What Healer Harald is proposing is that we strike at these traitors by cursing each of them. I'm sure that any chants we have available cannot be near as deadly as whatever they are using and are going to use, but if we can even give them all belly aches, that could gain us some time. This battle will be dangerous, because they will surely strike back at us. Lars, I think you are the youngest—speak."

Lars glanced disbelievingly at Eadig but then said, "Hit 'em!"

Eadig nodded. Lovise nodded.

Elvire and Harald and I all nodded at the same time.

"The Ayes have it," I said. "Harald, if you will find your malediction, I will find the one I brought so we can compare them. Lars, can you saddle Ruffian? Lovise, do you have a piece of parchment that I can use to write to Sir Vernon in Nottingham?"

To Vernon Cheadle, Kt., at Nottingham Castle, from Sage Durwin of Helmdon, at the house of Healer Larson, in Lincoln, written on the day after the Feast of the Birth of the Blessed Virgin, in the

Year of Our Lord 1166, being the 12th Year of the reign of King Henry the Second:

Greeting.

The bearer of this letter, being known to you, will relate a true story of most dastardly treason and black magic being perpetrated in His Grace's Castle of Lincoln by Satanist Corneille Boterel. Sir Neil d'Airelle and his squire have been imprisoned and tortured, and their servant Francois has been injured, perhaps to his undoing. Sir Courtney of Blanche, whom they sought to greet, is dead, most like murdered. I beseech you to send word of these crimes to His Grace's regent and justiciar, the noble earl of Leicester, and also to warn the Lord King in France, for I fear even worse crimes are imminent.

Farewell.

I had considerable doubt that my advice would be taken. Sir Vernon Cheadle was much more likely to put his head down and charge like a bull, straight at the gates of Lincoln Castle. He would certainly never quit the field himself by going in search of the justiciar, although he might dispatch a latter to him. He might not even consult Baron Everard, the sheriff. I had not dared mention the likelihood that Sir Neil and his brother would be turned from loyal servitors into potential accomplices by black magic, because I was certain that Vernon would reject that idea out of hand.

I gave Eadig the letter and advised him that, once he had delivered it, he should ride back to Helmdon and tell the faculty what was happening, although I couldn't imagine what they could do.

Eadig son of Edwin never lacked courage, and he proved it by vaulting up on Ruffian's back in that cramped little courtyard. Lars and I were hanging on to the big fellow's cheek straps; he roared his disapproval and lifted us both off the ground. Then he staved in the water butt with his hind hooves. This terrified the old gelding, Methuselah, who backed into the privy, knocking it over. That exposed a gaping pit, in which either horse could easily break a leg. Lars roared back at Ruffian and punched his nose. Ruffian very nearly bit Lars's ear off. At the second buck, Eadig shot straight up in the air. He came down on Lars's side; Lars caught him and lifted him out of harm's way.

But then Lovise, who was watching in the doorway, began to sing. Ruffian's ears swiveled. He steadied visibly, and in a few minutes she was out there, stroking his neck and he was calmer than any millpond. Had it been physically possible, I believe he would have curled up on her lap and purred like a kitten. Eadig listened intently to the words and melody, and gradually joined in. Grinning, then, he swung back up into the saddle and Ruffian barely seemed to notice. After a few minutes, I opened the gate and stood clear. Ruffian happily pranced out into the street and set off downhill, still entranced by Eadig's singing.

"It's a lullaby," Lovise explained. "Works well on colicky babies."

chapter 16

We restored what order we could to the yard, and I sent Lars off to the cooper with money to buy a new water butt—not that it could be properly filled until the winter rains, but water could be purchased from the water cart. The rest of us went back indoors to consider our attack on the evildoers.

This was when I wished Sir Neil had warned me that our mission might encounter treason. Back at Helmdon I had maledictions that would call down pain, nausea, blindness, impotence, and delusions on their subjects. The only one I had brought with me produced massive confusion, but its wording made me doubt that it would work at a distance or last very long. Those are not the sort of spells one tries out on people.

The normally unused grimoire that Harald brought down from his attic contained a curse that was longer, older, and fiercer. It was also less specific, calling for mistakes, misfortune, and misadventure. Since these are as common in the world as fleas, they are easily summoned, and with some luck on our side, the conspirators might not even realize for a while that their misfortunes had been sent. If so they would be slower to retaliate.

Also, our spell might even prevent their spells from working correctly, which would be a big gain for us. So we agreed to use the horrible thing. To chant it would be a breach of the sages' oath I had sworn, but I felt no guilt doing so in self-defense—Corneille and his gang had started the violence.

I easily located two trip wires in it, and with great difficulty convinced Harald that it was necessary to remove them. We made fair copies of the parts and, with Elvire's help, a list of our chosen victims: Quentin of Lepuix; Corneille Boterel, Walter of Froyle, Tancred de Umfraville, and Henri Morlaix.

"Eadig mentioned a giant who seems to be in their pay or under their control," I said.

"Odell," Elvire said. "I know who he meant. He's known as Odell Little. There are a couple of other Odells in the castle."

But Odell seemed to be more a victim than a conspirator, so we omitted him from our bane. Harald, Lovise, and I went into the sanctum, closed the door, and launched our counterattack on Corneille's treasonous coven. We felt acceptance every time, although not strongly in the case of Henri Morlaix. His house was farthest away, Harald said.

I was left with a soiled feeling I had never known before.

When we rejoined Elvire and Lars in the kitchen, we had to discuss what we did next, but it was obvious that Lovise and I should go to the castle to see if we could restore the constable to health. If we could, then he should be able to rally the garrison and bring back the rule of law. Moreover, Elvire was anxious to report to Nicholaa, who would be worrying. The sun was already in the west, and vespers could not be far off.

Lars supplied a tunic and hose that he had outgrown a year ago, and with those I dressed as a porter. Lovise had no trouble making herself look like a servant, since that was exactly what she was most of the time. In my eyes she looked just as attractive in worn old rags as she did dressed as a lady enchanter, beauty being always in the eye of the beholder. I lightened my pack by removing all the parchments that seemed irrelevant, but I left my cape in there, and added a white one that Lovise brought. Then I stuffed a robe in to pad it out so it looked more like a man's load. I slung it on my back and we were ready to go.

Almost ready to go. I made a quiet visit to the privy—now back where it should be—and quietly chanted the *Fiat ignis*. That is a release spell, which needs renewing every few days. It is more a handy tool than a weapon, but setting a man's shirt on fire will usually distract him.

Lars wistfully wished us luck, I warned Harald to be wary of reprisals by the conspirators, and we set off up the hill. Elvire strode along in front, of course, and we followed as her attendants. We went up to the cathedral's west door—the only part of the old church that was to survive the earthquake—and that is only a small distance from the drawbridge at the castle's eastern gate. The guards all knew Lady Nicholaa's principal servant and were much too busy admiring Lovise to notice me.

Da-dum-da-dum-da-dum- . . . It was quiet and slow, a gentle caution, not an urgent alarm.

Any first-time visitor must be impressed by the size of Lincoln Castle, for a small town could fit easily within its curtain wall. Elvire led us straight to the constable's private quarters in the Lucy Tower, and there we found Nicholaa in her private parlor, a cosy little room with a glazed window overlooking the inner courtyard. She was seated on a padded chair, embroidering, while a clerk on a stool read out a list of accounts for her to approve or disapprove. The clerk was dismissed and introductions made.

I was astonished at how young Nicholaa was—nubile but only just. As Lovise had already told me, her ancestors had been constables of the castle for a hundred years and she had no brothers, so it was natural that she should be in command while her father was indisposed. She could not hold a candle to Lovise in looks, but she did have astonishing poise and confidence for her age. Her youth and gender must have helped Sage Quentin bypass her authority, and yet they might aid us, if the conspirators underestimated her enough.

Once I had been presented, I explained the situation. I told her that I had sent Eadig with a letter to Sir Vernon, and hoped that he would report the problem to the justiciar himself. "He may not, of course. Belted knights have a strong disinclination to appeal to anyone for help, so I shall not be surprised if he charges in here tomorrow with his army to rescue Sir Neil."

"I will make him welcome, Sage," she said at once. "I only hope that the coven, as you call them, do not wreak further evil in the meantime."

"Corneille has probably sent word for his helpers to assemble here tonight. You could order the guards not to admit the town healers."

She was seated and I was standing, but her frown made me feel suddenly small and stupid. "Quentin and Corneille will hear of it. Then they will simply have my father overrule me. My father is totally in Quentin's power and does not know what he is doing, Sage."

She did not add that the Satanists might work some evil spells on her also, but that was obvious. Although I appreciated her predicament, I needed her help too urgently to give way.

"Please understand the stakes here, my lady. Quentin has painted a pentagram on the floor of the sanctum. That means that he uses, or intends to use, the worst sort of demonic black magic. For that he needs five chanters: himself, Corneille, and the three new healers from the town. *With* them he will be able to enchant Sir Neil and his squire into believing anything or doing anything that he tells them."

That startled her, as well it might. She looked for support to Elvire, but the older woman merely shrugged. Then she added, "From what the adept said, they have already enslaved Sergeant-at-arms Odell."

"I don't know if they used their pentagram to do that," I admitted. "If they did, they would have had to make him stay still while they chanted at him, which sounds unlikely from what I hear about his size. If they didn't, then they would have been limited to a two-man incantation, and their hold on him will be temporary, and weaker. He probably wouldn't commit murder for them, for example."

"Have you evidence on what they plan?"

"Nothing I could lay before the sheriff's court. But the king was sufficiently impressed by Sir Courtney's letter to send men all the way from Brittany to investigate, and my own arts warned me that we would encounter high treason. Rebellion may not be exactly the form it will take, but it seems the most likely."

"William of Addington holds the gates today?" Nicholaa asked.

"Yes, ma'am," Elvira said.

"And he will know the healers by sight?"

"Yes, ma'am. They might have special postern passes to enter after curfew, because I saw Healer Tancred here last night."

"I signed no passes!"

"But your seal or signature could be forged," I said.

Nicholaa's eyes flashed. "Go and tell William that they are not to be admitted today or tonight under any circumstances, by my father's order."

Elvire bowed her head in acknowledgment and departed without sparing me a glance. I felt I had won a significant victory. If our maledictions did not hinder the coven's assembly, then this must at least delay it: the pentagram would not work without five chanters.

"I am grateful, my lady. I have two further requests. First, with your permission, I should like to examine your father to see if his disablement is natural or not."

Nicholaa was on her feet in a flash. "I will take you to him, although I warn you that even I am not always allowed in to see him. As his healer, Sage Quentin can forbid visitors."

"I brought my sage's cape, my lady. Perhaps if I dressed the part?"

"If I can't get you in then no one can," she said firmly. "The guards likely do not know what a green cape signifies, and I had rather that Corneille and Quentin not learn of your presence in the castle yet."

"Wise advice, if you will not mind my attending your father without it."

"And what is the second thing?"

"You must have some men you do trust?" I knew she had, because she had managed to intercept Eadig on his way out that morning. "If you could round up four or five as an escort, ma'am, then as soon as I have visited your father, I should like you to accompany me to this jail that Corneille uses, so we can release Sir Neil and his squire."

"The jail is now a sanctum. It is warded."

"I can deal with wards. Even my cantor got in last night."

"And I do not know where the keys are."

"I can deal with locks, also, ma'am."

For the first time she smiled at me. "You are just the sort of avenging angel I have been praying for, Sage Durwin. Elvire, see if you can find Master-at-arms de Grasse, or one of the men we set to find the boy this morning. Come this way, Sage."

Lovise and I followed. As I expected from Eadig's story, Nicholaa led us to the solar, the highest point within the Lucy Tower. I braced myself for my usual struggle with a spiral staircase, but none appeared. My climb was easy, although I am slow on any stairs. Just before I reached the top and the room Eadig had described, I heard stools being pushed back, then Nicholaa's voice

"How is he, Tom?"

"A shade better than this morning, I think, ma'am, but still not as good as yesterday. He refused any nourishment at noon."

I emerged and saw the father-and-son team that Eadig had met the previous day, the two Tom-son-of-Toms. A glance at their chessboard told me that whoever was playing black was by far the better player—unless white had spotted him his queen to start with.

"And who is with him just now?" Nicholaa asked quietly.

The elder Tom said, "No one right now, ma'am. The sage looked in 'bout an hour ago. Didn't stay long."

"Good." She sounded relieved. "I would prefer that we not be disturbed, even by the sage." She tapped on the door and opened it without waiting for a answer. Lovise and I followed her in.

I suspected that the two Toms, however eager to please Nicholaa they might be, would not have much success in keeping Sage Quentin out if he appeared.

chapter 17

Despite his display of temper in the Larsons' yard, Ruffian was a lot less sprightly than usual. Even after Eadig had ridden him out of the town and given him his head, he did not roar off like a whirlwind along the highway as was his custom. This was his fourth day on the road, and even he must be feeling in need of a holiday. Eadig's own horse, poor old Bon Appétit, had been practically crawling on her knees, begging for mercy by the time she reached Lincoln yesterday.

It was another fine day for a ride, a little cooler than before, and Eadig was confident that he would reach Nottingham before curfew if nothing happened to delay him. The roads were almost empty, because the farmers would have delivered their produce and not yet have left for home.

He was still annoyed at being relegated to the job of messenger boy. He had done wonderfully well as a spy last night, and again this morning by finding Durwin and reporting what he had seen. Durwin had admitted all that and praised him highly. But he had also insisted that Eadig could best serve now by getting the word out to stuffy, hedge-faced Sir Vernon. Durwin was always fair and almost always right. He was undoubtedly right this time. True, but irksome.

Once the king heard the news, Sage Quentin's goose would be thoroughly cooked, but how long was that going to take? At least two weeks, maybe a month, to pass the news, and at least as long for the royal orders to get back here. By that time the enchanters might have jumped on their broomsticks and vanished, their evil deeds done.

Flying broomsticks would be really handy things . . . . maybe he could invent them when he was a licensed sage.

About halfway to Newark, Eadig paused at a swampy pool so that he could stretch his legs and Ruffian could drink. Something was niggling. Something he had forgotten? Something he should have told Durwin but hadn't? Something he should turn back to attend to? Of course not, that was ridiculous. And why was that soft tap of warning from the *Tambour* magic back again? He looked around nervously, but no one or nothing was creeping up on him.

But when he had mounted again and directed Ruffian back to the road, he felt a compelling urge to head back to Lincoln. *Oh, Satan's claws!* He recognized the problem now—he was being summoned.

Durwin? Had Durwin changed his mind? That wasn't likely. Some of the Helmdon sages were as jittery as chickens, but never he. The alternative was that Neil and Piers had been tortured some more, until they told Corneille Eadig's real name. That was much more serious and much more likely. If Eadig abandoned his mission and turned back, then Sir Vernon wouldn't hear the news. He wouldn't start wondering until tomorrow evening, because it was only tomorrow morning that Durwin was supposed to meet the others at the cathedral. Even then, Vernon could not set out until dawn on Saturday, and would not arrive until late that day. By then anything might have happened.

But Eadig had no choice. There was no one there to chant an antiphon, and the itch was growing stronger by the minute. He must either go back to the person who had summoned him, or go insane. And when he went insane he would still go back. He debated for a moment whether he could kick Ruffian into a gallop and hope to escape out of the spell's range before its grip on him became irresistible. The question answered itself when he realized that he couldn't force himself even to try.

He still had Durwin's letter. If Corneille caught him, he must not get the letter, because it named the Larsons' house. Putting off his inevitable surrender for a few moments longer, Eadig rode back to the pool, untied the letter, and dropped it in the water. The ink had probably not set well yet, and ought to smear enough that anyone finding it would not be able to read what had been written.

Then he turned Ruffian again and started his ride back to Lincoln. He would find out who had summoned him when he entered the town and rode up the hill. Either he would turn off to go to the Larson house, or he would continue to the castle at the top.

The castle it was, the east gate, and by that time the drumming in his head had driven him almost insane. He wanted to scream at it that he knew there was danger ahead but he couldn't do anything about it. Two enchantments pulling him in opposite directions—and nothing he could do to stop the torture except cut his own throat. He was almost glad to see the gate ahead of him and know that at least he would get some relief when he surrendered to the conspirators.

He crossed the drawbridge and reined in when the guards

challenged him, looking with grave suspicion at a peasant boy on what must surely be a knight's horse. If Eadig were refused entry, he would be in serious trouble, for the summoning really would drive him insane then.

He slid out of the saddle, staggering slightly from weariness. "Brought a message for Sage Quentin. This fellow's name is Ruffian. See he's properly attended."

"And your name?" one of the men growled.

"Eadig son of Edwin." There was no use pretending to be Ereonberht when he had been summoned by his true name.

The guard now holding the reins looked to another man, who nodded as if that were the right answer, and said to admit him. A stable hand took charge of Ruffian, and Eadig proceeded on foot into the castle to meet his fate. He was torn between relief that he had been allowed in and mounting terror of what would happen now. The enchanters must be mad enough at him for having escaped them last night. Since then they had somehow learned his real name, and if they also knew how he had witnessed them doing those horrible things to Francois and the d'Airelle brothers, they would be feeling even less well disposed toward him. He could be of no value to them, so they might just kill him out of hand, or turn him into a mindless serf, like Odell.

His feet led him unerringly through the clutter of buildings to the sanctum. The door with the pentacle stood open, so he need not worry about the warding on it. In the first room, which he thought of as the guard room, the trap door at the far end was open, as before. The door to the other room, the one with the frightening warding spell on it stood ajar. It had been closed on his earlier visits.

Still wearing an adept's cape, Satanist Corneille sat at the table, writing with one hand and stroking his beard with the other. He looked up at the visitor and smiled contemptuously. At that moment, the summing compulsion vanished and Eadig was free again. He felt a huge relief, and the drumming faded back to a quiet tapping.

"So, little man, you have answered our call! It took you long enough. Where were you?"

"On my way back to Nottingham, sir."

The sage wiped his quill and laid it down, while regarding Eadig with a sinister interest. How much did he know? While gloating last night, he had told Neil and Piers how he had found a cantor's cape in Eadig's pack, so the pretense of being a page wasn't going to work this time. Corneille folded his hands on his paunch.

"Why?"

"Because I didn't know where the others had gone. I got lost following you last night, and when I asked around, no one knew anything about them. I slept in the hall with the pages, and this morning I went looking for my master in the town and couldn't find him. So I decided to walk home."

The villain smiled even more widely than before, as if he was enjoying plucking wings off this helpless fly he had caught. "You smell of horse, Eadig."

"I rode all day yesterday."

Corneille stood his pen in the inkwell and stood up. "You are a vicious little liar. Come here." He took up the lantern that still stood on the table, lit it with *Fiat ignis*, and pointed to the trap door. "Down you go."

Did they know yet that he had been down there last night or didn't they?

Eadig said, "Why? What's down there?"

"You'll see. You're an adept, so you know I can make you do what I say."

That wasn't quite true unless he had a release spell prepared, but he was a lot bigger, and Eadig had no realistic alternative. Corneille could grab him and throw him down that hole if he wanted. Eadig turned around and went down into utter darkness.

He went backward, like descending a ladder, and stepped aside at the bottom. Phew! There was a disgusting stink in the cellar that hadn't been there yesterday. Corneille followed him with the lantern, facing forward, and blocking off the daylight from the trap as he descended.

When the cantor was two steps from the floor, Eadig pointed at his eyes, and shouted, *"Mori Vermes!"*

Durwin had said it would feel like hot vinegar, and certainly Corneille screamed loud enough. Clutching his eyes, he dropped the lantern, lost his footing, and came down with a blasphemous oath, a graceful swan dive into the flagstones. The lantern smashed and all went dark

Eadig jumped over him and flew up the ladder faster than a swallow in fly time. He slammed the trap shut—there was no bolt, unfortunately, but Corneille would need a few minutes to pull himself together after that fall.

The outside door stood wide open but the door to the other room offered an alternative. It was still ajar, so its warding would not be active. Eadig slammed the outer door loudly and shot in through the other, then looked around quickly for a place to hide.

This room was obviously the real sanctum, furnished with a desk, several large chests, and high shelves laden with jars and bottles. It was more luxurious than any such study Eadig had seen in Helmdon, with weavings on the floor, tapestries on the walls, three high-backed chairs with fat cushions on them, and a bed whose drapes hung open to show that there was no one in it at present. A man could hide in that, but it was too obviously the place to look for him. So Eadig just stood behind the door, where he wouldn't be seen unless Corneille came right inside.

Then he waited. And waited.

There came a crash as the trap was thrown open. Peering through the slit between the door hinges, Eadig watched the adept emerge from the trap and come limping in his direction. He had a bloody nose, and bloodstains on his cape. He looked madder than a wild boar with tusk ache.

He did not peer into the other room, or even pull the door closed as he went by. He left the building and shut the outer door.

Now what? Eadig had escaped for a while, but someone—either Quentin or Corneille—would be coming back there to sleep tonight, or torture someone, or both. It was also a long time since the dinner that Lovise had prepared. She was quite a piece, that one. No wonder Durwin turned into a simpering owl every time he looked at her.

He decided he must first check on the prisoners downstairs. The trap was still open. Come to think of it, the cellar had been strangely quiet. He would have expected Piers and Neil to cheer when Corneille fell.

Not daring to shout, because the window shutters were open and he might be heard by people outside the building, Eadig went down. *Phew!* The stench made his eyes water. The place smelled like Hell's privy.

"Hello? Anyone here?"

No answer.

In a moment his eyes adjusted enough to show him the ruins of the lantern. He extracted the candle. *Fiat ignis . . .* Flame burned up to show that the cellar was empty. No Neil, no Piers, no Francois.

Now what? Eadig was stunned. He blew out the candle, put it back where he had found it, then scrambled up the stairs to get out of the horrible stink.

He could not imagine where Neil and Piers had gone. They couldn't have been rescued, or Corneille would not be at liberty. If Corneille was at large, Quentin must be also, so the evil folk were still effective rulers of the castle. To fall into their hands again would not be advisable under present circumstances.

What to do? Eadig might go in search of Lady Nicholaa, but he could hardly hope to reach the Lucy tower and walk into her bedroom unchallenged. She might also be a prisoner by now, and even if she weren't, he mustn't lead the traitors to her and let them guess that she's already helped him once. Durwin it must be, and most likely Durwin was still at the Larson house. If he wasn't, Eadig had no idea where to start looking for him. That was the safest place to head for. From force of habit, he closed the door to the inner sanctum; he had been taught that such places should never be left open and unattended. He also closed the outer door, for the same reason. The sun had set already.

He could claim Ruffian and hope that the guards wouldn't question him going out, since they had let him in, but he almost certainly couldn't reach Sir Vernon before sunset, and he had destroyed Durwin's letter. So it might be smarter to head over to the west gate and hope that the traitors wouldn't look for him there? He might have a long walk because he'd have to go all the way around the castle, and probably all the way down to the bottom of the hill and back up again, but the important thing was to escape out of the castle. He headed west, zigzagging between buildings.

Da-dum-da-dum-da-dum-da . . .

Oh, saints! It was starting again. What an idiot he was not to see that of course they only had to summon him again. A summoning, at least the one he was familiar with, was a very short, simple, single-voice chant. He would walk right up to Horrible Corneille, who probably smash his face in for what Eadig had done to him with *Mori Vermes*. It was hopeless.

Or maybe not! He had suffered the summoning for an hour or so the last time. Maybe if he could retrieve Ruffian and gallop down to the Larsen house, Durwin would be able to take the compulsion off him. He spun around and began to sprint back eastward. With luck the same men would still be on duty at the paddock by the gate, who would not waste time with questions.

No such luck, the man at the gate was not the boy who had taken Ruffian.

"My horse, please. Stallion called Ruffian."

"What's your name, son?"

"Eadig son of Edwin."

The man nodded as if this information confirmed his worst suspicions. "That accurst troublemaker! We had to put him in a stall." He pointed to the stable. "At the far end."

Eadig ran. The stable was dark, full of horse smells and noises. Then he realized that he *wanted* to go in here, wanted to go to the far end . . . The man who loomed up in front of him had a black beard. He said something that Eadig did not catch. It was probably *Endormirez!* or something similar, the trigger word for the Release spell that put him to sleep instantly.

chapter 18

The solar seemed bright and welcoming after the gloomy anteroom. There was no one there, and Nicholaa went straight across to a drape and pushed it aside. Lovise and I followed her into the bedchamber beyond.

One wall of the room was built of massive masonry, the outlines of the blocks showing through a cover of plaster. Its three windows were mere arrow slits, so this was part of the keep's defenses, although at present being used as pleasant living quarters. Another wall faced inward, so it had a large window, like the solar's. The chamber was pleasantly cool on a hot summer evening, but had no fireplace, so it would be cold in winter. On the bed lay an elderly man, his eyes closed, the sheet over his chest barely moving. His hair and beard were snowy white and needed combing; his face was the color of dead grass. Nicholaa went to the chair beside him.

"Father? Father! . . ." And so on, but there was no response at all. She looked up at me in despair. "He's worse!" she whispered.

I nodded and took her place. I felt his forehead, but if there was a spell there, it was so faint that I could not trust myself not to be imagining it. If this were a normal sickness, I would not expect him to last a week. I gestured for Lovise to try, which clearly surprised Nicholaa.

Lovise laid her hand on the constable's forehead and then nodded. "Very faint, but I think so."

"Does he have conscious moments, my lady?" I knew that he had been capable of speech when Eadig saw him just the previous day.

"Yes. Usually he does. He did yesterday, but I don't think I have ever seen him as bad as this."

I wondered if Sage Quentin had done more damage during his brief visit, but did not say so. If he was as skilled an enchanter as I thought he was, he would be able to raise or lower Lord Richard's condition like a flag on a pole. Now the scoundrel wanted the constable firmly out of action, so he was moribund.

"If his affliction is natural, my lady, I can think of no potion or incantation that will benefit him. But Lovise and I both suspect that he may have been cursed, and in that case we can chant an antiphon that may do him some good. It cannot do any harm, so with your permission, I should like to try it."

She studied me in silence for a moment. She could not be certain that I was not in league with the traitors. "And if his ailment is natural, what are his chances?"

"Less than a week." That was an optimistic estimate.

Lovise said, "I know my father would not even try to treat a patient so grievously smitten in the way of nature."

Nicholaa nodded. "You may proceed, then."

I bowed, admiring her courage, for that was no easy decision she had made. I opened my pack to find the two capes and copies of the *Abi maledictum*.

"Cantor Larson," I said, "I suggest one small change. Let us assume that the evildoers have cursed him more than once, and amend the *maledictum* to the plural, *maledicta*."

Lovise nodded, and we began. I skipped over the super-fluous *nemo*. A few versicles later I felt acceptance, saw Lovise smiling, and then we were done. We looked expectantly at our patient. He took longer to react than Harald had the previous day, for this situation was graver. I had almost decided that the enchantment had failed us when his eyelids flickered and then opened.

Nicholaa gasped as if she had been holding her breath the whole time. "Father?"

Lord Richard blinked a few times. "Nicholaa?" His voice was barely a whisper, but his words were those of a man in full possession of his faculties. "Who are these people?"

"Friends sent by God, Father."

"Whatever they just did, tell them to do it again."

Startled, Lovise and I looked at each other. Obviously the decision must be mine, and I had never heard of repeating a spell that had worked. It probably would do no good at all, but I could not see how it would do any harm.

"As you wish, my lord."

I hummed a note, Lovise nodded, and we began again. If I felt acceptance, it was very faint, but perhaps the mere sound of the chanting raised our patient's spirits, for this time his eyes opened fully, and he said clearly, "Thank you."

Nicholaa practically threw herself onto the bed to kiss him. Lovise and I tactfully withdrew to the solar and closed the drape. Hearing voices outside, I opened the door, and found that three men-at-arms had joined the two Toms in the anteroom. I was relieved to see them, but they regarded me with grave suspicion.

"The constable is much better already," I said. "I expect he will have some orders for you in a few minutes." Rarely have I seen frowns blossom into smiles so dramatically. "And if Sage Quentin or Adept Corneille should appear, do *not* let them in.

In fact, you should arrest them. And if you do, be sure to gag them as quickly as possible so they have no chance to lay curses on you."

Rewarded with a chorus of, "Ayes," I closed the door again.

I returned our scrolls to my pack, but retained my cape, for the hardest part of the day was about to begin. I regarded Lovise with misgivings.

"I think you should go back home. I'll ask Lady Nicholaa to give you an escort." Seeing her jaw clench, I added, "We cursed every other healer in town. Your father must be swamped with new patients."

Her eye glinted blue fire. "And what are you going to do?"

"I'm going to attempt to rescue Neil, Piers and Francois. I can open the warded doors without a cantor, and the castle men-at-arms will do all the rough stuff for me. Much as I appreciate your help so far, love, I don't think I—"

"And if Neil and the others have been cursed? If the man Francois is too injured to move? Then you will need a cantor. And when did I give you permission to call me your love?"

I moved closer and gripped her shoulders. "When you bewitched me. When we have done with the traitors, Lovise, will you marry me?" I'm not sure I had intended to say that, and she did look startled.

"We met just yesterday!"

"Yes, but I've been very busy." I kissed her before she could say more.

Our embrace was interrupted by a cough from Nicholaa. We parted and I expect I blushed as red as my newly betrothed beloved. Blushing is the dark side of a fair complexion.

But Nicholaa was far too happy to take offense at our unseemly display. Her father was with her, leaning on her shoulder and barefoot, but gowned. His hair and beard had been hastily combed. Although he looked weak enough to blow away like a seeding dandelion, his eyes were bright and there was purpose in the set of his jaw.

When his daughter had helped him settle in a chair, I bowed. "My lord."

"Sage Durwin? I appear to owe you my life." He spoke softly, but clearly and deliberately.

"I did naught but my duty to the king and my profession, sir."

He nodded. "And what happens now?" He was smart enough to realize that he must husband his strength, not waste it in ceremonial chitchat.

"There are some of your guards outside, sir. I suggest that you give them orders to arrest Sage Quentin and Adept Corneille, and to liberate the prisoners they have chained up under the sanctum."

He nodded and glanced at Nicholaa, who could not shake off her delighted grin. She went to the door, peered out, and then opened it wide.

"Master-at-arms de Grasse, Father."

In walked one of the men I had spoken to shortly before. He was of average height, but broad and deep-chested, with a jaw like an anvil, a piebald beard, and icicle eyes. An ancient white scar ran from the base of his right ear up to his forehead, narrowly missing his eye. Not a man to trifle with, yet at that moment he was smiling. He saluted the constable.

"Captain, go and release the men who are being held prisoner in the sages' sanctum. Arrest Sage Quentin and Adept Corneille on a charge of treason and lock them up in the new jail."

"Aye, my lord!"

"This is Sage Durwin. You can trust him. Follow his advice on how to deal with the sorcerers and the hellish arts they have

been using, on both me and others. Report back to my daughter
. . . And you had better post guards on me until you have those
two traitors safely chained up."

"Aye, my lord!" The captain's smile was even wider, however
incongruous it seemed on such a face.

Lord Richard murmured, "Proceed," and sagged back in his
chair, his duty done.

De Grasse glanced expectantly at me, and then headed for
the door.

"I prescribe some nourishing soup and a few days' rest, my
lady," I said. "Do not let your father overtire himself."

Nicholaa smiled at me blissfully. "Truly God sent you to us
in our hour of need, Sage."

I was no stranger to gratitude, for I had restored health to
many patients, but I knew that I had come very close to disaster
in this project. "Even sinners can serve him, my lady, and the
glory is His." And we were not out of the forest yet. Indeed, we
were still in the lions' den.

I bowed, Lovise curtseyed, and we withdrew.

More men-at-arms had arrived, crowding the anteroom. De
Grasse looked to me. "I suggest we assemble outside, Sage, and
you can instruct us on how to deal with the traitors."

I nodded, while I recalled Eadig's description of the sanctum and cellar. "We shall need lanterns, rags to gag the prisoners, also shackles and chains, of course."

He began to issue orders, designating men to guard the constable. Lovise and I went downstairs, and found our way to the
main door and the stairs down to ground level. The solar had
still been fairly bright, but down among the shadows, twilight
reigned.

Soon de Grasse joined us with half a dozen men, who eyed
me suspiciously.

"The constable is recovering from his malady; he has ordered us to arrest Sage Quentin and Adept Corneille. Sage Durwin, here, is going to tell us how to go about it."

All eyes turned to me, glanced at my cane, my boot, and finally my face. I wished I had my cape with me, although Nicholaa had probably been right when she said that it would mean nothing to such men.

"I was sent here by His Grace King Henry," I said. "This is Adept Lovise Larson and you can all take your lustful, lecherous eyes off her, because I saw her first. The two traitors, Quentin and Corneille, have captured Sir Neil, the king's officer, and his squire, also one of his men. They are holding them prisoner in the cellar below the new sanctum, which I believe is known as the old jail."

"They've painted a pentagram on the door," de Grasse said.

"I can deal with that. Let's go!"

chapter 19

i made another vain effort to convince Lovise that she ought to go home then, because she naturally wanted to be in at the kill, when Corneille and Quentin were arrested. Again I pointed out that her father would be worried about her and might need help with his patients.

She set her jaw stubbornly. "I am not your wife yet, Sage Durwin of Helmdon, so I do not have to take your orders."

"If I promise never to give you another order as long as we both shall live, will you accede to my wishes and go home now?"

The men-at-arms were waiting by then, clutching chains and shackles and the other things I had ordered. They were amused that this wizard lad might be able to work miracle cures and storm warded sanctums, but he had no more skill at dealing with a stubborn woman than regular god-fearing mortals like them. I found their grins and chuckles intensely annoying, and I could see that Lovise did, too, but she was not going to give up.

"No," she said, "because my wedding vows will override your promise, so let's get started or there won't be any wedding vows. Not that I've agreed to them anyway."

"She doesn't sound too enchanted to me, lads," remarked one of the men-at-arms, and I had to surrender.

"Proceed, then, Master-at-arms," I said, and went with de Grasse as he set off through the maze of buildings. "I wish I knew where those two devil worshipers have gone," I added.

"I checked with the gate watch, Sage, and they haven't been seen leaving. Can they turn into birds? Or make themselves invisible?"

"No. They can do some nasty things, but not those. And the healers in the town are in league with them, all except Healer Larson. All together, I mean all five of them together, could raise the Devil, but just two are not so dangerous."

I thought I knew everything back then, and I was grossly underestimating the likes of Corneille Boterel.

We came to a door marked with a pentacle, recently painted from the look of it. Everyone else then stood back and waited to see how the constable's new magician would deal with this.

I tested it as Eadig had, and decided like him that it was fairly harmless. I was much more worried that Corneille and Quentin might be waiting inside with spanned crossbows aimed at whoever entered, but I murmured the Lord's Prayer and lifted the latch. The door opened, and nothing more happened.

I led the way inside. As Eadig had described that room, it had an inner door by the entrance and an open hatch at the far end; it was furnished with a table and some stools. Someone had been writing at the table, leaving his quill standing in the inkwell. There was a foul stench in the air that I could not identify.

I said, "Leave someone on watch up here, if you please, Captain. Men, do *not* touch that inner door. It isn't marked, but it is warded, and will damage you. A lantern?"

A man handed me a lantern and produced a tinderbox. I took my second opportunity to impress my audience by lighting the candle with the Repeat spell I had ready. Confident that I now had them all sufficiently convinced of my supernatural credentials, I went over to the trapdoor. The cellar below was dark, but was obviously the source of the smell. Wishing I had enough hands to hold my cane, the ladder, the lantern, and my nose simultaneously, I scrambled down.

The stench was reminiscent of many things—rot, feces, gangrene—and the only good thing about it was that it was too strong to be coming from corpses less than one day dead. There were no bodies, dead or alive, only bars, chains, and so on, as Eadig had described—and of course the ominous pentacle on the floor. But no Neil, no Piers, and no Francois. Had they been magically convinced that there was no treachery brewing in Lincoln, and sent off back to report as much to the king? That seemed too good to be true.

De Grasse had followed me down. He said, "What in hell makes this stink, Your Wisdom? Boiled dog shit?"

"I think it may be the smell of Hell itself, Captain. I fear some horrible evil has been done here. Send a man to the paddock, will you? Ask if Sir Neil d'Airelle's horses that arrived yesterday are still there. And let's you and me get out of here before I lose yesterday's dinner."

Upstairs I found Lovise studying the warded door, while the rest of the men-at-arms studied her. She grimaced. "This is more intense than anything I've ever met, Sage."

I joined her and recoiled when I tested the door. "Or I! Captain, it will take us some time to open this one. Would you please leave a couple of men on guard outside here and get everyone else available onto the hunt for Quentin and Corneille?" I also explained that it would be quite safe to knock on the door if they wanted me. Then I closed it behind them.

Lovise, seated at the table, was studying what had been

written on the small piece of parchment that had been lying there beside the inkwell and pen.

"I can't read this," she complained. "What language is it? Greek?"

I took it and held it to the fading light from the window. "Not Greek. Nor Hebrew. I'd recognize the letters if it were either, although I couldn't read the words. It's in no alphabet I know." I tossed it back down on the table. "Let's get the warding curse off that door, shall we?"

Her smile could have melted iron. "Go ahead. I shall be interested to watch. Very instructive, I expect."

"The only antiphon we have with us needs two voices."

"But you wanted to send me home. You said you didn't need me any more here."

I was quite sure I hadn't said that, not exactly. She was playing, of course, and I would happily have spent hours with her in such meaningless chatter, remembering later not a word that was said, only her smile, her lips, her eyes.

Unfortunately our discussion was interrupted by a knock on the door. Captain de Grasse had returned to report that Sir Neil and Squire Piers had collected their horses at dawn and left the castle. They had ridden two and led the other two. I thanked him, but the news was bitter. My own Bon Appétit had gone, but that was the least of my worries, for we were playing for much higher stakes than one palfrey. Neil and Piers were still alive, which was a relief, I thought I knew what had happened to the man who had ridden her yesterday—I assumed that Eadig was probably close to Nottingham by now, astride Ruffian—but what had happened to Man-at-arms Francois? I wondered if they might be inside the other, warded room.

Lovise saw much of that in my face when I closed the door. "They're still alive, though—Neil and Piers?"

"After a fashion, maybe. I cannot believe Neil would have left here voluntarily. I was thinking that Corneille and the coven were planning to work their evil tonight, but they must have done it last night, after Eadig left. He was asleep on the wood-pile, poor kid, and didn't see or hear the sorcerers returning around midnight. The d'Airelles have a whole day's start on us."

"But what are these traitors planning? Is Neil heading home to tell the king that there isn't anything wrong, here in Lincoln? Could they make him do that?"

"Of course they could," I said. "You've seen fairground swindlers working deceptions like that—convincing customers that their magic pickled snake eggs will make boys grow muscles or bring girls the men of their dreams. On that scale it's just slick patter, a cheap swindle, but I'm sure Corneille's black arts could convince Sir Neil that he was the Queen of Sheba. That's not the point!

"Think of how it started. The letter to the king was a forgery. Elvire told us that there were no mysterious visitors, and old Sir Courtney conveniently died before he could be questioned. You don't commit forgery and murder just so you can later send the king a message saying that there was no truth in your previous letter. The letter was carefully designed so that King Henry would take it seriously but not too seriously. He didn't send the justiciar north with an army, he sent one of his *familiares*."

In fact he had sent two, and neither of us had shone so far.

"I still don't follow," Lovise said.

"When Neil arrives at the king's camp to report on his mission, he'll be granted a private audience, and he probably won't have to surrender his sword first, because he's a *familiaris*. Even if he does, he'll still have a knife on his belt. He may even be able to take his brother, Squire Piers, in with him, and he too may be armed."

Her eyes widened. "Oh, no!"

"Oh yes! And we don't know where he's gone: back to Nottingham or straight to Dover? We don't know where the king is. Neil does, and he certainly carries a royal warrant giving him royal authority, which I don't."

It was too late in the day to set out in pursuit, so our next step must be to catch and de-claw Corneille and his gang. Tomorrow we should have to begin the chase.

I found our spell-removing text in my pack, and this time Lovise made no objection to helping. We chanted at the warded door, and we both felt only a faint acceptance.

"Our villainous friends take no chances," I said. I tested the door again, and it was still warded. As we had for Constable Richard, we tried the chant again. This time it seemed to have more effect, and at a third attempt we cleared the final spell and it was safe to enter the inner sanctum. Triple-warded! The conspirators took no chances.

We had no idea, of course, that Eadig had been in there less than an hour before us. We saw what he had: a bed, a desk, shelves of medicines, chairs, and some chests, at least one of which should hold the Satanists' grimoires.

I closed the door, wishing it had a bolt on that side. "Let's see what's lurking in those boxes."

"First let's light some candles and close the shutters," Lovise suggested, ever practical, so we began by doing that.

All four chests were warded, so we had work ahead of us. The first three chests contained nothing of interest to us, except a battered old grimoire. A quick glance inside showed that it contained healing spells. It might have belonged to the evicted and murdered healer, Bjarni, but he would have taken his books with him, so more likely it was Quentin's, for he would need such recipes to act out his role as in-house healer.

"We'll have to go through this," I said, "in case some of these spells are not what they seem to be. But let's hope fourth time lucky."

The fourth chest was even more heavily warded than the door, and put us to a lot of trouble before we could lift the lid and peer inside. The first thing we saw was a fleece, or rather several fleeces sewn together to make a bedcover for winter nights. It was bulky and heavy, and the sort of thing that would be dumped tight at the bottom of a storage chest so it need not be lifted out until the cold weather came. I wasn't going to be distracted by that fancy, though, so I hauled it out and found myself looking at boards, the bottom of the chest.

Disappointed, I stepped back and studied the matter. Why ward a bedspread? Was this just a distraction? The sight lines looked wrong . . . the bottom of the chest must be very thick . . . I reached in, hunting for concealed hinges or a catch to unlock a false bottom, and instead my fingers went right through the boards as if they weren't there at all. They weren't. I touched something that felt like a book, and lifted it out. It was exactly what I had hoped to find: another grimoire. Its covers were made of stout black oak, its clasps of solid brass, and it had a pentagram stamped on it in gold, with the number IV in the center.

"You know, I've been thinking," Lovise said quietly. "If you'll swear me a solemn oath that all your children will be as clever as you are, then I probably will have to marry you."

"With you as their mother, they'll be three times as smart."

"Flattery is not what I asked for."

"I'll promise anything under the sun if it will make you marry me."

"That statement does not inspire confidence in your veracity."

"Stubborn wench! Then take this and I'll see what else I can find that may move you." I reached back through the box's illusory floor, and ultimately brought out four more grimoires. At the cost of dirtying my fingers, I felt around every inch of that chest and could find nothing more.

But what I had found was more than enough to confirm all our fears. The books were identical, each much smaller than Harald Larson's huge volume, smaller even than most in the Helmdon library, but beautifully crafted with pages of fine lambskin enclosed between oak covers held by shiny brass clasps. They were numbered from I to V. The text was a single incantation for five voices, in old Church Latin. Although it was written in an ancient minuscule hand, this was so finely done that it was not difficult to read. However, with five voices— Primus, Secundus, and so on—the logic was devilishly hard to follow.

We opened Book IV on the desk and began to study it—in silence, because I was afraid to speak a word of this foulness aloud and would not let Lovise do so. The text was the heart and core of Corneille's evil. It could only be the black magic that had been invoked the previous night over the wretched prisoners then chained in the cellar. By the second page I felt physically ill: demons, devils, and human sacrifice! Whatever had we done to bring such iniquity into our land?

The text referred to "servants", "offerings", and "recruits". It was obvious that the "servants" were the five Satanists chanting the incantation. The "offerings" were the victims they were now tendering, body and soul, as a price for the "service" they requested, meaning enslavement of the "recruits" to serve Satan in future in whatever acts the prime servant directed.

"Why are so many of the words underlined?" Lovise asked.

"Because . . . um . . . er . . . because," I said triumphantly, "the only words underlined are 'offerings' and 'recruits'. The 'servants' must always number five, but the 'offerings' and 'recruits' may be one person or more, so the forms of the words will change, singular or plural."

"That must make it the very devil to chant."

"Too true, but we are dealing with experts here, love."

So now we could guess that Francois had been offered up as the price for the two d'Airelles' enslavement. Had Eadig been discovered, he would have been dragged bodily to Hell also. I flipped to the final page and confirmed my conclusions: Neil and Piers would be turned into puppets, unable to resist any commands that the principal enchanter gave them.

I slammed the grimoire shut. "That's enough!"

"Too much!" Lovise agreed.

"Let's take these over to the kitchens and burn them," I suggested. "Then no matter what happens, this monstrous evil will not contaminate the world again. Not hereabouts, anyway."

Lovise took two of them, I tucked the other three under my arm and led the way to the door.

As I said, even then I was greatly underestimating the evil-doers. Constable Lord Richard had been enchanted several times over, as had the door and the chest, so I should have been more cautious. I was in such a hurry that I barely heard the sudden thunder of the warning drum. Never before had I heard of a door being warded on both sides, but that one was. The moment I touched the latch, the curse hurled me backwards. I landed flat on my back in a heap of grimoires, totally unconscious.

Lovise was left by herself, with no way of removing the curse from me or the door. She was effectively locked in, and all the windows were barred.

chapter 20

"*Retournez!*"

Eadig was frozen, aching all over, and really, really, really in need of a pee. It was dark. He was lying on straw, but not much straw, on cobblestones stinking of horse dung. Huh? Then he remembered coming to the stable to get Ruffian . . . Corneille . . . *Oh, shit!*

"Get up!" The voice was familiar.

He struggled to obey. It wasn't easy. His feet began screaming pins-and-needles at him.

"Need to pee!"

"Do it, then, but if you aim it at me I'll have Odell smash all your teeth out."

The horses wouldn't like it. Human pee didn't smell right to them, but Eadig was past worrying. What time was it, anyway? Oo, that felt good . . .

The moment he pulled his britches back up, the voice told him to put his hands behind his back. It was Corneille's voice, but that wasn't surprising. The bastard roped his wrists tight enough to hurt. Then a rag was forced between his teeth and tied even tighter.

The enchanter said, "Bring him, Odell. If he causes any trouble, hit him."

A hand the size of a saddle wrapped itself around Eadig's neck and moved him. Causing trouble just wasn't on the agenda. Staggering along on pins-and-needles feet was. Out of the stable, into the night . . . It was even darker out there, but the man in front, who must be Satanist Corneille, was setting a fierce pace, and the giant behind was keeping up, so Eadig had to. The hand around his neck was holding him up more often than it was pushing him forward. Could both men see in the dark? All Eadig could see was stars above the buildings. The Dipper the right way up meant it must be near midnight, and a pentacle at midnight meant black magic, and so whatever had happened to Sir Neil and Squire Piers was about to happen to Eadig son of Edwin.

Eadig the late son of Edwin.

They arrived at the sanctum. Two men-at-arms were standing outside, keeping guard over the door, but they were chatting and did not react at all to the new arrivals. Eadig was not taken close enough to them to lash out with a kick, and when he tried to make noises through his gag, Odell squeezed the pressure points under his ears hard enough to make him squeal like a tortured rabbit. The guards did not seem to hear anything. Eadig could—the *Tambour* drum was going crazy inside his head: *da-DUM . . . da-DUM . . . da-DUM . . .*

Either the door had been left ajar or its warding had been removed, because Corneille just pushed it open, without pausing to speak a password, and went in. Odell the giant pushed Eadig inside after him. Even the candles in the guard room were bright when your eyes had been working in darkness. The door to the inner sanctum was open, with more light coming from there. Quentin and another men were at the guard room table, chattering away in French . . . Quentin's snaky eyes gleamed when he saw the prisoner arriving . . . a pile of books on the table, probably grimoires . . . the outer door thumped shut.

Odell delivered his prisoner to the trap door and let go. Eadig swayed, but the pins-and-needles had almost stopped, so he didn't fall head first into the hole.

"Your choice, pest," Corneille said. "You can go down by yourself or be thrown down. And you're not going to hide under the desk tonight. Tonight you will be entree, or perhaps dessert. Yes, make that dessert. Sweet, tender dessert."

Eadig wanted to point out that the stairs were very nearly as steep as a ladder and his hands were not only tied behind him but tied so tightly that they were almost numb already. He couldn't say so, though, because of the gag. The Satanist already knew all that and would probably enjoy watching him hurtling down into the cellar—feetfirst, headfirst, in my lady's chamber . . .

Having no choice, Eadig sat down, lowered his feet into the opening, and then wriggled in after them. Struggling to grip the slats with his hands, he slid downward, step by step, until he was standing on the flagstone floor. That Satanic stink was still there, and he supposed now that it was about to get much stronger when tonight's abomination was completed.

All five lamps above the pentacle were lit already, and the five lecterns set in position at the points. One man was busily dressing himself in one of the black robes, while another was starting to strip, ignoring the fact that there was a woman sitting . . . *Oh, Lord, save us!* It was Lovise Larson, bound and gagged, seated in the middle of the pentacle. She hadn't seen him, because she had her back to him, and was looking at—

Worse! The man chained against the far wall, where Sir Piers had stood yesterday, was Durwin. Only then did Eadig realize that he had secretly been hoping that Durwin would somehow appear to rescue him, leading in a band of men-at-arms to slaughter the devil-worshipers. But if both Lovise and Durwin had been captured, then there wasn't any hope at all.

Durwin was staring at Eadig with equal dismay, because Eadig was supposed to have been safely away in Nottingham hours ago, letting cats out of bags.

Corneille had come down the stairs. He said, "Move!" and gave Eadig a hard shove. Eadig staggered forward, then stopped. He wasn't going to cooperate in his own last rites in any way at all! His stubbornness made no difference—he was pushed through the gate, into the pentacle. Lovise looked up and her eyes widened. Unable to say anything, Eadig just shrugged.

"Sit!"

Eadig shook his head, so then his legs were kicked out from under him, pitching him down on floor. Hard!

Corneille knelt at his feet, holding a rope. "I owe you a hard kick in the face, brat, and if you give me any trouble at all, that's what you'll get, understand?"

Eadig nodded, and offered no resistance as Corneille began to bind his ankles.

"Oh, brave man!" Durwin said. "Brave, brave man! A child half your size, bound and gagged and helpless, and you threaten to kick him in the face? Is there nothing you won't stoop to?"

The Satanist looked around at him. "I don't know. I might try to find out in an hour or so. Like ordering you to cut off your own balls, for instance. And you'll do it, you know."

Footsteps on the stairs announced that the rest of the gang were assembling.

"Odell!" Durwin shouted. "Go and tell the master-at-arms that Durwin's chained to the wall down here! They're going to raise the Devil here, Odell. You're on the wrong side, you're helping Satan, Odell. Your soul—"

Quentin ran forward and backhanded him across the mouth, then turned to look past Eadig at the giant. "He's lying, Sergeant. Don't believe anything he said. You can go home, now. Go to bed now."

Eadig heard the ladder creak as the giant began to climb.

Satisfied, Quentin inspected the trickle of blood from Durwin's lip. "He does what I tell him, you fool. Just me, no one else. Only two of us enthralled him: Walter of Froyle and me. We have to renew the spell about twice a week, but that's nothing compared to what's going to happen to you, with five of us chanting. We had the d'Airelle brothers down on their knees licking the floor."

"You will burn in Hell for all eternity."

"Not I!" Quentin snapped. "Henry will arrive in Hell before I do, but he will burn and I shall not. At the Dark Lord's side, I shall sit in comfort, watching that Plantagenet dog writhe in torment through all eternity."

"You really believe the Devil's promises, you idiot?"

"What I believe doesn't matter. And just in case the d'Airelle brothers fail, we now have a second string to our bow—you, *Familiaris* Durwin. You, too, have access to the king."

Durwin laughed. "Me? Access to the king?"

"Oh, yes. It was Neil who warned us of that, and he cannot lie to me. Henry really ought to choose his friends more carefully. You won't even need a dagger, because you know how to chant, and we shall arm you with a malediction that will stop his foul heart."

Eadig looked around to see what the others were doing. Quentin and Corneille were undressing and the other three had already put on robes. Everything else, even shoes, went into the chest. Two of the enchanters began carrying books around, one to each lectern.

"To your places, if you, please, brothers!" Sage Corneille was the only one whose face was visible to Eadig. He frowned as he regarded the layout. "The offerings are too close to the center. Henri, Tancred, move them please."

Hands gripped Eadig's shoulder and dragged him nearer the edge of the pentagon. Another of the robed men moved Lovise, and no more gently.

"Better!" Corneille said. "Tonight of course, fellow *Savants*, we shall again chant the *Adeste daemonia*. I remind you that we have a couple of minor changes of wording. Last night we had one offering and two recruits. Tonight we have two offerings and one recruit. So the—"

"You don't need the woman," Durwin shouted. "Kill the boy if you must kill somebody, but leave Lovise out of this abomination."

Eadig nodded vigorously to show that he approved of this idea, although it wasn't the program he would really prefer, which would be to cut all the enchanters' throats with a rusty saw. Slowly.

"If you interrupt again," Corneille told Durwin, "I shall have to gag you. I prefer not to, because we shall be able to judge by the timbre your screams when you are genuinely being possessed—not that I expect you to have much opportunity to fake your response. You should consider yourself honored to witness this magnificent demonstration of conjuration. I am sure the self-styled wise men of Helmdon never taught you anything as advanced as the *Adeste daemonia*."

He cleared his throat. "Now, brothers, do please remember: *two* offerings and *one* recruit. *Sacrificia* plural, *tiro* singular. If anyone wishes, we can do a read-through. That will take some time, and I am sure we are all anxious to get to bed, after two busy nights. No?

"As before, we use the plural second person when summoning the guests. It is," he told Durwin, "never possible to know exactly how many of these, um, entities is or are present."

"Too many, either way," Durwin said in an astonishingly calm voice.

"Quite. They also have a distinctive odor, which will permeate our clothing, and that's why we change into these working costumes. You, Durwin, will survive the ceremony, so if you wish to undress, we can pack your garments away in the chest to preserve them. Otherwise you'll have to burn them tomorrow."

"Very kind of you, I'm sure, but I find this dungeon rather chilly. You, on the other hand, are playing with fire. Why don't you get on with the farce and we'll see who laughs last?"

"You threats don't worry us, Sage Durwin of Helmdon. Your spells don't work. You tried to curse all five of us, but we had taken precautions. We are all completely curse-proof against anything you could throw against us. But don't worry. You will be very happy with your new slave status—you will feel as if you are achieving your life's ambition." He glanced around his accomplices. "Ready, brothers? You are all quite happy with omitting a read-through first?"

Four cowled heads nodded and mumbled agreement.

"Very well, then. At the beginning." He blew a note on a pitch pipe, and launched into the enchantment.

Adeste daemonia called on demons to attend. As its title proclaimed, the spell was in Latin—old Church Latin, so far as Eadig could tell. It was also by far the longest and most complicated enchantment he had ever heard. Corneille was first voice, singing the equivalent of versicles. Sometimes the other four had solo responses, but not always all of them, nor in the same order. Sometimes they chanted together, as a choir—a choir of Hell, for they were summoning major devils. Eadig recognized many of the names, having been taught to shun any incantation that mentioned even one of them: Lilith, Iblis, Azazel, Beelzebub, Minos, Rhadamanthus, Aeacus, Pluto, Samyaza, Puck, Angra-Mainyu, Set, Loki, Rahu, Baal, although never Satan, but there were dozens of others that he had never heard of, and those must be devils also.

Gradually the demonic summons began to work. The light faded as if the lanterns were being obscured by smoke; the dreadful stench of dung and rotting meat grew stronger. *Something* was happening in the center of the pentacle, although it was hard to make out exactly what. The air above it glowed, usually faintly, but sometimes bright, as it writhed, grew, shrank, changed color, varied from one to many. The floor was shaking, the lamps swinging, the ground making ominous noises, like belching or farting.

Eadig wanted to pray, but he found that he couldn't, that somehow the words were being blocked. He was both shivering and sweating at the same time.

With a sound of grinding rock, something oozed up through the floor at the center of the pentacle, between him and Lovise. It might be a giant's head, or a bundle of decayed corpses, or just an enormous suppuration—it was hard to look at, and never stayed quite the same for more than a moment. It, or they, shone in disgusting greens and yellows. At times it had eyes, two or more, and one or many fanged mouths. That might be a vast arm resting on the floor as it heaved itself higher, and if so it had claws like scythe blades.

The incantation ended in a triumphant chorus. Five grimoires were shut, and the chanters leaned on their lecterns as if recovering from a long exertion.

"By what name are you conjured?" Corneille cried, still speaking Latin. His voice faded away in strange echoes.

We are Legion.

That answer seemed to originate inside Eadig's head, and yet it reverberated through the cellar as the singing had; it was both an intimate whisper in his ear and an echoing thunder from far away. The vision was never still, changing constantly, both too horrible to look at, and yet impossible not to look at, for it reeked of evil, hatred, and infinite power.

"Legion, I bid you to enthrall the prisoner Durwin of Helmdon to me so that he shall always do my bidding, fanatically serve my purposes, and never betray me."

Yuuuh? Legion gurgled as if its mouth or mouths had filled with vomit. *And what price do you offer for this service?*

"I give you Healer Lovise Larson and Adept Eadig son of Edwin, body and soul, to feed your hate."

Two enormous eyes rolled around the monster and came to a halt staring down at Eadig.

Two virgins without enough sins to be crunchy. Still, two for one is better than you gave us last night. Let us hear what Durwin bids.

All five enchanters shouted out in anger or panic, with Corneille the loudest. "No! It was we who summoned you by the ancient call!"

Silence! Legion's whispered command stopped every sound. *At the end of your song you offered us this choice. Speak, little Durwin, and speak well, because we are offered two virgins. You, if you will excuse my mentioning it, do not qualify in that category.*

Durwin seemed surprised, but certainly agreeable. "I offer you all five of these traitor Satanists, body and soul, to feed your hate."

But the worshipers are already ours, given time. However long any of them may live, we can wait; 'twill be no loss for us, for we are eternal.

"Five are better than two."

This is true. What services do you demand in return?

"Nothing! Nothing at all. I do not bargain with the likes of you. Take them and begone."

Five black sinners as a free gift instead of two virgins as price for a possession? That smells like a better offer. What do you think, Corneille of Lepuix?

"You cannot!" The sage's voice was almost a scream. "You are bound by our enchantment!"

You should have done the read-through. You sang words that were not there last night. Have you no better offer?

"Yes, yes!" Corneille screamed. "Take them all but me! I give you Durwin, Quentin, Walter, Lovise, Henri, Tancred, and Eadig, but leave me so that I may continue to serve you here, in the world of sinners, forever."

The demon, or demons, found that amusing. He-they guffawed, making the whole building rock. *We think not, little Corneille. We like Durwin's offer better.*

"But I am offering you seven souls, seven bodies, to feed your hate, and I ask nothing in return, nothing."

True, the demons said thoughtfully, *but we had rather leave Durwin here, in the world of sinners, until some other night. In time he may serve us better than you will. We accept your price, Durwin of Helmdon, and laud your lover's cunning. Come to me, dear Quentin of Lepuix.*

A vast, slobbering maw opened in Legion's shivering, shifting image, emitting a belch whose stench that made Eadig's head swim. Screaming, pleading, and cursing, Quentin approached it, fighting every step, but drawn inexorably. When he arrived, a black tongue lolled out like a welcoming carpet, and he climbed aboard. He and the tongue vanished inside. Legion made some disgusting chewing noises, and then spat out a soggy mess that might once have been a black gown.

Again Legion belched thunderously, then metamorphosed into a scrambling mass of smaller demons like cockroaches, struggling and tearing at one another with sickle claws, each one trying to reach the top of the heap.

Walter! they screeched. *Walter of Froyle, come to us.*

As reluctant as Quentin, another robed enchanter dragged himself inward to meet his fate. The pack sucked him in, ripping his gown off him in bloody shreds, and then devouring his naked body while he screamed. At the end, when only his head was left, they played with it, tossing it up and catching it, and somehow, even lacking lungs to breathe with, it screamed and screamed. Then they ate it also, and spat out the teeth in a tiny hailstorm.

That left Henri Morlaix, Tancred de Umfraville, and Corneille Boterel. One after another they went, and each death seemed more horrible than the last. Corneille took the longest to go, burning and melting like a lump of soft fat, bubbling screams all the time. Lovise Larson was weeping and sobbing prayers. Durwin just watched, grim and ashen-faced. Eadig wished he could faint.

Finally there was only Legion itself, or themselves. Now they reeked of roast meat; it sweated gravy. *Very tasty! Will there be anything more, Boy Enchanter? The stench of pity in here is quite sickening.*

"Nothing more," Durwin said hoarsely. "You have done. In Christ's name begone."

Then I wish you a fond evilbye, the monster said. *I know we shall meet again, some dark night.* It dwindled and vanished with a disgusting sucking noise.

The lanterns brightened.

chapter 21

i have already admitted that I underestimated Corneille Boterel and his accomplices, but no one had ever warned me about *Le Salon de Satan*. I had no idea that such an organization existed. "The Sons of Satan" was what we called them later as we hunted them all across England. It was years before we were able to catalogue all the chants and tricks Quentin and Corneille must have used to avoid capture that day, to smuggle the town healers into the castle when the guards had orders to forbid them entry, and eventually to assemble in the sanctum building right under the noses of the men-at-arms guarding the only door.

Nor have I ever claimed credit for foiling the Satanists' efforts to enthrall me. That was all Lovise's doing. Finding herself locked into the room upstairs with me an inanimate lump on the floor, she remembered what I had told her about trip wires and proceeded to add six words to each copy of the final chorus in the enslavement chant. As Legion gloatingly told the Sons, they should have done a read-through, for then at least one of them must surely have noticed that deadly addition.

So the conspirators had gone and we three had survived, but the danger was by no means past. Neil and Piers had a clear day's start and were undoubtedly riding hell for leather on their way to find King Henry and kill him. The night was halfway gone and we were all exhausted.

I dredged up from memory the text of *Cambrioleur*, a solo-voice spell to open locks. I chanted it and my shackles fell free. With my muscles all tangled by pins and needles, I staggered over to Louise and knelt down to untie her bonds. Eadig made frantic noises through his gag.

"I'll get to you in a moment," I snapped, struggling with the knots.

He made louder noises, rolling his eyes and jerking his head. As soon as I had the sense to realize what he might be telling me, I started playing the question game.

"There's a knife?"

Nod—nod—nod. More head waving.

"In the chests?"

Nod—nod—nod.

So I went to the chests and located the writing supplies he had discovered two days before, which included a penknife. That solved the first problem, releasing the prisoners.

The second problem was the unbearable stench that had saturated our clothes. The only available substitutes were the clothes the Satanists had discarded—for which they would never have any use again. They were all men's garments, of course, but Lovise was tall. She selected some and went off upstairs to change. Eadig and I did what we could with the rest. Our skin and hair still reeked, of course, but that was far down our list of troubles.

At this point a truly romantic hero would have leapt on his trusty warhorse and galloped off to cut down the would-be assassins on the palace doorstep, or at least warn the king that they were on their way. But eight years of study in the rural peace of Helmdon had not trained me to be a Lancelot, Roland, or Beowulf. I was at the end of my tether, out of my depth, dead on my feet, and I freely admit it.

I also faced some practical difficulties that heroes in romances never seem to. The young moon would long since have set, so I couldn't leave before first light. Ruffian needed several days' rest and Neil had taken our other horses, which meant that I would have to beg some substitutes from either Nicholaa or her father. Worst of all, I had no idea where the king was and I had no warrant to provide me with authority. I should have to travel as a freeman on his own business, and that would take more money than I possessed.

When the three of us gathered upstairs in the inner sanctum—with the door stoutly wedged open—I said, "The next thing we must do is get word to Master-at-arms de Grasse. I suppose there will be guards on the gates."

"There should be two right outside," Eadig said, between yawns.

I had forgotten them. "Still?"

"Corneille walked right by them and me too and they never even saw us."

I proceeded to open the shutters and peer out. There, to my delight and astonishment, I saw the sentries I had ordered the previous evening, although naturally not the same men. One was seated on a stool, leaning back against the wall and dozing under a rug, while the other paced up and down in the cold. I did not recognize either of them, but clearly Master-at-arms de Grasse had his squad well trained.

"God bless," I said. The man walking spun around, the other scrambled to his feet.

They chorused, "Sage Durwin?"

It crossed my mind then that, so far as they or any other

outsiders were concerned, I must have spent the last ten or twelve hours locked up with the delectable Lovise, refusing to answer knocking on the outer door. How they must envy me! Then Eadig popped his head out beside mine, giving them something else to wonder about.

I said, "I assume Master-at-arms de Grasse is in bed and asleep, like any good Christian?"

"Aye, sir," said the taller of the two.

"I urgently need to speak with him. If you don't have authority to waken him, bring me whoever does. You can tell him that Sage Quentin and Adept Corneille are both dead. And I must speak with Mistress Elvire, also."

"My reputation is utterly ruined," said a quiet voice behind me.

I spun around to take her in my arms. "Now you have no choice—you will have to marry me."

"I could enter a nunnery."

"Over my dead body." I kissed her.

"You don't need me," Eadig said, while dragging a rug out to the guard room. Neither of us answered.

"Besides," I gasped, breaking off a kiss that was becoming too compulsive to pursue further outside of holy wedlock, "you saved my life, all our lives. What exactly did you write in their grimoires?"

"I don't remember." Releasing me, Lovise went over to sit on the bed. "Waken me when it's Michaelmas."

"Don't sleep here! Your father will slaughter me. Elvire will find you somewhere to rest."

"She had better be quick."

I began pacing up and down, struggling to stay awake and battling with the problem of how I could send a warning to the king.

In an amazingly short time, a shout outside the window announced the arrival of Captain de Grasse. He was untidily clad in civilian clothes and his hair was a rook's nest. With him was Elvire, looking immaculate by comparison. I roused Lovise, who was still awake, if only just, and led her out through the guard room where Eadig was already snoring.

Both de Grasse and Elvire recoiled when they caught a whiff of us.

"We are unharmed," I said, "although we had a very narrow escape. I think the lady Nicholaa should be informed, for I need her help on a matter of the greatest possible urgency. Maid Lovise needs rest, and I know she must have new clothes, because her old ones will have to be burned."

"We can manage all that. Come, dear." The ever-efficient Elvire took Lovise by the hand and led her away.

I told de Grasse, "I must report to Lady Nicholaa as soon as possible, but I had better clean up first. What you smell on me is the stench of Hell. The immediate danger is past, but the future emergency is not. Indeed it is more urgent than ever."

As the fine warrior he was, he accepted my words without question or argument. "I'm due for a bath myself this week. At this hour the water won't be as hot as it should be, but why don't we clean up together while you tell me what's happened?"

How much I told de Grasse in the bathhouse, and how much he believed me, I cannot recall. Granted that I had just had a very narrow escape from what I can only think of as the worst form of abject slavery, is it surprising that my mind was not at its sharpest? Even worse, I was now certain that I was the only person capable of saving the king's life. He ruled so much of Europe, that his death now, before his heir, Lord Henry, reached adulthood, might throw half Christendom into chaos.

But that night held yet another miracle, for I was able to

unload my troubles onto the shoulders of a fifteen-year-old girl. Nicholaa de la Haye was destined to be one of the most remarkable women of her era, second in my mind only to Queen Eleanor, and she showed her mettle that day. She received me and de Grasse in her parlor, with Elvire present for propriety. I told her the whole story as well as I could.

While I talked, I somehow worked out details that I had missed earlier. Quentin had done the preparatory work—evicting Healer Bjarni and installing his other accomplices in the town. When all was ready, their leader, Corneille had arrived, making the coven complete. With their pentacle operational, they had been able to foresee the king's men's arrival.

The forged Courtney letter about treason had mentioned the possibility of magic, so the king would surely send a sage, who would be their greatest danger. So they set a trap for me, and I fell right into it by lifting the spell they had laid on Harald Larson, the only man in town who could assist me or even enlighten me on the situation. By Wednesday night they knew where I was, and by Thursday dawn they had ensorcelled Neil and Piers. Neil, now their eager accomplice, would have warned them that I, too, had the king's ear, so I was both a potential danger and a potential second string to their bow if the D'Airelles' attack failed for any reason. He had willingly told them my name so that they would be able to summon me.

It must have been a very muddled account, for I can recall Nicholaa's frowns and quiet questions when I left something out or contradicted myself, but in the end she sighed and turned to de Grasse.

"Well, Master-at-arms? Do you believe him?"

"Not easily, my lady. It's a nightmare."

"With the king's life at risk, do we dare disbelieve him?"

The old warrior smiled. "Certainly not, my lady."

"Then you will lend me a second horse?" I asked, half in hope and half in dread. At that point I would rather have been chained up in dungeon, so that I could not be blamed for whatever was going to happen.

And this was when the lady Nicholaa truly began to show her quality. Faced with an epic choice, she kept her head and made the correct, but hard, decision. "No, I will not. Not right now. What do you say, Captain? Is the sage fit to ride?"

"No, my lady. I've seen men go to sleep in the saddle. They either fall off and break their necks or they get dragged, which is worse."

"You are only human, Durwin," she told me. "You need rest."

"But the king—"

"Yes, I understand. You have told me four times about Sir Neil being enthralled to seek him out and assassinate him. You have asked me three times to send a message to Healer Larson as soon as the gates are opened. You need to rest, Durwin. Grandiose heroics will do no good now. Your only weapon is your enchantment skill, and for that you must have the use of your brains. You must outsmart the enemy, not outfight him. At the moment you are incapable of out-maneuvering a mushroom. At sunrise I will send to the square tower to ask if the sheriff is back and, if he is not, to learn when he will be back and where he is now. I will consult with my father, but only if I think he is strong enough to take on the burden. In the meantime, you are going to eat something and then go to bed. Is that clear?"

I nodded and said, "Yes, my lady. That is clear. And thank you."

"I will find you a room somewhere in the tower."

"No need, my lady. The bed in the sanctum will be fine. Bang on the outer door if you need me. The warding will only act if you try to open it."

I have no memory of going to bed. When I awoke the sun was shining and there was food on a nearby table. I drank something, probably ate something, and went straight back to sleep. Rest is the greatest medicine, but it needs time.

"Are you dead or alive?" Eadig asked.

I opened one eye. "Mind your own business." Then I sat up and said, "Omigod! What time is it?"

"About an hour short of sunset."

Panic! "But I have to go, should have gone long since!"

He poured some wine into a beaker and handed it to me. The food, I noticed, had gone. So had the heap of clothes on the floor. The room itself was tidier than it had been. Eadig had enjoyed much more sleep the previous night than I had.

"Lovise?"

He flashed the little-boy grin that was as distinctively Eadig as a coat of arms. "I was told that Lars was dozing outside the castle gates when they were opened at dawn. He took her home, but a little while ago she came calling on Lady Nicholaa, to ask how you were."

As I threw off the cover, he grinned again. "Shouldn't you put some clothes on first? I mean at least until you're properly married? Besides, what will Lady Nicholaa think?"

He had found some clean garments for me. I needed a shave, but that would have to wait for another day. Time, time! I had slept away a whole day when I should have been riding in pursuit of the killers. What sort of *familiaris* was I turning out to be, sleeping when my liege lord was in such danger? I headed for the Lucy Tower at a pace that had Eadig running to stay with me.

Now the little parlor was crowded. Lady Nicholaa sat in her personal chair, which wasn't a throne but somehow seemed to be. The second chair was awarded to me. Lovise and Eadig both had stools, while Lars sat on the floor, squeezing his bulk into a corner. Elvire was absent, possibly because the room was packed to capacity without her. Wine was handed around. We established that we were all in good health.

"How is Lord Richard?" I asked.

"Making progress," Nicholaa said. "He was relieved to hear that you had solved the Quentin and Corneille problem, but I did not burden him with the details. And did my prescription heal the healer?"

"I am much improved, thanks to it, my lady. But it was not I who dealt with the Satanists. It was Lovise."

Lovise just smiled at me.

"She claims that you taught her how," Nicholaa said. We all knew that the problem we faced was grave, and yet I sensed that Nicholaa was enjoying herself. She was very young and could not compare to Lovise in either beauty or intelligence, but she had been born to command, her father was out of danger, she was running the castle once again. She would decide what happened next.

Eventually we had to discuss business.

I said, "I feel guilty, my lady. I should be on the road. I have wasted an entire day."

"It wasn't wasted, Sage. At our last talk you could barely keep your eyes open or complete a sentence in the language you began in. By tomorrow you may be functioning again."

"By tomorrow my horse should be rested also, and ready to go."

Nicholaa smiled. "Go where?"

"To find the king and warn him!"

"And where is the king?"

Um . . .

The king was in France—somewhere in France. I knew that France was a very big place. Brittany probably, but Brittany also was a very big place. I had a good horse, but Neil had taken Bon Appétit, and I would not by choice leave Eadig behind in Lincoln to walk home to Helmdon, although in such a crisis I might have to. I had very little money, and no knowledge of the road to the ports, or how much it would cost me to cross the sea. I had only to look at Nicholaa's smile to see that she had worked all this out already.

"I think, my lady, that I had better head over to Nottingham Castle, and consult with Sir Vernon Cheadle. He must know where the king is, or at least how and where Sir Neil was told to report to him."

"Indeed?" Nicholaa sipped her wine with the grace of an troubadour plucking a harp. "Adept, tell him what you told me."

Eadig shot me a guilty look. "He won't believe you, master."

I thought of Vernon with his monster mustache and fancy piebald steed. I imagined me explaining that his commander, the king's friend Sir Neil d'Airelle, was now a devoted servant of Satan and currently on his way to—

He wouldn't believe me if I talked for a century.

"From Adept Eadig's description of the noble knight," Nicholaa said, "I would strongly suggest that you do not go anywhere near Nottingham Castle, Sage. My guess would be that Sir Vernon is much more likely to judge you guilty of murdering Sir Neil and his brother. He may well have Sheriff Everard throw you in the dungeon."

I could escape from a dungeon, unless I were gagged, but then I would still have no horse, no money at all, and with the addition of a price on my head. Plan Two?

"Today is Friday, isn't it?" That morning I had been due to report to Sir Neil at the door of the cathedral, and if he did not turn up—which he obviously hadn't—then I was supposed to head over to Nottingham. Which I obviously hadn't.

Eadig said, "I think Sir Vernon will be here by noon tomorrow."

Nicholaa nodded agreement. "Or soon after. And here he cannot arrest you, because I won't let him. So enjoy another night's sleep, and then decide what you will do if Sir Vernon doesn't believe you and refuses to tell you where the king is."

I wanted to argue and could not think of any way to refute her case. Curfew was at hand, so she sent the Larsons off home. I walked Lovise to the east gate. Lars and Eadig followed us, a tactful distance back.

"I owe you my life," I said yet again.

"I would have done what I did for anyone. I thank God it worked."

"I love you."

She smiled without looking at me. "Yes, I know. And it's catching. Except . . . what did Legion mean when they said you were not a virgin?"

"Satan is the Father of Lies. You mustn't believe a word that nightmare said."

"How many?"

"Three," I admitted. "A long time ago. The first time wasn't my idea, and I was terribly clumsy."

"Um."

"Father Osric gave me absolution."

"I suppose experience must count for something."

"Then you will marry me?"

"My father wants to know where you live, what prospects you have, and by what means you can support a family."

My turn to um. "I can't answer that yet. I am truly one of the king's *familiares*, which should guarantee me a good living." Of course I might find myself tucked away in some corner of a castle in France, endlessly copying out spells for Enchanter General Aubrey de Fours.

"Provided you can warn him in time, else you will probably get a quick trip to the gallows for failing to do so."

"I intended to imply that I want us to marry after I have saved the king's life, not before. And I will be executed with an ax, not a noose."

"An ax is faster, but messier."

We had reached the gate. I must leave in the morning, and I still had not persuaded her. "If I do save the king and if he does provide me with an honest living and if I can answer all your father's other questions to his satisfaction, will you marry me?"

"In a flash."

There in the twilight I kissed her. Eadig and Lars were watching. The guards were waiting to close the gate. But the kiss did not end until the spectators all began to clap.

chapter 22

ot surprisingly, I could not sleep that night, twisting and turning and trying to decide what I must do. Back on Wednesday—which was only three days ago—Sir Neil had told me what to do if he missed our rendezvous on Friday morning, but he had not told me what instructions he had left with Sir Vernon. Was he supposed to wait where he was until he received further orders, or rush over to Lincoln, or send a warning message back to the king . . . or seek out the regent . . . or what?

That was one set of problems. Another was that I did not know what the demonized Neil and Piers had done after leaving Lincoln. Had they ridden straight off toward France, or had they gone around by way of Nottingham? If the latter, had they taken Vernon and his men south with them, or . . . or what?

That line of thought led me to consider Corneille and Quentin. After enslaving Neil and Piers, they had expected to catch me and treat me the same way. They could have forced me to seek out the king, but what about Vernon and his men? The Satanists would not have wanted that force blundering around in Lincoln, raising Cain in a search for their lost leader. In all this fog I eventually decided that Corneille would have ordered Neil to go back to Nottingham, which would not have taken him far out of his way.

From there he might have led his escort south with him, as if all were normal and he had completed his mission—it would be easy enough for him to invent a story to explain why Eadig and Francois and I had remained behind. The argument against that plan was that two men could travel a lot faster than a platoon, and it left me, assumed to be another traitor by now, to find my own way to France. Or possibly one of the Satanists might have planned to accompany me. But why not let Vernon serve as my guide?

By dawn I had convinced myself that Eadig and Nicholaa were correct: Vernon would turn up in Lincoln by noon. Either he would be coming to find Piers, which seemed the least likely reason. Or he would be coming to escort me south. Or Piers might be with him, planning to carry on as if nothing had happened, and he had refuted the rumors of treason that had brought him there in the first place.

So my best course of action was to wait for him to arrive and make my decisions then. With that I rolled over and drifted off to sleep, just as the roosters began to crow.

If Sir Vernon were coming, he could not arrive much before dinnertime. I had to work out what I must do if he did not appear at all. The answer, if there was one, might lie in the sanctum, which had become our comfortable lodgings. The bed was only wide enough for one, but Eadig had slept well on a double thickness of fleece on the floor.

"There must be a clue in here somewhere," I said. "Ideally, the king gave Neil his instructions in writing and he left them behind somewhere here."

"Because he couldn't read them anyway?"

I was tempted to cuff his ear, but he was right, of course.

With the help of Master-at-arms de Grasse, we inspected the cellar one last time, and then nailed the trapdoor shut with an iron spike.

Upstairs we did find some documents, but of course they had belonged to the coven, not Sir Neil. I had already burned the five spell books containing the summoning spell, as I had told Lovise I intended. The ancient grimoire that I had found with them might have been in the castle almost since it was built, a century ago; it contained only legitimate healing spells, but we discovered some loose sheets in one of the chests, hidden above a false lid. There was also the scrap of parchment that Corneille had been writing on when Eadig responded to the summons. Possibly one of these documents included the spell that had been used to enthrall Odell. Others might show how the conspirators had come and gone unseen. But none of them helped us, because they were all written in the alphabet that I could not read.

I emptied my pack and studied every spell I had there, and not one could provide any help in telling us how we could find the king. Then I recalled that I had left some of my scrolls at the Larson house, and suggested that we go and see if I could help with the healing.

"That's as good an excuse as any," Eadig said snidely.

"Or we could try the *Hwá becuman* chant. That would tell us if Sir Vernon's on his way."

Eadig lost his smirk. The *Hwá becuman* had given him the headache of a lifetime exactly one week before.

"All right," he said gamely.

Then I laughed. "But let's go and ogle some pretty girls first."

I was curious to discover whether Nicholaa's guards would even allow us to walk out the castle gates, but they saluted me respectfully and asked no questions. Had I tried to take my horse with me, I might have had more trouble. We walked halfway down the Danesgate hill and turned off to the Larson house. About six or seven people were lined up outside, which meant about as many again waiting in the house. Obviously I could expect no private talking time with my love.

We found Harald chanting over a patient in his sanctum and Lovise doing the same in the kitchen. Lars seemed to be alternating between them, depending on which needed a cantor. I retrieved the scrolls I had left there, and the precious futhorc tiles. I managed to obtain another quick inspection of the grimoire that Harald never used, but nowhere did I find a spell that would be the least help to me in my current predicament.

Eadig and I set off back up the hill.

"Why can't you just make up a spell to find the king?" he asked.

I laughed. "You mean write an entire chant from scratch?"

He said, "Yes!"

I found his faith touching, but utterly unreasonable, and said so.

He said, "Why?" That is the world's most powerful word.

"Because all the spells we know have been handed down from the ancient philosophers, who lived centuries ago and were far wiser than we are."

"I think you're as smart as any of them old fogies."

"I am flattered but not convinced."

"Why not?" *Not* is the second most powerful word.

"Son of Edwin, you are about as stubborn and annoying as Lady Nicholaa! Nobody in Helmdon has ever tried to compose an original chant. I suppose that possibly, in theory, I just might one day manage to put together some simple charm that would work, but I am certain that it would take months, or even years, of study and labor, and hundreds of trials to get it right. And we don't have that sort of time. You know what's going to happen." The street was crowded and I dared not speak aloud the disaster we foresaw.

The Saturday crowds were even thicker in the market space at the top of the hill, between the castle and cathedral, and it was not until we were through the gates that we were able to walk side by side again.

"And besides," I said, "the king is hundreds of leagues away, across the sea. I don't know of any enchantment that works at such a distance."

"Well, why can't you just make some changes to a spell you know that does something else?"

"That's absurd! No one can do that nowadays."

"Lovise did!" Eadig said with a wicked gleam in his sky-blue eyes. "Didn't she? Which one would you start with?"

"Oh fie!" I said. I was tired of stupid questions that I couldn't answer. "Lovise didn't know any better."

Which reduced the argument to absurdity, and Eadig knew enough to leave it there.

To reach the sanctum we had to pass the kitchen building, and its tantalizing smells were a reminder that the sun was high and it was almost time for dinner. Half the day had gone, with nothing accomplished. Neil and Piers d'Airelle would be twenty or thirty miles closer to their quarry.

A worried-looking page was pacing up and down in front of the sanctum. He lit up with relief when he saw us, and came running.

"Sage Durwin, Your Wisdom, Lady Nicholaa wishes to see you in the solar."

I turned and ran, fearing that the constable had suffered a relapse, but he had not. The news was good.

No householder ever welcomes an invasion by a squad of armed riders, but those who live in castles have ways of keeping such people out. The lookouts on the Lucy Tower had recognized the approaching dust cloud for what it implied, and had sounded the alarm—for the first time since the king's last visit three years earlier, Nicholaa told me.

Of course when the king came visiting, there would be flags, trumpets, and cheering crowds. The constable would come out to greet him, bearing the keys to the castle. Sir Vernon Cheadle was not the king. When Sir Vernon Cheadle arrived at the gates, soon after I received my summons, they were closed and archers lined the battlements.

Queried through the spy port, he identified himself as being on the king's business and requested audience with Constable Richard. Informed that the constable was indisposed, he demanded to meet with his deputy. Both he and his men then had to suffer the indignity of surrendering their weapons and, once they were admitted, of attending to their own horses, although that was predictable for so large a party.

Neil and Piers were not with him, which ruled out one of my guesses. And he was not asking for them, which ruled out another. Neil, then, must have called in at Nottingham and issued fresh orders. That conclusion cleared the board considerably.

Master-at-arms de Grasse conducted Sir Vernon to the solar at the top of the Lucy Tower, and presented him to Nicholaa, who was genteelly embroidering. I rose from my stool and bowed. Eadig was listening behind the bedroom drape with Lord Richard.

Vernon glowered. No one would have spoiled the joke by warning him that the acting constable was female and a mere slip of a girl—not even Sir Neil, because he had not met her during his brief visit.

She looked up with a regal smile. "You are most welcome, Sir Vernon. Do please be seated. Sage, if you would be so kind . . ."

I did the honors, pouring and passing around the wine that had been set out. de Grasse declined both a seat and a drink, and took up position alongside the door.

Nicholaa raised her goblet. "*Bonne santé*, Sir Vernon . . . How is dear Sheriff Everard?"

Vernon strained some wine through his floor brush mustache. "Past his best. The king ought to replace him."

"Then I hope that you will so advise His Grace. To what do we owe the honor of this visit?"

"Sir Neil D'Airelle asked me to convey his apologies to your father for his impetuous departure. He believed that the message he must convey to His Grace justified the most exigent urgency."

"Mercy me!" Nicholaa's eyebrows rose and she took another sip of wine. "My father took no offense. He understands the necessity of hiring more archers for the Breton campaign as soon as possible. It was most kind of you to ride all this way for so piddling a purpose."

"There is more," Vernon growled. He might be starting to realize that his hostess was wiser than her years, and perhaps wiser than his years too. "He instructed me to conduct Sage Durwin to the king to report on whatever magic he discovered in Lincoln."

Nicholaa and I exchanged glances. Of course Neil would have been assuming that I was now possessed like him. Or would he? How much Satanic guidance could he call on now that he had been recruited into the forces of darkness? Had he been somehow warned that the conspirators' attack on me had been turned back on them? And if he had, had that happened in time for him to instruct Vernon accordingly? I must always keep in mind that the d'Airelle brothers were now servants of Satan, and might wield dark powers stronger than anything I had available or even knew of.

A trickle of ice water ran down my spine as I tried to work out the tactics here. It was past time for me to say something, anything. "That was a kind thought. I am presently ministering to Lord Richard. I am happy to say that he is making progress, but I cannot in good faith abandon him yet. And then I shall have to see Eadig safely back home to Helmdon. Just tell me where the king is exactly, and I am sure I shall be able to find him."

Vernon was no intellectual giant, but he had a warrior's cunning, and I should not have blurted out my prime concern so soon. His expression became foxy. "Sir Neil will leave up-to-date orders for us where we disembark in France."

I could hear no warnings from my tambour enchantment, but that was probably because ancestral survival instincts were already screaming at me that I must not trust myself to Vernon's tender care. "Your offer is welcome, sir, but I needn't keep you from your duty. If you just give me some instructions, I am sure I can find my own way to the king."

"Sir Neil's orders were for me to escort you there—even if I have to put you in chains," he said. Now it was his turn to blunder.

"What!?" Nicholaa lowered her embroidery. "Why on earth? What is Sage Durwin supposed to have done?"

"Murder."

Nicholaa threw her embroidery on the floor. "Murder? Sage Durwin? What sort of nonsense . . . ?"

"He killed Francois, a man-at-arms, my lady. Sir Neil and his squire both saw it."

"Then they had better report him to Sheriff Alured."

"No, he's a king's man, so Sir Neil thinks the king will want to judge the case himself. I am to take him with me, back to France."

Nicholaa looked to me. "You'd better tell him the whole story."

I had no option, I knew, but I was also certain that he wouldn't believe it. "Did Sir Neil say he'd spoken with Sir Courtney?"

"Didn't ask."

"Did he tell you what he had discovered here in Lincoln that required him to report to the king with such urgency?"

"Not my concern." Vernon drank some wine.

"It is very much your concern," I said, "and I shall tell you why. Sir Courtney died the very day the warning letter was sent, and it was a forgery, full of lies. Sheriff Alured and Bishop de Chesney are both out of town, Constable Richard was smitten—not by a sickness but by a curse, which I was able to remove. The castle was at the mercy of Sage Corneille, a Satanist, and they deceived His Grace into sending two of his *familiares* here to investigate. Both Sir Neil and his squire are now possessed by devils, and they are heading to France to kill the king."

The sky is green. Pigs can fly.

Vernon drained his wine and set the goblet down. "And where is this alleged Satanist now?"

"In Hell, where he belongs," I said. "He and his collaborators tried to bind me to their evil purposes as they had Sir Neil and his squire, but my helper at the time, a local healer, managed to deflect their enchantment, and the Devil took them, instead of me."

Vernon said, "Ha!" with utmost scorn. "Do you believe this rubbish, my lady?"

"I certainly do. Master-at-arms?"

"So do I," said de Grasse.

"Of course. You are bound by loyalty." Vernon was veering very close to calling de Grasse a liar, risking challenge and combat. A girl's opinion was not worth a thought, of course. "So when is the sheriff due to return?"

"Not for another week," Nicholaa said.

"Then I require you to deliver this man to me in shackles, so that I may bring him before His Grace for judgment."

Nicholaa bristled. "By what authority do you give me orders?"

"By the authority of Sir Neil D'Airelle, one of His Grace's *familiares*."

"Sage Durwin is another *familiaris*."

Vernon turned his angry glare on me.

"That is so," I said. "I, too, am a king's man. Two years ago I put my hands between his and swore to serve him as a *familiaris*. You know that the first thing Sir Neil had to do in England was to include me in his mission. You cannot give me orders, Sir Vernon."

"Nor me," Nicholaa said, rising. "Master-at-arms, see that Sir Vernon and his men are given food by way of Christian charity, but then they must leave the castle and are not to be allowed back in."

chapter 23

The moment the door closed on Vernon and de Grasse, Constable Richard emerged from behind the drape with Eadig right behind him.

"That was beautifully done, my dear. I think I shall retire at once and advise the king to appoint you constable in my place."

He took the seat Vernon had just quitted. I handed him the goblet that de Grasse had refused. I had examined him before Vernon arrived, and been pleased by his progress. He was still frail after his long bed rest, but fully alert now. That he should leave the negotiations to his daughter had been his idea, not mine, although I approved of his decision. I was sure he was not joking when he foresaw Nicholaa succeeding him; he was training her for her future duties.

"He was a horrible man," Nicholaa said. "Had he been as beautiful as Durwin, I could never have insulted him as I did."

"Quite!" The constable cleared his throat disapprovingly and turned to me. "Sage, I applaud your wisdom in not following any orders that originated with Sir Neil."

"Indeed not, my lord. Or even orders that Sir Vernon says originated with Sir Neil. And I am grateful to your daughter, for had she not stopped me, I would have ridden to Nottingham yesterday and fallen into Sir Vernon's clutches. She would not have been there to defend me as she did just now."

"However, we still don't know how you will find His Grace to warn him of the assassins' approach."

My chances of arriving in time were already very slim, and would disappear altogether if I didn't set out soon.

"I can't see any use in trying to follow Sir Vernon," I said. "I do not know for certain that he is on his way to the king. I would lose him at the coast, because I would have to take passage on a different ship."

Nicholaa said, "And he could have the wit to lie in wait for you on the road. Not likely, but possible."

The constable set down his goblet and clasped his hands. They were still the large hands of a warrior, but now they were knotted and twisted by age.

"The best help I can give you is a letter from me, confirming that you are on urgent business for His Grace, and requiring all persons to assist you to meet with the justiciar, the earl of Leicester. He is usually in London, often in Winchester, but his secretaries will honor my seal. We'll send our courier, Iden, along with you. He knows England like his mother's face."

I thanked him, for his offer of a letter bearing his seal was very encouraging; it would give me a hearing at least. "Tell me, my lord, when the king held his great council at Northampton, two years ago—the one where the traitor Archbishop Becket fled by night and quit the realm—did the justiciar attend?"

"Undoubtedly so. All the great barons of the realm were there."

"After the council ended the king went hunting, but he stopped briefly at Barton. That was where he swore me in as his man. Would Earl Robert have been there, do you suppose?"

"Like the king, he is a keen hunter, so very likely."

Better yet! As the chief officer in England, the justiciar must have watched King Henry accept homage thousands of times, but his acceptance of a crippled Saxon yokel had made the courtiers twitter like a basket full of sparrows. He would remember me.

What else? "I shall need to borrow a horse for Adept Eadig, because Neil stole one of mine."

"We'll give you a horse!" Nicholaa said. "We owe you at least that much for all you have done."

"And money, too," her father said. "You will need to eat, and fare for the ferry. When will you leave?"

I thanked them and was about to say that I would leave right after dinner, but Nicholaa forestalled me. "Wait until tomorrow, Sage. If Sir Vernon's intentions are as sinister as you fear, I would not put it past him to linger in the town, hoping to ambush you."

"Again, wise advice, my lady. And I shall put this afternoon to good use, I hope. I have one faint hope of an enchantment that might guide me directly to the king."

I chivvied Eadig all through dinner in the hall. As he wanted to hear everything that had happened with Sir Vernon, I got less eaten than he did before I took him off with me to the sanctum. I did not quite drag him by an ear, although that was the general effect.

"You've thought of something!" he said.

"Something I should have thought of a long time ago—the *Hwæt Segst*."

I had been trying to find a spell that would tell me where I could meet up with the king, and there was no such chant, not here in Lincoln and not in Helmdon, so far as I could recall. But the *Hwæt Segst*, if it worked, would predict a person's destiny.

It had done so twice before for me, and once for Eadig, in Northampton, when it had warned us of High Treason.

So we reached the sanctum, where we had already changed the password on the outer door to *Nicholaa*, and taken all curses off the inner one. We settled across the table from each other. Eadig quickly read over the scroll to remind himself of the text, and then tied on a blindfold. I spread out the tiles. Eadig chanted, and smiled as he felt acceptance. I waited with chalk poised over a slate.

His hand moved, and pointed: *feoh . . . æsc . . . gyfu . . . eh . . . rad . . .* In the Latin alphabet that would be *fæger*, meaning "beautiful". Then came another word, followed by the blank tile, signing off.

Eadig hauled off the blindfold. "What'd they say?" His smile faded as he saw my disappointment.

"Fæger munt," I said. Beautiful mountain.

"Sounds possible, doesn't it? They might have told us if that's in Brittany or Normandy or . . . No?"

"It's not a place," I said. "It's a name. Robert de Beaumont is the justiciar, the earl of Leicester."

Eadig was young enough to ignore the clouds and concentrate on the silver linings. "Well, then the Wyrds are predicting that we'll meet him, aren't they? If you have to guess between London and Winchester, it sounds like you'll guess right."

I nodded as I began putting the tiles back in their bag. "We can probably pass close by Leicester town on our way. I don't know if he has a seat there or not. If he does, then the garrison will be able to direct us to him."

But it meant more delay. Neil would have three full days' start on me. Of course the weather might prevent him from reaching France for weeks, but it might also favor him and then delay me. For several minutes we sat in silence. Then I glanced up and saw Eadig's glum expression. I knew I was somewhat of a hero to him and the other Saxon varlets at Helmdon. He had known me as the boy who shoveled out the stable. He had seen my dramatic rise to royal *familiaris* and astrologer to the queen. And now, in his eyes, his champion was quitting the field.

I banged my fist on the table. "*All right!* I'll try. I've got nothing better to do with what's left of the day. But I'll need ten thousand slates and twenty thousand wood tablets. And ten gallons of ink!"

Grinning widely, Eadig jumped off his stool. "Yes, master!"

"Just don't expect it to work," I growled.

An enchantment is a lot more complicated than a psalm or a drinking song. It must be rhythmic, yes, and its form is set—within limits, for some seem to break all the rules and yet work well. It can appeal to many of the ancient spirits or to very few, but their order is important, for even very minor deities can be touchy about precedence and their respective prerogatives. Above all it must be beautiful, in a way that is hard to define. Ugly enchantments never work. That is why tiny flaws like the trip wires can render them ineffective, and also why even those texts have been preserved for centuries.

Eadig had suggested earlier that I could base a new chant on one of the traditional ones, and there was some sense in that. One that I had brought with me was the *Ubi malum*, "Where Is The Evil?" which I had used with dramatic effect at Barton, almost causing a murder. It invoked a whole cosmos of entities. On the other hand, some of those it called upon were malevolent themselves, and would have to be omitted.

After more head scratching, I realized that my greatest successes in curing damaged chants had been the *Hwæt segst* and the *Hwá becuman*, both of which had been addressed to the

Wyrds. Perhaps they liked me. Perhaps they were lonely now, when almost no one spoke to them anymore. I decided to appeal to them.

Besides, while I could read many dialects of Latin or French, writing a correct text in one's mother tongue is much easier, and the Wyrds might not respond to any other language. I would begin my pretend spell with, "*Loc hwær he sie*", meaning "Wherever he may be," so *Loc hwær* would be its name.

Eadig laid out at least a beginning of the supplies I would need in the inner sanctum and promised to keep me undisturbed for the next year or so.

Once or twice I heard voices, but the connecting door remained closed. Once I heard Eadig chanting something, but he had the resident healing spell grimoire out there and was quite competent to deal with a bellyache or a bad tooth. How long this situation continued I do not know, but it was close to sunset when he tapped on the door and peered in—very cautiously, as if he feared I might throw the inkwell at him.

I laid down my quill, yawned, and stretched my arms. "Almost done."

"They're singing evensong, master, and Lady Nicholaa has called for you to join her and her father at sup in the tower."

I growled. Certainly I needed a break, but I had been planning to make a quick call on Lovise. Yet I could not refuse the constable's daughter, and the gates would be closing soon. I sent Eadig off to the servants' mess to make up for what I had dragged him away from at dinner time, and told him that when he returned he could look over what I had written.

Five of us supped in the Lucy Tower solar that evening: Nicholaa, Constable Richard, mistress of the robes Elvire, me—and Iden Attewell, the courier. Iden was about my age, but no taller than Eadig, and built like the racing dog they call a *grighund*. He would be little more of a burden for a horse than the letters he carried. Everything about him was quick, from his eyes to his feet.

We did not talk of my business during the meal, mostly we listened to Iden's merry chatter. Despite his youth, he really did seem to have been everywhere between the Scottish border in the north and Aquitaine in the south. Talking did not stop him eating as much as I did. I marveled that he stayed so thin.

When we finished, I was itching to return to my attempt to invent a new enchantment. I asked Iden how long we should need to reach London.

"Three days easy," he said. "Lord Richard has picked out Peregrine for your lad. A bay gelding. He's fast and always willing. Can't see that Ruffian brute of yours letting himself be outclassed, and I'll be riding Whirlwind, as usual." He obviously foresaw no chance of being out-ridden by a couple of glorified clerks.

Nicholaa picked up my hint. "You'll be wanting to make an early start, Sage?"

"I'll try not to waken the roosters, my lady."

Iden nodded. "First light? Meet you at the stable, sir?"

"I'd rather you stopped by at the sanctum. We could use an extra hand with our baggage."

That was agreed and then I must make my farewells. I thanked Lord Richard for the gift of a horse and remembered to tell him the password on the sanctum door. I suggested that he have the pentacle on the cellar floor covered over with tiles, but he said he was going to raze the whole building. Healer Fulk in Nottingham was sending a new healer, who would set up in the old sanctum that Healer Bjarni had used.

And after all that I could rush back to the sanctum. Dark was falling, and I had an enchantment to try. I found Eadig there, frowning over my efforts. He had written out the responses on a separate sheet of parchment, ready for a trial performance.

"Speak up," I said. "I value your comments."

He simpered at my flattery. "This verb should be *willaþ*, not *wilt*, unless you intend that to be a trip wire, also the third and fifth versicles don't scan. Apart from that, as fine an assignment as you've handed in in years, varlet."

I swung a slap at his ear and he ducked.

"Very well, Sage Eadig, let's try it. It's late," I added, glancing at the window, "but there's nothing too risky in the text. We won't be summoning any evil spirits." I hoped I was not mistaken.

I corrected the flaws he had seen and we did a read-through. It seemed to flow well, considering we were working backward. So we began at the beginning and sang it through.

We felt not a trace of acceptance. We talked it over, changed a couple of details, and tried again. Still nothing.

I had wasted half a day attempting the impossible. I should have known better.

"You did warn me," Eadig said sadly. "But the *Hwæt segst* promised that you would meet with the earl of Leicester."

And that would have to do. "Early start in the morning," I said. "Let's pack and catch up on sleep. We've got two hard days ahead of us." And I had a letter to write.

chapter 24

"**W**ake up!" I repeated, "or I'll dribble hot wax on you."
Eadig groaned, rolled over on his back, and blinked up
at my candle. "It can't be morning yet. I won't allow it."

It wasn't quite. "The sky's changing. We have an early start
to make, and before that we have to chant again. We forgot
something!" That wasn't fair, because I was the one who had
done the forgetting.

"What?"

"The queen."

"She's a whom, not a what." Eadig's voice was muffled as he
pulled on his shirt, so perhaps I was not supposed to hear that
impudence.

"The king would recognize me and believe me. Possibly the
earl of Leicester was there in Barton and saw me swearing loyalty to the king; if so then he may believe my wild story backed
up by Lord Richard's letter—or he may not. But the queen was
certainly there that day, and young Lord Richard with her. She
commissioned me to draw up his horoscope. If I can find Queen
Eleanor, she will know who I am and will certainly believe our
story."

"She's in England?"

"Sage Gilbert in Northampton told us that she is."

I set up candles on the table and found the necessary scrolls in my bag. In a few moments Eadig joined me, half dressed and blinking, barely awake. "What d'you need me t'do?"

"Start by reading over this incantation." I handed him the cantor's part of *Oculos deceptus*. That spell isn't black magic, but its purpose is to deceive, and therefore at best it could be called gray. I had first met it and used it two years earlier, at Barton, with results close to disastrous, and I had brought it along with me to Lincoln purely by accident, because the parchment had been rolled up inside another.

Eadig's own *oculos* grew wider and wider as he read. He was only seeing half the text, of course, but he could tell enough from that to know that its purpose was well on the shady side of enchanters' ethics. When he finished he gave me a very troubled look.

"What are you planning to do with this, master?"

"Get by Sir Vernon Cheadle."

Eadig said, "Oh!" in a very small voice.

"Isn't it obvious? He knows we're here and Sir Neil gave him orders concerning us. He said he was told to escort us to the king. That may well be true, but I think it will only be true when I give him the password."

"What password?" Eadig was still not quite awake, and I had been chewing over my problems half the night.

"I don't know what password. Corneille and Quentin would have given it to me after I was safely enslaved. It would change Vernon's memory of what he was supposed to do with, or for, me. Since I didn't get the password, the first instructions remain in effect and he believes I am a murderer."

"That's crazy."

"No, it's just foxy. We were dealing with very clever men. It took a woman to out-think them. So I think that Vernon truly believes that I murdered Francois. Remember that Neil and his brother have been 'recruited' as Satanist agents, so they may have dark powers of their own now, at least enough to deceive Vernon. He will be waiting for us on the road, Friend Eadig, sure as fleas jump! So we have to sneak by him in disguise. Now, who would you like to look like? Someone you know well would be best."

"Adept Maur?"

Maur son of Marc was his closest friend at Helmdon, and also much taller.

"Excellent idea. And when I've sung it for you, you'll sing it for me and I'll try to be Sage Marcel. Be warned, this is a ramshackle sort of spell. I mean it doesn't work very well, especially in sunlight, but in this case we don't need a perfect likeness. As long as we don't look like ourselves, we should pass by the ambush quite easily. You need us to read it through together first?"

Eadig shook his head, rubbed the last of the sleep out of his eyes, and moved one of the candles closer. "Pitch, please, master."

So we chanted the *Oculos deceptus* and when we reached the end, the gangling Adept Maur was sitting on the other side of the table from me. I was very impressed, because the spell had produced a much more stable illusion than the one it had provided for William Legier and me at Barton two years previously. Perhaps that was because the candlelight was dimmer here, or because we were limning a living person, not a dead one.

The fake Maur had Eadig's grin, though. He stood up and looked around from his new, higher point of view. "Mm ... This has possibilities," he said in Maur's deeper voice.

"That's why it isn't taught to adepts. *Dimitto!*" That brought him back to his normal appearance. "Now me."

We exchanged scrolls so that he could take the enchanter's role and I the cantor's. The second attempt did not go as smoothly. We had to start over a couple of times, but when we reached the end, Eadig was staring at me in awe. I was fascinated to see my wrists bearing little black hairs that had not been there before.

Eadig said, *"Dimitto!"* and they disappeared. I was Durwin again.

Time was fleeting. Iden was due very soon and I wasn't ready to leave yet.

"My *Loc hwær*," I said. "I don't think we gave it a fair trial last night. The king is far away and over the sea. But what about the queen? She knows me. She'll believe me. If she's still in England, then this should tell us where she is, and she can send a warning to the king much faster than we could take it."

In fact I had been wakened by a vivid dream of Queen Eleanor. I don't much believe in prophetic dreams, being more inclined to agree with Sage Guy's opinion, which was that not all your brain goes to sleep when you do. It leaves a night watch on duty, and often the night watch can find answers that your waking brain missed. I should have thought of the queen much sooner.

Eadig said, "Mmph," with a disappointing lack of faith in the incantation that he had persuaded me to invent.

"I think we'd better write in the changes."

"Mmph."

He took up a pen reluctantly and we went over the two parchments, changing "king" to "queen" and all the necessary pronouns and adjectives. Then we did a read-through. We found one adjective I had missed. We chanted. Half way through I found another mistake. We started over, and this time I felt a strong acceptance. Eadig's voice took on the ancient croak I now recognized as the voice of a Wyrd. When we finished I waited anxiously.

"Hwær æðling cirmane oðer sona!" Eadig closed his eyes. For a moment I feared he was going to be smitten with a headache, as had happened when we chanted the *Hwá becuman.* But then he opened them wide. "What did I just say?"

I thumped both fists on the table in triumph. "You said Beaumont!"

Blink. "No I didn't."

"But you meant it. You said, 'Where a prince cried, another soon will.' There are two Beaumonts, Eadig! One is a name— Earl Richard de Beaumont, the justiciar, and the other is a palace, just outside Oxford. When the queen commissioned a horoscope for Prince Richard, she told me when and where he was born, and the 'where' was Beaumont Palace. That's what the *Hwæt segst* was telling us, too. The Wyrds just had you inform me that the queen is with child again and has gone back to Beaumont Palace for her confinement. We'll go there and warn her, and she can send the message on—far faster than we could take it."

Eadig beamed. "Then you did it, master! You wrote a new spell."

Great Heavens! So I had.

chapter 25

Very soon after that, in the clammy colorless light before dawn, while the castle roosters were screaming for their harems, Iden tapped on the outer door to lead us to the stable. We loaded him up, collected everything else we needed, and then followed, shivering and laden.

Despite the early hour, Iden was as chattery as ever. He nattered to the ostlers as they saddled up Ruffian and two others. Ruffian was difficult on principle, so I went over and lectured him. Knowing that I was good for a fine ride, he calmed down and stopped trying to eat the stable hands. Iden introduced Eadig to Peregrine, and I paid my compliments to Whirlwind, who was lean and built for stamina, like his rider.

Iden gave me the constable's letter to the justiciar. I gave him mine to Lovise, with a penny to bribe the stable hand he trusted most to deliver it for me. I had written very little except that I would come back for her if I had to crawl all the way, because I loved her more than life itself. My words were far from original, but heartfelt all the same. I don't suppose I expected her to believe them, but I hoped that she would hope.

When the day watch arrived to open the gates, the three of us were mounted and ready to go.

The bells had not yet rung for Sunday mass, and the market square was deserted. I cried, "Whoa!" and reined in. The other two looked at me in surprise.

"Iden, yesterday a man named Sir Vernon came calling with a troop of knights. He wanted to escort us to the king, or so he said. Not trusting his intentions, I declined his invitation, and Lady Nicholaa sent him away. It is possible that he will lie in wait for us and try to seize us on the road. Now, where would you expect him to make such an attempt? At the town gate perhaps?"

Such problems were not in the regular day's work for a civilian courier, and Iden frowned for a while as he thought it over.

"No, Sage. Too many witnesses there. Just past Brayford Pool, I'd suspect."

Gratified because I had already come to the same conclusion, I said, "Excellent. So Eadig and I are going to perform a little magic here to disguise ourselves. We may look blurred or fuzzy, but the main thing is that we shan't look like ourselves, and if we keep moving fast, we should not be recognized. I hope this won't alarm the horses. Eadig first. *Fac sicut dico!*"

The horses barely flicked an ear, even Peregrine, although the genuine Maur must be a lot heavier than Eadig. Iden went so white I feared he would fall out of his saddle in a swoon.

"All right?" I asked. He licked his lips and nodded.

The spell was far from perfect. No one who knew Maur would mistake that facsimile for him, although there was certainly a likeness. That did not matter, because it was even less likely that anyone would see Eadig son of Edwin there either. It was good enough! Then he bespelled me with the same command. Ruffian did sense the change, and shied, but I brought him under control before he alarmed the other two or did any damage. I wondered if I even smelled wrong.

So we went on our way, out of the square and down the hill. Very few people were around yet, just a few humble souls making an early start on their way to the cathedral or one of the other churches. I was busily calculating how I would set up my trap if I were Vernon. I decided I would post some men out of sight somewhere just inside or outside the gate, and the rest some distance along the road, most likely just beyond the Brayford Pool, as Iden had suggested. Plus a watcher to identify the quarry as we left town. Then the watcher could rally the first group to follow us and signal to the second group—with a flag or a horn—to block us. We would be trapped with the lake on one side, fences and buildings on the other. So everything rested on whether or not the watcher recognized us.

Even before we reached the town gate, I saw a horse standing there, and a youth behind it leaning against a wall. Soon I was almost certain that he was one of the squires who had ridden with us from Helmdon to Nottingham. If he was, then Vernon might have made a mistake. It should be Vernon himself waiting to make the call in the moments it took us to ride past, for he knew me. Almost all the time during our journey together, Eadig and I had ridden at the rear, and the rest of the troop had not needed to pay us any heed.

Then I realized that I was riding Ruffian and a smart young squire would not have failed to notice so splendid a stallion. To him, my horse would have been far more memorable than my face. I discarded a few delirious thoughts of enchanting Ruffian to look like a mule. I also resisted the urge to turn my head away as we went past the spy—I must trust the magic and leave him in no doubt that I was not the man he was looking for.

Twenty yards along the road I said, "Is that lad with the horse following us?"

Iden glanced back and said, "No."

We weren't quite out of the woods yet—or into the woods, which might be a better metaphor. At the far end of Brayford Pool I saw Vernon himself, sitting with another man at the roadside and eating something. He looked at us, but did not react.

"I think we've made it," I said. "Saints be praised!"

It was a fine morning for a ride through a quiet, sleepy England. We pushed the horses as hard as we dared, but Iden was an expert and knew how to get the best out of them. The race was joined at last, but the killers had a three-day start. My sense of urgency ate at me like a canker.

After a couple of hours, our disguises wore off and we were our own handsome selves again.

About then Iden asked cheerfully, "London or Winchester, Your Wisdom?"

"Beaumont Palace. You know it?"

"Aye. Got a good friend lives near there!" He would probably have been happy to lead me to Jerusalem, had I asked him to. When a man performs his labors well, he usually enjoys doing so.

"A female friend, of course?" Eadig demanded.

Iden smiled as smugly as I ever did see. "That's the only type that interests me."

"And one in London? Another in Winchester?"

"Can I help it if I'm so lovable?"

"No, but you can give me some lessons on the way."

I was sure that Iden was bragging, but he certainly had Eadig thinking wistfully.

Iden on a horse was a joy to watch—he fitted there like the top half of a centaur, and the prospect of an exhausting three-day ride obviously inspired him as much as it depressed me. I had thought I knew everything there was to know about horses, but just watching him during our journey together was to teach me a lot about long distance travel.

"Must we take three days?" I asked him soon after we had passed Vernon. "Could we do it in two?"

He studied me for a few minutes as if assessing both me and my horse. "Aye," he said at last. "I could get you there in two, Sage, but you'll be no good at all for two days after you arrive. I've gone that far in one, but it damned near killed me, and I needed four fresh horses on the way."

At first we headed south along Ermine Street, the old Roman road that runs past the turnoff to Newark and goes all the way to London, but around noon Iden lead us off on a series of lesser trails that he knew would be passable in this weather. I would never have traveled so fast without his guidance, for I should have had to ask my way at every hamlet and village. He never did. He laughed when I asked if there was a tree in England that he didn't know.

"Not many, Your Wisdom, but the bushes keep changing."

Travelers usually overnight at monasteries or with friends, but Iden could do better than that. The first night he led us to an isolated manor owned by Lord Richard, not far from Leicester. There we were made welcome by the steward, fed, wined, and bedded. By then even Ruffian was willing to be grateful.

The second night Iden did almost as well at an estate where he was known. The owners ran a hostelry as a profitable side-line, and we changed our mounts there, on the understanding that we would be coming back the same road in a few days. The country thereabouts had a familiar look, so I asked how far we were from Pipewell. The answer was just, "An easy ride," and I was sorely tempted to demand a detour, so that I might visit with my mother for the first time since I was fourteen, but to delay for even an hour would have felt like treason by then.

The sun was in the west on the third day when we came in sight of a group of spires, a sure indication of a sizable town ahead. Iden reined in at a junction.

"Oxford, Your Wisdom. And that way leads to Beaumont Palace. You and the adept want to put your capes on now, sir?"

I was weary, sore, and as dusty as a threshing floor, but the sudden prospect of unexpectedly dropping in on the queen of England concentrated my mind. I agreed that capes would be a good idea.

Iden was as grimy as I was, but he showed a perfect set of teeth in a smile. "Then if I call on you in the morning for orders, that would be agreeable?" Judging by the lecherous gleam in his eyes, he had not been bragging about at least one of his girl-friends.

"Certainly." I hoped that I would not have to do any hard riding for several days.

"Give her my love, too," Eadig said.

"Never. Mine is as all she can possible want." Laughing, Iden rode off along the town road, looking as fresh as he had at dawn. Eadig and I headed for the palace.

chapter 26

Beaumont Palace, known locally as the King's House, is not a castle, but any royal palace will be surrounded by a high wall and have guards on duty at the gatehouse. Important visitors, having sent harbingers ahead to arrange a reception fitting their station, will arrive with an armed escort. Thus the guards could hardly be expected to extend a warm welcome to two unknown young strangers turning up unexpectedly close to sunset. I was well aware that there must be a servants' entrance somewhere else with a doorstep we could sleep upon until morning.

Asking whether the queen was in residence was not likely to elicit a straight answer, and few men-at-arms can read, so I simply held up Lord Richard's letter with the seal dangling on its ribbon, and demanded urgent audience with Her Grace. We might have been in serious trouble if my enchantment had deceived me and Queen Eleanor was somewhere far away. To my relief, the seal worked its own magic and a gate was opened for us.

Back then Beaumont Palace comprised several buildings of various sizes and ages, some of stone, some of wood. The

grounds were shaded by giant beeches and patrolled by con-
ceited peacocks, although they had much less to show off with
than they would have had a few months earlier. Hostlers came
running to take charge of Ruffian and Peregrine; porters followed, to carry our baggage. It was all very efficient. An elegant
young man in grandiose livery solidified out of nowhere to bow
and inquire my name and station.

"Sage Durwin of Helmdon, to see Her Grace on a matter of
great urgency." I proffered Lord Richard's letter.

He unrolled it and read it through in a fast mumble. Then
he regarded me with spine-chilling suspicion. "This says that
you were sent to the Earl of Leicester."

"If his lordship is also present to hear my news, then even
better. I asked first for Queen Eleanor because she knows me
personally. In the past she has commissioned me to cast horoscopes for her sons." Specifically one, count them, one sons, one
horoscopes.

That claim produced a frosty stare, but my steadfast innocence under it eventually thawed the ice. "Then if you would be
so good as to step this way, Your Wisdom."

After three days in the saddle I could barely stagger, let
alone prance as he did, but we followed along him a paved path
to the largest building in sight. We mounted three steps of marble and entered a high-arched hall, where two young pages were
lighting scented candles set in tall and ornamented candelabras.
This was my first view of the interior of a palace, a world of high
ceilings, tapestried walls, tiled floors, and glazed windows. It
amazed me, and left Eadig literally wide-eyed. Somewhere in
the distance, a man was singing. Our guide excused himself and
a lesser servant showed us into a cloakroom, where visitors could
make themselves presentable.

A few cloaks hung on pegs, indicating that guests were

present. There were also stools and a table with basins and towels. Eadig sank gingerly onto a seat and sighed.

"This is how kings live?"

"When they must. I expect they usually find better lodgings."

"Why is it that after three days on my ass, sitting's the first thing I want to do?"

I settled beside him. "Please yourself. Personally I'd rather go for a horn or two of beer, a hearty snack, and eight hours on a soft mattress. But the hard part may still be ahead of us."

"You really think we're really going to meet with Queen Eleanor?" Eadig's eyes were permanently as big as horseshoes.

I did not have to answer that, because then pages brought hot water and towels so we could wash our hands and faces. I combed my hair in front of the largest mirror I had ever seen and wished my stubble did not grow so quickly.

I had barely finished adjusting my cap when the doorway was filled by a large man, with a chest like a water barrel and an unforgettable battering ram of a nose. He was elderly, with a silver beard and a slight hump that made his great head thrust forward. His robes were a splendid scarlet color, trimmed in ermine despite the summer heat, and he sported a gold chain around his neck to indicate that he held some important office. In a massive hand sporting a gold signet ring, he clutched my letter of introduction as if trying to crush it to death. His fierce warrior eyes looked me up and down. I did not recall seeing that nose at Barton.

"Durwin? Leicester. What's this urgent message you want to give me?"

"It concerns a Satanic plot to kill the king, my lord."

I expected to see the droopy-eyelid, stretched-mouth signs of disbelief, as if I had told him that King Arthur had just arrived back from Avalon and was recruiting knights for his round table, but his reaction was the exact opposite—alarm. "Wait here!" the regent snapped, and was gone.

I returned to my seat. I said, "Yes," to Eadig's question of a moment before. "If she weren't here, he would have taken us with him."

Our liveried flunky soon returned. "Her Grace will receive you now, Your Wisdom." He looked down askance at my companion coming forward with me.

"Adept Eadig son of Edwin is a witness to some of the dread events I must disclose to Her Grace."

Faced with having to make a decision, Glorious chewed his lip for a moment and then nodded. I got the impression that this unscheduled business was all highly irregular and improper and we should be ashamed of ourselves for interrupting the royal leisure. He led the way out to the hallway, and along a corridor. The singing had stopped. At the end he announced us.

"Lady Queen, by your grace, I present Sage Durwin of Helmdon and Adept Eadig son of Edwin."

The chamber was large and still bright, with sunset shining through high glazed windows overlooking a small park. The walls were hung with colorful tapestries, the floor tiled with variegated slate. I saw at once that we had interrupted a social evening. Only the queen and the earl were present, but they sat amid a group of eight or ten empty chairs, arranged to face the other side of the room, so we had interrupted a musical soirée. A side table held wine and many goblets.

Eleanor looked no older than she had two years earlier, at Barton. As then, she wore a heavily embroidered robe, whose skirt fell in pleats to the floor. This time it was of forest green, but she could wear any color in the rainbow. Her hair was concealed by a French hood and her neck by a linen wimple. From the cursory glance that was all I dared give her, I could not have told by looking at her that she was again with child, as the Wyrds had told me. At forty-four she was unlikely to be, but she looked years younger than most women of her age.

I bowed to the queen first and then again to Earl Robert of Leicester.

"You are welcome, Your Wisdom," the queen said as I straightened up, "but your news may not be, if it is so urgent. You have come poste haste from Lincoln?"

For a moment I thought she must be aware of why I had been sent to Lincoln, and then I remembered who had signed my credentials. "I have, Lady Queen."

"In three days?"

"Aye. We left at Sunday's dawn."

"That is hard riding," the justiciar said. "You went there with Sir Neil d'Airelle?" So the king must have informed him of the Courtney affair.

"I did, my lord, and it is of him that I bring most terrible news."

Queen and earl exchanged cautious glances.

"He is dead?" she asked, frowning.

"Worse, my lady. He and his squire, Piers d'Airelle, have both been ensorcelled by the blackest of Satanic magic. They left Lincoln last Thursday morning, intent on heading to France to find the Lord King and kill him."

I had expected a strong reaction to that over-dramatic announcement. Instead, they showed no reaction at all. I had never considered the possibility that even the queen would not believe my warnings. Sudden thoughts of dungeons and thumb-screws filled my mind.

"You must be weary," she said calmly. "Sit down, both of you. Tell us your story, Sage."

For two days I had been planning just how I would do that, but for a moment my mind went as blank as a snowdrift. I said, "Um," twice, and then it all came out in a rush. I did not mention that I had foreseen Sir Neil's arrival at Helmdon, nor that the Wyrds had later predicted high treason, for that would have sounded like bragging, while the rest of my tale was to be a confession of failure. I did mention that I had not taken my most powerful spells with me, but I blamed myself, barely hinting at Sir Neil's failure to take me into his confidence.

That brought me to Nottingham, at which point the earl rose and went to the table, returning with goblets of wine, first for the queen, then for both me and Eadig. Never before had I been served by an earl, and it hasn't happened often since.

It was at Nottingham that I had persuaded Neil to continue to Lincoln without his armed escort. Would things have turned out differently if he had ignored my advice? I didn't know and still don't, but on the whole I think it made no difference. Corneille would have planned some way to enslave him without his followers' knowledge.

I described the situation we found at Lincoln—the sheriff and bishop both away, and the constable stricken. That provoked the first interruption and, surprisingly, it came from the queen.

"Did either you or Sir Neil speak with the old knight who wrote the letter, Sir Courtney?"

"Sir Courtney died on the day that letter was written, Lady Queen. Which happened first I do not know."

She frowned. "Continue."

"From what I have been told of that letter, my lady, I believe that it was carefully designed to be sufficiently incredible that His Grace would not send an army, but alarming enough to justify investigation by one of his trusted *familiares*, someone who would later be admitted to report to him privily. The purpose was always to set up an opportunity for assassination."

Then I had Eadig tell how he saw Neil and Piers captured, and how he witnessed their torture in the dungeon. I picked up the story with Harald Larson, and the replacement of all the town healers by strangers. It was when I named them that I received the biggest surprise of the day so far—although there was worse to come. My audience had been watching me intently, but suddenly their attention shifted to something behind me.

"Describe this Corneille Boterel!" roared the king.

chapter 27

there was another doorway, on the far side of the room, normally concealed by a tapestry. Henry must have been standing there all the time, with the man now following him out—Master Aubrey de Fours, the enchanter general.

Eadig and I leaped off our seats so we could kneel. Leicester rose. The queen smiled at the drama. Eadig had spilled his wine over his britches.

Henry II by the grace of God and so on, had grown a beard since I had seen him two years earlier, but that was just his campaigning style. It was even redder than his hair. His rather protuberant eyes were still that brilliant, piercing blue. He wore garments no grander or cleaner than mine, suggesting that he had not bothered to change since he last rode a horse.

"He was about Your Grace's height, Lord King," I said, "but fa . . . inclined to stoutness. He wore a long black beard."

The king swung around to Master Aubrey. "Well?"

"Sounds like him, Lord King. Repeat the other names, Durwin."

He and I had met briefly at Barton. As master of all the king's enchanters, he had been piqued when Henry did not consult him before swearing me in as a *familiaris*. Now that I had become a certified sage, our future relationship was likely to be stormy.

"Corneille of Lepuix, Henri Morlaix, Tancred de Umfraville, and Walter of Froyle."

"Froyle, yes," the enchanter general said, nodding in his fussy way. "Some relative of Roul Froyle? A brother perhaps."

"So it's into England now?" the king bellowed.

"It would appear so, Lord King," de Fours said with unusual humility.

Henry's apoplectic rages were legendary. He wasn't into one yet, but he was dangerously unhappy. Not having the slightest idea what he was talking about, I was glad not to be in de Fours's shoes. But the royal anger turned on me.

"Where are they now, these devil worshipers? Still in Lincoln? Where did they go?"

At least I could offer him good news, if he would believe it. "They went straight to Hell, Lord King. They tried to enthrall me as they had enthralled Sir Neil and his squire, but a local healer who was helping us had tampered with their spells, and when the Devil came, he took them all."

The king's face flamed even brighter red. *"Are you lying to me, boy?"*

"No, no, Lord King! As I hope for salvation, that is the truth!"

"Ha!" This time the royal roar was one of triumph. "You hear that, Enchanter General? This hayseed, as you called him a little while ago, has done more against *le Salon* than you have achieved in the last seven years!"

The look I then received from de Fours was the sort that should be reserved for mortal foes. "So he claims. He describes a plot to insinuate a puppet assassin into Your Grace's presence.

Possibly that objective has now been achieved? None of us here is armed, but he carries a stout stick. Wielded with demonic strength, that would be capable of inflicting a fatal blow. I advise extreme caution, sire."

All eyes turned on me. I handed my cane to Eadig. "Ask Her Grace to take custody of this."

Eadig scrambled up and carried it over to the queen, where he dropped to one knee to proffer it. She smiled graciously and accepted it. Eadig bowed and returned to kneel at my side.

The king had watched the byplay sourly. "Now I want the whole story. In detail! Start talking, Saxon. If any of you hear anything false in this testimony, question it. I will have the truth of this if we have to stay here till dawn."

He began to pace, and the justiciar moved aside to give him room. Henry II was almost never still. He rarely sat down anywhere except on a horse, and when he did, he had to keep busy— famously he would continue mending his hunting gear while hearing reports or petitions. Few except the queen ever sat in his presence. By now the room was dim, lit only by the candles in half a dozen tall candelabras. The king stalked back and forth, detouring around Eadig and me, once diverting to help himself to wine.

"In detail, Lord King." Realizing that I might now be on trial for my life, I began again. This time I did describe how we had foreseen Sir Neil's arrival and were waiting for him when he arrived. Aubrey de Fours snorted disbelievingly, but said nothing. I stressed that Neil had not taken me into his confidence, so I had not been able to prepare properly, and my first intimation of high treason had come that evening, when Eadig and I had cast the futhorc tiles. This time de Fours sighed.

The king turned on him. "Stop making those animal noises. If you have a question, ask it!"

"Yes, sire. What spells are these that you use to see the future?"

"The *Hwá becuman* and the *Hwæt segst*," I told him.

"Ah, old Saxon gibberish!" de Fours shrugged dismissively. "If you are such a wonderful prophet, how do you explain the mess you now find yourself in?"

"I am aware of no mess," I retorted. "I consider that I have triumphed in a nigh-impossible mission against enormous odds."

"You see, sir? I do urge Your Grace to have this man restrained before he does even more harm."

But Henry nodded to me. "Continue, Sage Durwin."

And so it went. I explained offhandedly how I had lifted the curse on Harald Larson by correcting an old spell, making that sound run-of-the-mill simply because I knew that de Fours was one of the old school who did not believe that this should even be attempted. He glared at me but that time did not interrupt.

I talked; the king paced. When I called on Eadig he told his parts magnificently. When we got to the climax, where the conspirators summoned Legion and it took them instead of Eadig and Lovise, Aubrey de Fours exploded.

"Oh, Lord King, Most Gracious Liege! Must we listen to this farrago? *Le Salon* has defeated the best efforts of Holy Mother Church and the united sages of Christendom for ages, and now we are being told that five of its senior mavens were outwitted by the juvenile daughter of a back alley healer? Let Her Grace call for one of her Provencal troubadours to sing to us of Lancelot and the Fisher King, but do not let this Saxon churl belabor our ears with—"

"My ears feel far from belabored," Queen Eleanor said sharply. "This is the most fascinating and exciting adventure I have heard in years. Please continue, Sage Durwin. We are all anxious to hear how you escaped."

Gratefully I bowed my head to her in acknowledgment and continued into the tricky part of telling what we did next. It was the earl of Leicester who saw the chasm I was attempting to bridge.

"You say the D'Airelle brothers were sold to the Devil early on Thursday morning? Then why did you wait until Sunday before you set off in pursuit?"

"Partly, my lord, because the Satanists were attempting to convert me likewise, make me into a second string for their bow. I was rescuing the constable from their clutches and struggling to preserve my own body and soul. Even after I had won that battle, I did not know where Sir Neil had gone. He had not told me where or how he had been ordered to report to His Grace. I hoped he would have told his deputy, Sir Vernon. I wanted to ride to Nottingham to confer with him, but Lady Nicholaa, the daughter of Constable Richard de la Haye, insisted that I remain in Lincoln until—"

"Ha!" said de Fours. "Another virgin enters the forest in search of unicorns."

"Stop this childish carping!" the king snapped. "If you have nothing useful to say, be quiet!"

The enchanter general shrank like a startled snail.

I described Vernon's arrival and his refusal to believe my story. Then I set a trap for de Fours and he fell into it perfectly.

"So I took Lady Nicholaa's advice, and turned to magic to solve my problem. I believed that you were still in France, Lord King, so I decided I must inform your regent of the danger, because he could send a warning to you much faster than I could hope to reach you myself. Of course I did not know where his lordship was either. Adept Eadig and I first tried using the futhorc tiles that Master Aubrey dismisses so readily. Alas, I misunderstood their response."

"Surprise?" de Fours murmured.

"Folly on my part, Master Enchanter. The tiles spelled out *'Fæger munt'* which means 'beautiful mountain'. I assumed that they indicated Lord Richard de Beaumont, not the palace. In other words, I thought that they were simply confirming my own intention, not providing guidance."

He scowled. "So how did you know to come here?"

"Having no other enchantment available to try, I wrote a new one of my own, *Loc hwær*, asking where the king was. It failed to give me an answer."

de Fours rolled his eyes. "Ignoring the fact that no one has presumed even to try creating new magic since ancient times, you not only expected it to work at all, but you thought it would reach across the sea and find His Grace in France?"

"With His Grace's life is threatened," I said, "I was frantic. Also, I have never heard a learned sage openly affirm that magic will never work across water. Is that truly the case, sir?"

"There may be exceptions," de Fours muttered angrily.

"This is irrelevant!" King Henry snapped. "How did you know to come to Beaumont Palace?"

"Early on Sunday morning, Lord King, I recalled that your lady queen knew me from Barton, because she commissioned me there to draw up Lord Richard's horoscope . . ." The king frowned as if he had not known that and did not approve. Not daring to look at Eleanor in case I had let slip a secret, I hurried on. "So I thought she would be more inclined to put credence in my story than would someone who had never met me. The adept and I tried the new spell again, asking where she was, and it told me to come to Beaumont Palace."

"This was an entirely new enchantment that you had composed yourself?" The king's disbelief showed that he was far from ignorant about theories of enchantment.

"Aye, Lord King."

"And it worked?"

"Very well, Lord King. Of course the answer was somewhat cryptic as they often are. What it said was that, 'Where one prince first cried, another soon will.' I knew that this could only mean Beaumont Palace." I bowed again to Queen Eleanor, as well as I could while on my knees. She raised a hand to her mouth to hide a smile.

The king seemed momentarily nonplused. A fourth son would be bell-ringing good news all across his wide dominions, but he must naturally suspect that I was trying to pull wool over royal eyes. Aubrey de Fours was shaking his head as if my tale was utterly beyond belief.

It was the old warhorse, the earl of Leicester, who saw the opening and promptly couched his lance and charged. "You are telling us, boy, that you have invented an enchantment that will locate any man or woman in England?"

The enchanter general smiled as if he had not done so in years. "This will be extremely valuable, Lord King."

"It did find Her Grace for me," I admitted, "but not His Grace."

Henry strode closer to glare down at me, making me wish I were a few leagues away, astride a good horse. "When was it that you tried to locate me?"

"Saturday evening, Lord King."

"We were still at sea, then."

"So the spell could hardly be expected to describe your location then, Lord King!" de Fours exclaimed. "Oh, I am eager to see this new wonder demonstrated."

"Can you show us this enchantment?" Leicester growled.

My heart sank at the thought of trying it out again before such witnesses. We all knew that many spells were erratic and unpredictable, and I could guess that my precious *Loc hwær* would not be given the benefit of much doubt.

I said, "The texts are in our baggage. Fetch them, Eadig, please?"

Eadig looked aghast. "I don't know where they are, master."

The king snapped, "There will be servants outside the door to show you."

"Oh!" Eadig was halfway to the door before he had even straightened up.

The king tapped a foot, angry at having to wait for anything at all.

The queen said, "Sage Durwin? While we are waiting, would you be so kind as to bring the wine around?"

I was happy to oblige, although my limp was worse in the absence of my cane. Of course de Fours had to be served last, and he had no goblet. While I was fetching one for him, he took another jab at my veracity.

"I am most anxious to hear how you overcame the Satanists."

"Have you ever heard of a door being warded on both sides, Lord Enchanter?"

He smiled pityingly at me. "It is a favorite trick of *Le Salon*."

"You have the advantage of me. I had never heard of *Le Salon* until His Grace mentioned it a few minutes ago. I still have no idea what it is. I was investigating Sage Corneille's sanctum in the company of cantor Lovise Larson, who had assisted me in freeing Constable Lord Richard from the spell that had incapacitated him. There we found five copies of the hellish enchantment they used to summon devils. I decided to take those right over to the kitchens and burn them before they could be used to do more evil, but the ward on the door stunned me. Unable to escape from the sanctum, Maid Lovise tampered with the texts;

the Satanists failed to notice her changes and unwittingly left themselves exposed to the devils' spite."

"Then the maid is the heroine of the whole affair!" Queen Eleanor exclaimed. "I trust that she is witty and beautiful as well as sagacious?"

"She is indeed, Your Grace, all of those and brave as a battle-hardened veteran. As soon as Lord King grants me leave, I plan to race back to Lincoln and claim her as my bride."

"We shall contribute a worthy gift. Won't we, my lord?"

The king eyed her quizzically. "A volume of romantic poetry, mayhap? If you are wearied, dear heart, we shall understand your wish to retire."

"I wouldn't miss this for all the music in England, such as it is."

There is tension in any marriage, and must be much more when the husband is lord of a third of Europe but a third of his realm came to him by way of his marriage. Eleanor was an extremely determined woman, and Henry an extremely determined man. Like flint and steel, they struck sparks. And yet, even after fourteen years of marriage, sexual fires still burned. There was more lightness than heat in their banter.

When the king said no more, de Fours went back to jabbing at me. "So a back alley healer's daughter in rural England cannot merely chant spells, but even write them? Who taught her this incredible ability?"

"I did. It is a very simple skill, Master. I will be happy to instruct you in it tomorrow. We teach it the adepts at Helmdon. They don't find it difficult, so I am sure that you . . . When her father, Healer Larsen, was smitten by the Satanists, which was partly an act of spite but mostly a trap they laid for me, I had to correct the text of the antiphon they were trying to use. I showed her what I was—"

Eadig entered. Someone closed the door behind him as he hurried over to me. I accepted one of the scrolls he had brought, and asked him to bring the nearest candelabra closer.

"You may stand," the king said. "Now tell me where Sir Hugh de Cressy is tonight."

I struggled not to show my resentment at a challenge that felt bitterly unfair. Eadig and I were both exhausted by three hard days' travel, our texts were blotched with changes from "king" to "queen" and masculine to feminine grammar and the light was poor. I had never heard of Sir Hugh de Cressy, although I was later to know him and respect him highly as another of the king's *familiares*. But needs must when the devil rides, as they say. The one bright spot in all this was that none of the audience would understand a word of what we were chanting.

de Fours said, "Ten marks if you can do it in within three attempts."

I gave Eadig a comforting smile, for he looked even more terrified than I felt, "Five each!"

He nodded, wide-eyed. Five marks seemed like a small fortune to both of us in those days. The chant was not going to be easy, though. The scrolls had already been altered from so much that they were a mess, and we would have to try to keep the beat steady while looking a line or two ahead. I gave him a pitch.

So we began the *Loc hwær* again. Annoyingly, the king came to stand right behind me and peer over my shoulder. Henry was unusual among the sovereigns of Christendom in that he could read. He did not speak the old tongue, or very little of it, and might never have seen it written down. I found his presence disconcerting, and promptly made a mistake.

"Hold!" I said. "Sorry, cantor. Start again."

"That's one," de Fours said.

I forced both him and the king out of my mind and

concentrated on my singing. I felt acceptance! We chanted through to the end. We finished. So where was Sir Hugh de Cressy? I looked expectantly at Eadig.

He blinked a couple of times and then in the harsh croak of his Wyrd voice said, *"Hwær Arður cyning slæf."*

"What!?" I stared at him in horror. Nobody knew where that was! At any other time or place I would have thought he was just trying to be funny, but there and then what he said felt like enough impertinence to get both our heads cut off, or at the very least two royal floggings.

"What did he say?" the king demanded, and there was enough disbelief in his tone to suggest that he had at least an inkling of the answer.

"He said nobody knows where Sir Hugh is, Lord King. I expect he's out of reach of the spell. Perhaps if Your Grace would choose someone closer . . ."

"He did not say that!" Henry's eyes were a startling blue at any time, and a king's glare is more terrifying than a bolt of lightning.

"Lord King, he was merely using an expression common among the vulgar folk that means 'nobody knows', sire."

Henry stepped even closer and showed me his teeth. "Give me the exact words!"

I dared not lie. Breathing a silent appeal to my Redeemer, I answered. "He said, 'Where King Arthur sleeps,' Lord King, but—"

Henry II by the grace of God uttered a huge roar and thumped me so hard on the shoulder that I almost fell headlong. "You did it!"

"Indeed he did!" echoed the queen.

"He did?" barked the earl of Leicester, looking as puzzled as I felt.

The enchanter general stared at me in horror, having just thrown away a fortune in silver and a huge chunk of his reputation. I confess—my smile at him contained much more triumph than Christian charity.

"Glastonbury!" the queen said. "We received a report that the monks of Glastonbury have discovered the grave of King Arthur. Sir Hugh was sent to Glastonbury to investigate."

"And he has apparently arrived," the king agreed. I could see his nimble mind buzzing as he worked out applications for this new magic.

"And the reports are apparently true, my love!"

So we weren't contumelious Saxon churls! We were heroes. Eadig's face was a blend of delight and amazement. He looked about twelve.

"I am most impressed," de Fours said sourly. "Congratulations, Sage. Now perhaps you can enlighten us as to the whereabouts of the two assassins you described so graphically?"

A moment's silence as everyone considered this suggestion . . .

"Oh, come!" said the queen. "You can see the poor boys are worn out. They've had two very hard days. Surely that can wait until tomorrow?"

In retrospect, I can see that she duped me into the giving the answer she wanted. There was no greater man-manipulation expert in Christendom than Eleanor of Aquitaine.

"Oh, we can try, Your Grace. I cannot guarantee that it will work again so soon, but we certainly can try. Right, Eadig?"

Eadig of course agreed. I glanced to the king for a nod of permission, and we launched once again into the *Loc hwær*. By then I could almost have chanted it without the text. Where, we asked was Sir Neil d'Airelle?

Again acceptance! Then the answer came in a single word.

"*Utane!*"

"Outside?" I said. "Just 'outside'? Outside what?"

Eadig's face crumpled. "Dunno. Just 'outside', Sage!"

de Fours couldn't resist, of course. "Outside is a rather large place, unfortunately. It doesn't really narrow the—"

Something crashed against the door. It flew open. Outside was shouting and the ringing of swords. In stumbled Sir Neil d'Airelle. He was clutching his chest with his left hand, blood spurting between his fingers. He favored his right leg, which was also bleeding. But his right hand held his sword, and he came in a sort of clumsy gallop, half running, half limping, across the room toward the king, with candlelight shining golden on his eyes and his teeth bared in a grimace of hatred.

The queen cried out in alarm. None of us was armed. Leicester grabbed up a chair to use as a weapon, but I was closest to the intruder. I stepped between him and the king and with a shout of "*Fiat ignis!*" set his face on fire.

chapter 28

Screaming a blast of flame, Neil dropped his sword, and clutched at his burning flesh. The earl of Leicester smashed the chair over his head, and he fell headlong to the place the king and I had vacated as we shied back. He lay there, wailing, writhing, burning, and spurting blood. Leicester snatched up the fallen sword.

"Through the heart, if you please, my lord," de Fours said.

The justiciar obliged, ramming the blade into Neil's back so hard that it went clean through the chain mail and I heard the floor slates crack. The corpse thrashed once more and then fell still. The pulsing torrent of blood dwindled and died.

The king's first thought then was his pregnant wife. "Are you all right, my love?"

"Quite all right, thank you for asking." She certainly seemed so, and her voice was steady.

"We have a couple of qualified healers here if you need anything."

"I would appreciate some more wine, when one of you noble gentlemen has a moment. Don't fuss, Henry! I am not fragile."

She was all right, but one of those qualified healers, me, was staggering around, struggling frantically not to disgrace himself by throwing up, and vowing that never, never, never again would he use that spell on a living being.

Through the door stumbled a man-at-arms, clutching a bleeding arm. "There was only two of them, Your Grace, and we got the other one."

"At what cost?"

"Three dead, four wounded. Fought like mad boars, they both did, Lord King. Never seen the like."

de Fours ran to attend the wounded and I hobbled after him.

Three of the wounded needed no more than some competent bandaging and a chant to hasten healing. While I saw to that, de Fours tended the fourth man, who had been run through, a belly wound for which I knew no treatment. The enchanter general did, though, having had battlefield experience. He chanted it from memory, and it certainly stopped the man's bleeding and eased his pain.

As we returned to the king's presence, I said, "Will he live?"

"No. But he will die in comfort. Your three?"

"They will survive. Will the king reward them?"

"Probably. If not, the queen will."

Neil's corpse had been removed, and a couple of flunkies were on their knees, washing away the blood. Leicester, surprisingly, was sitting beside the queen. The king was still standing, his hands resting on the hilt of the broken-tip sword. The mood was grim, for obviously the Satanic plot had come very close to success. Eadig was hovering in the background, trying to be invisible and almost asleep on his feet.

Henry regarded me for a long, nerve-testing moment. "I do not blame you for this, Sage Durwin. You have performed your duties magnificently."

I bowed. "You are very kind, Lord King. I truly thank God's mercy that you survived unscathed."

"So do I. I lost a good man in Neil D'Airelle."

"And in his brother, Lord King. His squire was practically hacked to pieces out there."

The king nodded. "And many good men died stopping them. Kneel!"

Chastened by the reprimand, I wobbled down to my knees.

"What is your heritage?"

"As humble as can be, sire. My father was a hostler for Pipewell Monastery."

The king looked puzzled, likely because I did not speak like a stable hand. "And your ancestors?

Ah! For the first time in my life, I could brag about them. "My great-grandfather was Thane of Pipewell, Lord King, and led his fyrd of fifteen housecarls to Hastings. Had King Harold won that battle, instead of William the Bastard, I would be his successor."

"Good breeding will always show in the end," the queen said.

The king said, "Where is Pipewell? Were you born there?"

"I was, sire. Pipewell is near to Rockingham." He knew the forest there, one of his favorite hunting grounds.

"We shall keep the thanedom in mind," Henry said with a smile. "But for now—" he reached out with Neil's sword, still streaked with dried blood, and tapped my shoulder. "Rise, Sir Durwin of Pipewell."

Oddly, my most vivid memory of that milestone in my life is of Eadig's face, with his mouth literally hanging open. Doubtless mine was doing the same. I staggered to my feet. The queen was smiling and holding out my cane, so I lurched over to her to accept it.

"One other thing before we give you our leave," the king said.

"Sire?"

"You are obviously the greatest sorcerer since Merlin. I am minded to appoint you our enchanter general for England. You will attend our council tomorrow, where we shall discuss this."

Life in a palace was an interesting novelty, which I was too numb to appreciate that first night. Our chamber was a dream, with a featherbed for me and a rollout cot for Eadig. Even the dramatic knighthood and prospective appointment were not enough to keep me awake.

Morning jumped in with birdsong and the inevitable roosters, backed up by the peacocks' discordant screaming. Incredible memories came drifting into view. The emergency was over, and I had won royal approval on a scale I had never even dreamed of. King Henry had a reputation for making fast evaluations of people and rarely changing his mind about those he favored.

A quiet voice nearby said, "What must I do for you today, *Sir* Durwin? Sharpen your lance? Polish your armor?"

I chuckled, because it was extremely rare back then for a civilian to be admitted to the brotherhood of knighthood. "You can write out the *Loc hwær* in fair, and then translate it into French, so I can give Sir Aubrey de Fours a copy—as a token of my respect and admiration."

"You really think the Wyrds will answer an incantation in French?"

"Not a hope in the world. That's the whole point."

Shortly thereafter our chatter was interrupted by the arrival of a valet to shave me, and then by fresh clothes for both of us.

"You'll get addicted to this, you know," Eadig said, admiring the softness of his robe.

"And you won't?"

He pulled a face. "Over my father's dead body." Then he hastily crossed himself and muttered a prayer for forgiveness. "Enchanter general for England?" he sighed, shaking his head. "Did you see dear Aubrey's face when the king said that?"

"No. I saw yours. Was he surprised?"

"Looked like he was going to puke."

That was a problem I knew I must try to mend. There being no sign of a summons from the king by the time we came downstairs, I told a page to locate Enchanter Aubrey de Fours and ask him if he would graciously grant me an audience.

The reply came that he would be delighted to meet with me in the rose bower. To which I could merely respond that I needed to be led to the rose bower.

I had not been there long before two men appeared around a hedge. One was a liveried page, who pointed to me and then disappeared, and the other was our guide from Lincoln, Iden Attewell. As he approached, I noticed how bowlegged he was. That explained how he fitted so well on a horse.

He bowed low. "*Sir Durwin?* When did that happen?"

"Somewhere between sunset and dawn. It still feels like a dream. Did you have a restful night?"

"Far from it, thank you for asking. My friend wasn't there, but her sister made me very welcome."

I laughed. "I shall not be leaving today. When will you start back northward?"

"Not today, sir. My horse needs a rest.

"Does the sister?"

"Not as much as I do."

"I shall have letters to go back to Lord Richard. If you could pick them up tomorrow?" And so it was arranged. I would also write to Lovise and Nicholaa, of course. But later. I needed to do just nothing for a few hours.

de Fours kept me waiting for quite a while, but it was a pleasant nook, the roses were remarkable, and so were the swans on the pond. I had plenty of things to forget about the last ten days and plenty of future to contemplate, so I was far from bored.

I was not surprised to see de Fours carrying a satchel when he arrived. I rose and bowed to him, and we exchange polite blessings. Then we settled side by side on the bench, both being on our best behavior.

"Congratulations on your promotion and appointment, Enchanter," he said with a passable attempt at a smile.

"Thank you, sir, but the appointment is not confirmed."

"It will be. He wouldn't mention it and then not do it."

"I feel as if he threatened to drop Lincoln Castle on me."

"Oh, no, no. The need for such an officer has been clear for some time. I had pointed it out to him several times, and even mentioned your name in that respect."

"Then I am truly grateful, sir," I said, meaning that I would be if I believed a word he'd said.

"I hate sailing," he murmured. There he might well have been sincere, and he could have added that he couldn't understand a word of the language. Having England lifted off his shoulders would be a great relief, especially if *Le Salon* had crossed the Channel. Whatever *Le Salon* was.

"Did you bring some blocked enchantments for me to look at, sir?"

He had, of course, and I again offered to explain my technique for unblocking them. I am not usually so saintly when it comes to ignoring previous slights, but at that point I needed de

Fours much more than he needed me. Besides, we served the same king.

"This one," he said, opening his satchel, "the two-voice *Ubi malum*. Two years ago you told me you had made it work?"

I studied the parchment he produced. It was badly faded and cracked, centuries old, so its text had never been considered worth copying out. "This is not blocked in quite the same way mine was, sir. The 'errors' were deliberate, you understand?"

Of course that had never occurred to him, or indeed to anyone except me, but he caught on fast enough when I explained what the trip wires were for and how to detect them. I showed him how to look for incorrect grammar, distorted rhythm, or preposterous meanings. After we had gone through six or seven scrolls he was almost giggling, foreseeing the treasure chest of old enchantments I had opened for him.

So much for tat, now for tit.

"Master Enchanter, please tell me what *Le Salon* is."

"It is short for *Le Salon de Satan*, a brotherhood of devil worshipers. They have sold their own souls, of course, and they wield Satanic powers. They understand that they will spend eternity in Hell, but they believe that they will be spared the usual torments in return for serving the Demon during their worldly lives. You witnessed one of their rituals, and you were extremely lucky to survive it without becoming possessed yourself. By wiping out an entire pentacle of Satanists, Sir Durwin, you have done more to set *Le Salon* back than the rest of Christendom has achieved in the last five years. Corneille Boterel was one of the ringleaders."

Oh. Then maybe *Sir* Durwin did deserve his new title and office.

"The credit really belongs to my future wife . . . You were surprised that my *Loc hwær* enchantment could locate people.

How do you explain how Sir Neil found the king? Had he been instructed to report to him here at Beaumont?"

de Fours glanced around to make sure we were not being overheard. "I doubt it. King Henry is as fickle as a bluebottle, Sir Durwin. He got bored besieging a castle and decided to make a flying visit to England to see how his wife fared. Nobody had prior warning of his intent."

"Then Sir Neil . . . ?"

"I expect he headed to Dover or Hastings and then was advised by the Fiend to change direction and come here."

So my *Loc hwær*, of which I was so proud, was a mere trifle compared to the powers of the Devil's agents.

"And when he got here," de Fours added, "he learned that you had preceded him, or perhaps he already knew that. Since he could no longer hope for a private audience with His Grace, he tried to force his way in."

Had I arrived an hour or so later . . . Better not to mention that.

"Obviously, master, if His Grace does appoint me enchanter general for England, I cannot hope to serve his needs without a huge load of help and advice."

Which de Fours was now happy to supply. Our rivalry was over. The ocean was to separate us, and I would not become a threat to him, a royal favorite ready to stab him in the back at every opportunity. We talked of the number of helpers I would need, how and where I should set up my headquarters, and how I should test all applicants for Satanic possession.

"I will send Sage Serge Silvain to advise you about *le Salon*," de Fours announced. "He is well informed on its aims and methods, and his mother was Saxon. He speaks your argot."

So he would be an excellent spy, able to report to de Fours on whatever I got up to in England. I saw that at once, and my guess was later confirmed, but at the time none of it seemed real to me.

In later years, de Fours and I met a few times and corresponded frequently, but I never saw the ten marks he owed me.

My hours with him that day were well spent, though, because just when everyone was ready to break their fast with dinner, we were summoned to the room where the previous night's mayhem had taken place. A large table had been added, but the only person seated at it was a tonsured clerk, who wrote only what the king told him to.

Around it stood the half dozen or so lords able to attend at such short notice, most of them still wearing dusty travel garb. They varied in age from a bishop a little older than I to a toothless geriatric who sat beside the queen near the fireplace. The king paced. He had cast off his military ginger beard, and for the first time I saw him in formal robes, which looked very hot in that stuffy oven of a room.

de Fours and I were recognized and our presence entered in the record. I was not told the names of the others; that had to wait until I was sworn in as a privy councillor, a few years later. I was grateful for an encouraging smile from craggy old Leicester.

"Tell them how you got here," the king said.

Knowing how limited his patience was, I outlined my adventures very briefly, from Sir Neil's arrival at Helmdon until he turned up where I was now standing, just inside the door.

Leicester took up the story without mentioning his destruction of a chair. "My lords, I assure you that I thought I was going to see our gracious lord struck down before my eyes. We owe the king's life entirely to Sir Durwin. None of us was armed. I was over there, by the window, and could never have moved fast enough to interpose my person. But Sir Durwin just snapped his fingers and the assassin immediately burst into flames! He may not be a conventional swordsman, but he is a doughty fighter!"

More applause. The bishop, I noticed, remained silent, but to everyone else I was the hero of the hour. I did not feel it. I should have protected Neil and his brother from the Satanists— why else had I been sent to Lincoln with them? Now I was being honored, and two fine, honorable men had already been buried in unhallowed ground with spikes through their hearts.

"Furthermore," the king added, "this latter-day Merlin has predicted that King Arthur is indeed buried at Glastonbury, and that my gracious wife is carrying a son!"

More wild applause. I wished the earth would open or the sky fall. Suppose I was wrong on either prediction? My reputation would be even briefer than a sneeze.

Then Enchanter General de Fours was questioned about *Le Salon*, and I saw that several of these English-resident councillors were as ignorant of it as I had been until the previous evening. He did go so far as to say that my success in Lincoln had been "remarkable".

"When compared to what has been achieved in France," the king snapped.

"And the rest of Christendom, Lord King," de Fours protested, and cringed under a royal glare.

"The attempt on my life that was made right here in this room," the king said, "must remain secret. You are all charged never to mention it, by speech or script. The events in Lincoln must already be public knowledge. Now, my lords, we are minded to appoint Sir Durwin our enchanter general for England, and task him to lead the battle against the Satanists here. What say you?"

One lord, who evidently had something to do with the Treasury, at once asked how large an endowment would be required.

Kings do not like to put a price on a favored project. "As much as is needed. Is anything more important than fighting Satan?"

The bishop immediately agreed, but then asked if he was correct in assuming that I would be required to operate under the oversight of the Church. This launched a discussion. Every time someone referred to me as *Sir* Durwin I had to stop myself from looking behind me. I kept my mouth shut, but I was convinced that the only contribution I could expect from the Church would be gags and shackles. There would be no cooperation, only suppression.

Then I noticed the queen looking at me. She raised one eyebrow very slightly. My nod was even slighter, but suddenly, without a raised hand or as much as cough, by some magic unknown in Helmdon, Eleanor had everyone's attention.

"Will someone inquire of Sir Durwin, my lords, just how he would propose to proceed, if entrusted with this vital responsibility?"

Grimly aware that most of the authoritative eyes in the realm had suddenly focused on me, I sent a silent prayer racing off to Heaven and said, "Enchanter General de Fours has already been most helpful in advising me on what I should need, Lord King, and I would certainly recommend that I begin by setting up a central library of enchantment. The sages in Helmdon have been meeting with much success lately in resurrecting the ancient native lore of this country, which has been sadly neglected of late. Indeed much of it has been lost. It was by means of such long-neglected enchantments that I was able to arrive here in time to forestall the attack on your gracious self."

Eleanor said, "You would train other enchanters in these skills?"

"Most certainly, Lady Queen."

"Have you given any thought as to where this school should be set up?"

"Not yet, Lady Queen." I did not know if even Helmdon would have a home after Dean Odo died.

"We have several unused buildings right here in the Beaumont grounds. If the space later proves inadequate, there is room for expansion in Oxford itself. And, as my lord bishop is aware, the Church already maintains several theological schools in the town, whose officials would be available for consultation on any controversial matters. And we have facilities here—stables and kitchens and others—that stand idle for years on end." She smiled a smile of virginal innocence—probably the same smile she had used when she talked King Louis of France into a divorce.

Her present husband strode across and stared down at her. "It is against the way of nature for a woman to be so clever."

"Oh, sooth, my lord! Are you implying that it is in the way of nature for men to be stupid?"

The laughter required at the queen's jest sounded a trifle strained. I wondered what she might be up to, and could see that everyone else did also. In fact I never discovered any dark motive in her suggestion. She had just seen a perfect solution, some hours before us men would have done. Beaumont was close to London and other important towns, but could provide a quiet center for study and meditation. She had even made it seem handy for the Church to keep an eye on.

Nobody came up with an objection. As my appointment did not sound unduly expensive or menacing to the nobility, it met with universal approval.

Thus, in a matter of minutes, my entire future life was determined, and the king's two enchanters general were thanked and dismissed. The council could then go on to discuss the exciting report of King Arthur's grave being found in Glastonbury.

chapter 29

No sooner had the council meeting ended than the king ordered his horse brought to the door, grabbed some food to eat in the saddle, and took off to Glastonbury with a small entourage.

Earl Robert of Leicester remained behind and ate in more civilized style with some of the other councillors. But then, having seen them off, he took me by the scruff of my neck—or so it felt—and led me on a tour of the palace grounds, accompanied by a couple of clerks. What size of establishment did I have in mind?

If the Glastonbury rumor proved false or the queen was delivered of a girl, I was unlikely to need much more than a six-foot grave. Since all I knew was Helmdon, I described a school of about that size.

"Double it," Lord de Beaumont grunted. "And double it again. You have all of England to worry about now. Think fifty or sixty sages, plus adepts and pupils. At the moment you have the king's ear and can ask what you will. In a couple of years his interest will fade and he may be less inclined to favor you."

We found a building that had once served as a monks' refectory, and decided that it could be divided to make classrooms.

Leicester barked instructions and the clerks scribbled. Then we found a derelict stable, which he ordered torn down and replaced with housing. The attendants' estimates of cost swirled in my head like flies around a dunghill. I had never thought in such terms.

Then the old warhorse fixed me with a glittering eye. "Why are you smirking, Enchanter?"

"I was trying not to, my lord. I was thinking that two years ago I was a stable boy."

"And now you're one of the king's senior officers! The king has a rare gift for finding good men and binding them to him with chains of steel. You don't look like a stable boy or speak like a stable boy."

For which I had to thank the sages at Helmdon, most of whom were sprung of noble stock. Guy Delaney had been reared in a bishop's household, Rolf de Mandeville had been a count's brother, and they had taught us varlets gentle ways.

"Well?" Leicester demanded. "If I order these buildings altered to suit you, can you fill them with enchanters?"

It was at that moment that I saw the obvious answer to my recruitment program. "Yes, my lord. You build the paddock and I will round up the livestock."

The old warrior laughed and clapped me on the shoulder. Nothing earlier had so demonstrated to me that I had joined the fraternity of knighthood.

That evening I supped with the queen and her ladies. She had me sing for them, and they agreed that I was as good as any minstrel. I decided that Eleanor just enjoyed watching me blush. Her Grace declared that I was now armigerous, and sent for a funny little man who wrote and sketched with his nose almost on his slate. Between them, they designed my blazonry, a crown within a pentacle.

I would need a house for my bride, Her Grace declared. There was a fine cottage in the grounds that would do splendidly—only five or six rooms, but when our family outgrew it, I would be able to afford something larger in the town. I did not enlighten her on the size of the kennel in which I had lived with my parents and three brothers.

Next morning Iden Attewell turned up again to announce that he thought Whirlwind would benefit from another day's rest, unless I had any urgent business for him. I did not, I said, but I played his favorite game by asking after his friend's sister.

She needed more exercise, he said, and strutted away whistling. I couldn't tell how much he was just making up, but I thought longingly of Lovise, and swore that I would head back to Lincoln the following day.

That presented more difficulty than I expected. Queen Eleanor was not as indefatigable as her husband, but she never lacked for energy, and she was screamingly bored at being confined to one place by her pregnancy. I was a new source of amusement for her. I also had business to attend to with the workmen. I had to obtain funds, which was no easy task until I appealed to the queen, because Leicester had gone off back to London.

Iden did set off for Lincoln the next day, carrying letters signed by my hand and making no mention of my new rank. I swore him to secrecy about that, too. The day after that I received my new signet ring, with my bearings, and *Magus Max Durvinus Pipveli Eques* written around the edge.

When I left Beaumont, the queen presented me with a finely polished oak cane. It is one of my proudest possessions and is with me still, although the engraved silver handle is now worn smooth.

At first Eadig and I rode north, retracing the way we had come, for our first destination would have to be Helmdon, or so I thought. It would be an easy day's ride. Beautiful clouds dappled the sky, and the air was sweet. I was a knight, on my way to claim my lady and bring her to live in a palace. God was in his heaven and all was right with the world. Or so I thought.

I turned to Eadig to suggest that we sing a song or two and saw that something was very wrong in his world. He looked as if the hangman were just adjusting the noose around his neck.

"You can't bear the thought of moving to Oxford?" I asked.

"It's not that, Enchanter. It's the thought of moving *back* here." Seeing my blank response, he added, "we came through Bicester on the way here, remember?"

Then I understood. "Your home?"

"I could go right by it on Monday, because I was on duty as your cantor and doing the king's business, but I can't go past it now and not stop."

That no longer seemed a problem to me. "You would rather continue your studies than stay at home and help your father?"

"A thousand times rather."

"Then I shall tell him that the king needs you. If necessary I'll *buy* you!"

He chuckled at that notion, but hope faded fast. "He's a stubborn man, Enchanter."

"So am I," I said. "If you want to, you can tell how the queen praised your singing last night. As long as you don't go into details, I think you can even mention that the king was greatly pleased with our efforts on his behalf, and has charged us with many important labors."

"Charged you, not me."

"But without your help, I would have failed dismally, so that distinction is irrelevant."

The grin returned. "That might help, I suppose."

Barely an hour after we left the palace, Eadig turned aside from the road and led the way to a sizable farmhouse, standing in an extensive orchard. Cows were grazing, bees buzzing, and hands were bringing in the wheat sheaves. I had known that his father was a freeholder, but not that he owned anything like that. He might not be gentry as the Normans would define the term, but clearly he was no peasant. I should have realized that a mere yeoman could never have funded an adolescent son to study at Helmdon.

Dogs barked, geese hissed, our horses fidgeted uneasily—a typical welcome. We dismounted, and immediately the dogs were all over Eadig, tails whirling like leaves in a gale. A dumpy little woman came scampering out the door, yelling his name.

I found myself holding two sets of reins while the long lost son was clasped to the family bosom, both literally and figuratively. I heard no laughter, and soon both mother and child were weeping copiously as the story unfolded. Edwin had died very suddenly, the day after returning from installing Eadig in the school at Helmdon, and no one had been able to remember where he taken his son.

This unlikely tale was supposed to explain why Eadig had never been summoned home to keep his father's accounts, but it was bad news for me also. I could hardly deprive a weeping widow of her only available son, the elder boy having long flown away to become the fully tonsured Brother Pious.

Then the situation changed dramatically, as a burly young man came striding out to see what was going on. Eadig was introduced to John Thatcher, the steward. By this time Widow Edwin had noticed me, so Eadig introduced me, and I caught my first glimpse of what it meant to be the king's enchanter general. Mother and steward seemed about to fall on their knees and

I had to move swiftly to offer goodman Thatcher a handshake. Although a steward must be literate, this one was no bookish clerk. He had a palm like a farrier's rasp and a grip like a vise.

The grouping had subtly changed. Widow Edwin was standing closer to Steward Thatcher than to her son, and I was suddenly uncertain whether she was still Widow Edwin or had now become Goodwife Thatcher. He was younger than she was, but King Henry was eleven years younger than Queen Eleanor, so who cared about that? The nature of their relationship was obvious, whether or not it had yet received the blessing of Mother Church.

Eadig had realized the situation also and was seriously off-balance. He had not expected this and he had a father to mourn. His first duty must be to visit the grave. And his second request would be to see his father's will, if there even was one. Under common law, all this property must belong to him. So where did John Thatcher come in?

I was offered hospitality—the finest cider in England and freshly baked bread with clotted cream and honey. Under normal circumstances I would have accepted gladly, but I excused myself, pleading a long journey ahead. I promised that I would look in again in a week or maybe two, when I was on my way back to Oxford. Eadig nodded, understanding that I was telling him he could make his decision then.

I handed him Peregrine's reins and mounted up. As I rode away, I looked back and saw his mother hugging him again and his step-father leading the horse away.

In the middle of the afternoon I rode into the academy yard. Sages, adepts, squires, and varlets came pouring out to greet me. I had removed my signet ring, but my fine new britches and doublet made it clear that I had prospered during my absence.

My first words, of course, were to ask after Guy, and their faces told me the answer.

"The day you left," Sage Laurent said. "He was alive at dinner time, but refused food. We continued to keep the watch, of course, and near to sunset we sent for his family and Father Osric. I don't think he was aware of anything by then, but we assembled everyone outside the cottage and sang for him until Osric came out and said that he had gone."

A new stable hand, whom I did not know, attempted to take charge of Ruffian. Ruffian disagreed, which was typical of his ornery ways, because he knew quite well that he would be given a rubdown and some oats as soon as he cooperated. The struggle was going to be unequal, probably leading to one damaged youth and even one damaged horse, if he were allowed to tangle his feet in his reins or a fence.

I took charge again. "Can you sing?" I asked the lad.

Surprised, he nodded. "Some, Sage."

"Listen." I started Lovise's lullaby. After the first few bars, Ruffian's ears, which had been horizontal, rose back to their correct place. Soon the boy picked it up—the tune seemed to matter more than the words—and the two of them went off happily together. The conversation resumed.

Dean Odo, too, was failing fast, I was told. When the old sage could no longer look after his own bodily needs, Lord Odo had been summoned, and had taken him off to be properly tended at the family home. His lordship had also confirmed that he wanted to take over the academy as replacement housing for his tenants.

Sage Laurent had assumed the role of spokesman. "We have until St. Andrew's Day to find alternative accommodation," he said glumly.

Of course, I could now regard this as good news, but I tried not to show my delight.

"In that case, Your Wisdoms, I have some relevant information for you, matters you will wish to consider in your debates. I would like to meet with you in private immediately."

Leaving the rest of the inhabitants to be devoured by curiosity, we trooped into the sages' dining room and sat down around the table. I noticed that Laurent put himself at the head, which had always been Odo's place.

"We were waiting until you returned, Durwin," Alain remarked, "to elect a new dean."

Alain and Laurent had never been the closest of friends. I had ideas of my own about who was going to head up the academy.

"That was thoughtful of you all," I said, "but I do not see myself remaining at Helmdon." I must admit that very few times in my life have I enjoyed myself as much as I was doing then. "First, Your Wisdoms, there is a grave shortage of healers in Lincoln. If we consider any of our adepts qualified to practice, we should send them there, even if only temporarily. Heads nodded: we could agree on that.

"Secondly, Eadig and I ran up against a major conspiracy of Satanists in Lincoln. With much good fortune and some remarkable assistance from locals, we both survived. We hurried south to report directly to His Grace the king." I let them assume I had gone across to France.

I still remember their faces. I never worked out which impressed them more—that I had wrestled with the Devil or that I had again spoken with royalty.

"The king was very perturbed by my news, because this same cult has been causing great distress in France and other parts of Europe. He is anxious that it not be allowed to become established here. Strictly between us, I suspect he is somewhat dissatisfied with the performance of Enchanter Aubrey de Fours.

His Grace therefore decided to appoint an enchanter general for England. The man he chose is planning to open an enchantment school very similar to Helmdon, but it will be much larger, and will be located in the grounds of Beaumont Palace, near Oxford."

"Who is this magical overlord to be?" Laurent demanded, but some of the others were starting to grin.

At that point I produced my signet ring and rolled it across the table to him.

And when the tumult from that news had died down, I explained that I was offering them all newer and much better accommodation, together with reliable employment in a noble cause.

Yes, I was showing off like the shepherd boy holding up the head of Goliath, but two years ago I had been their stable hand! Very rarely in my life have I gotten truly drunk, but that night I did. The whole academy joined in, consuming every bottle that individual sages had been hiding away for years, plus all the beer that the village alewife had brewed up for the week. There wasn't enough to intoxicate everyone, but I got much more than my share.

chapter 30

i rested up a day to recover and another one to make a start on all the problems that the great move to Oxford was going to create. On the third day, I set out in the company of Amé and Guiscard, two adepts whom the sages had agreed were now competent to act as healers in Lincoln, and who had happily accepted the opportunity to earn some money. We were a happy trio, all three of us looking forward to new lives. The only shadows on my happiness were the many deaths that had touched my life lately: Guy, Francisco, Neil, and Piers, good men all. Life was transient, but I was young and I had the world in my pocket.

I had absolutely no presentiment of danger.

The weather had cooled a little, which made for easier riding, but we were not pushing the horses. Of course my companions kept questioning me about my adventures in Lincoln, my audience with the king, and so on. I answered as best I could, but my mind was on the first stop I had planned, a return to Pipewell, to meet my family, none of whom I had seen since I was a child.

Soon we came to where the trail to Northampton runs through Burly Copse. A copse, of course, is an area of farmed forest, and Burly was mainly composed of ash trees. The original stumps may be centuries old, but the roots keep pushing up new shoots, which are coppiced every few years, the timing depending on the length and thickness of the poles required. Ash poles are especially prized for their length and straightness, and serve many purposes—scythe handles, bows, and arrows, to name but a few.

The breeze, such as it was, was in our faces. Ruffian whinnied just before we turned a slight bend and saw a line of three horsemen blocking our way about a hundred yards ahead. Their menace would have been evident even had they not been wearing helmets and chain mail. I did not bother to look back, because I knew the curve of the road would limit my view, but I was certain that more men-at-arms would now be closing in behind us.

The copse walled us in on either side, high fences of poles so tightly spaced that you could not have put a sheep between them, let alone a horse. We had ridden into a canyon, a wonderful trap, and the man in the center ahead of us was astride a piebald horse. As we drew closer, I could make out the bushy mustache below his nose guard. He was armed with a sword, while his two companions carried shields and lances. The lances were shorter than standard jousting equipment, probably inspired by the surroundings and improvised on the spot. In practice they would be perfect to block any attempt I might make to squeeze by, for I had no doubt that I was the intended prey.

"What's going on, Sir Durwin?" Guiscard muttered as we continued our steady approach to the barrier.

Ruffian whinnied again, angrily. I was going to have trouble with him if he got near to that piebald.

"Crap," I said. "I am going to try to talk my way out of this, because I don't have much option. If I can't, then you two will have to make your own decisions—go back to the academy or push on to Lincoln. Do not get involved, because he must have another six men behind us."

The number did not really matter. Vernon in battle gear on horseback could slaughter three unarmed scholars singlehanded.

"But why are they doing this?" Amé demanded.

"Because Sir Vernon Cheadle is a blockhead and is probably possessed. Such nuisances are sent to try us," I added, to raise my own spirits as much as my companions'. "But he can't know that I have been knighted. If he starts getting aggressive, Adept, I want you to announce me."

I looked to Amé as I said that. He was larger than Guiscard and had a more impressive voice.

The lancer on Vernon's right was one of the knights from Sir Neil's company, whose name I had never heard. The one on his left was the squire I had seen looking out for me at the city gate. When we came almost level with the ends of those improvised lances, I reined in, my companions doing the same. I heard a horse whinny some distance behind us, so the other jaw of the trap was now closing.

"Sir Vernon, by what right do you impede my progress? I travel on the queen's business." That was stretching the truth a bit, but not much. She had told me to go and fetch my bride.

"Sage Durwin, I arrest you for the murder of Sir Neil d'Airelle's man-at-arms, Francois."

"Hold!" Amé boomed. "You are addressing Sir Durwin of Pipewell, the king's Enchanter General for England."

I held up my hand again so that my ring was visible. In my pouch I carried a warrant sealed by the justiciar and letters from him to Sheriff Alured, but I didn't think they would impress the illiterate Vernon much.

"Hog shit," Vernon said. "Sir Neil saw you murder his man,

and by his command I am arresting you and taking you to the king for trial."

In the normal course of affairs, I could trust Vernon to obey orders, for he could never imagine doing anything else, but I did not trust whatever compulsion or possession Neil and Piers might have laid on him after they themselves became possessed. They would not have had pentacle magic available when the pair of them returned to Nottingham, but they could have still bewitched him with a spell provided by the Corneille coven. I could only guess at what such a compulsion might do. One possibility was that around midnight it would override his ethics and honor to make him kill me in cold blood.

"Sir Neil D'Airelle?" I said. "I saw him die a week ago. He was slain by the Earl of Leicester, the justiciar himself. What other witnesses do you have for this murder you accuse me of committing?"

"Squire Piers saw it also, and I don't believe a word of your lies about Sir Neil."

The stupidity of the situation was infuriating. Even without enchantment, Vernon was the embodiment of stubbornness, the ultimate blockhead, who would never be talked into or out of anything. All he knew was obedience. If anger were a weapon, mine would have struck him dead on the spot.

Then I thought of a way out. It was risky to the point of insanity, but safer than letting Vernon put shackles on me. Once that happened, I was as good as dead.

"You call me a liar? You accuse me of murder? By the saints, I will not tolerate this. By insulting me you insult the king, my master. I demand an immediate trial by wager of battle!"

Trial by combat was rarer than it had been, but it was perfectly legal. I saw a flicker of interest inside the helmet. "You, devil worshiper? You are challenging me? I don't fight with upstart Saxon trash."

"I am a royal *familiaris*, and as good a knight as you are, Vernon, dubbed by King Henry himself. If you refuse me, then I call you coward."

Of course I was hoping that he would refuse me and that his men would then insist that I be allowed to go free. That was the law, and Vernon was as aware of this risk as I was.

"You wouldn't fight fair, Saxon. You'd use your devilish powers on me, like Piers saw your boy do on a crow."

I could hear horses champing behind me, jingling their tack, shuffling hooves, so the rest of his train had caught up with us and we had a larger audience now.

"In wager of battle, God in Heaven judges the right. You think a mumbled word from me can blindfold the Lord? I call you coward—coward and no true knight."

"You wear no hauberk."

"My innocence is all the defense I need against your lies. Throw away your mail or keep it on, I care not. Give me one of those poles, you take the other, and we'll see who is unhorsed. Healer Amé, you will be my second."

Both my companions were chalky white with horror, convinced that I had just put my head on the block. But I still had the Release spells I had chanted the day Sir Neil came to Helmdon . . . Or did I? I had sworn I would never again use the *Fiat ignis* against a living person, however appropriate Vernon's mustache might seem as tinder. *Hic non sum* would be useless. There were a couple of others that might serve, but how long did a Release spell retain its potency before it must be chanted again? It varied, of course, and I did not know the answers for all of them.

Like a bolt from Jove came the sudden horror that my *Battre le tambour* enchantment had sent me no warning of Vernon's ambush. That spell had been classed as long-lasting and I had chanted it a day after the Release spells. I hoped that I was being too pessimistic. *Tambour* had done a lot of work for me in Lincoln Castle, so maybe it had just worn out, whereas the Release spells I hadn't yet used might still work, even after more than two weeks. Perhaps.

Obviously my life was going to depend on the answer to that question, because Vernon was already setting out the jousting field. He sent the men behind me back to the bend in the road, so we had the long straight stretch to serve as the list. He told Guiscard to go with them, and his squire to give his pole to Amé. Then he turned to me with his mouth set in a gloating smile.

"You start at that end, witch man. Jehan will be in the middle with the pennant. When he drops it, charge! Give my disregards to your master when you arrive in Hell."

"And may God see that right is done between us," I retorted. I turned Ruffian and urged him forward. Amé rode at my side, carrying my lance. His face was set in a funereal expression, carved in white marble.

"Enchanter, sir, the odds do not look good. Are you truly relying only on God to give you victory? I mean, I am as good a Christian as the next man, but . . ."

"Adept, I assure you that I am completely innocent of the murder of man-at-arms Francois." Although not without guilt in the deaths of Piers and Neil d'Airelle. "No, I am not solely dependent on the Lord in this event. I have a Release spell ready that I hope will give Him some assistance. If it doesn't," I added with sudden bitterness, "when you get to Lincoln, please assure Maid Lovise Larsen that I did love her, and if I am worthy, I shall meet her again in Paradise."

I kept thinking of that as we caught up with the rest of Vernon's men, near to the curve in the trail. I had been so happy before this happened, dreaming of seeing my mother again, and going on to Lincoln and Lovise. And now this blockhead Vernon . . . I brooded on the injustice of this encounter in the hope that it would raise my fury, which might stop me feeling so scared.

When that didn't work, I prayed.

We reached the spectators, I accepted the ash pole from Amé, and turned Ruffian to face the foe. The purpose of jousting is to break a lance on one's opponent and hurl him out of his saddle, but my pole was as green as green. An hour ago it had been happily growing in the copse, minding its own business, and Vernon's likewise. When its end struck Vernon, if I did manage to strike Vernon, then it would bend like string. It might also rip my hand apart, for I had no gauntlets. That wouldn't matter much if Vernon's pole was firmly lodged between my eyes.

I did not even have a helmet. Vernon had the advantage of me there, although he lacked a proper jousting helm. In the highly unlikely event that I managed to unhorse him, the helmet would protect his brains, such as they were, when he hit the ground. He also had a shield and a chain mail hauberk.

Should we by a miracle both be unhorsed, we would fight it out on foot, he with his sword, and me with my cane.

The squire, Jehan, was in place, halfway between us, holding up the pennant I had first seen in Piers's hand, that long-ago morning when Sir Neil came to Helmdon.

"Sir Vernon is signaling that he is ready, sir," Amé said in a small voice.

"I am ready," I growled. Ready as I ever could be.

Amé waved. Jehan swung down the pennant and backed his horse as far off the trail as he could so that one of us could go by him. I kicked Ruffian hard. Seeing a racetrack and a chance to show off, he shot forward.

Hooves thundered on the hard clay. *Pipewell and my family*, I thought. *Lovise, my darling Lovise, and a wedding . . . Oxford and overseeing all the enchantment in England . . . All gone now?* A great, seething, tide of rage swelled up in me as I watched Vernon rushing forward on his fancy piebald destrier—rage and hatred for his stupidity.

But otherwise my mind was blank. *Release spells! Release spells!* In the thunder of Ruffian's gallop and my struggle to keep my pole from waving around like a feather, I could remember none of them. *Ignis . . . Hwæt . . . Maledicto . . .* There was one that would bewilder him. Another would melt him with terror. I knew what they did, I just could not recall the words to release any of them.

I had the pole in my right hand, pointing out to my left, and the reins in my left hand. As we closed, as Sir Vernon on his piebald grew larger and larger in my horrified gaze, I pointed my left index finger at him and snapped the first words that came into my head, *"J'écrase vos testicules!"*

I missed. No one had ever explained the jousting game to Ruffian, so he assumed that he was expected to fight that great ugly piebald beast in horse style. That would involve both of them rearing up and boxing with their front hooves while trying to bite each other. The piebald sensed what was coming, and tried the same maneuver. Vernon was more taken by surprise than I was, because I knew all Ruffian's unruly ways. My spell failed to connect with Vernon, but it connected with his steed.

Vernon did not scream in agony as a man should when his genitals are crushed. But his stallion did. It tried to rear and turn and buck and kick, all at the same time. Vernon's lance hit the ground and he pole-vaulted past me like a missile. He only just missed me, and he broke his neck when he hit the road.

I fought Ruffian for a few minutes, and gradually soothed him. Only then could I go back to look at my victims—one dead man and one dead horse, for the piebald, also, had broken its neck. Guy, Francois, Piers, Neil, and now Vernon!

The spectators rode in closer. They looked at the bodies. They looked at me. I have never seen so many frightened faces. The adepts seemed even more shocked than the soldiers, for they lacked helmets to hide their expressions.

"God be praised for this righteous verdict," I said. "Do any of you dare to repeat this man's lies about me, Durwin of Pipewell, Enchanter General of England?"

Nobody spoke.

"Then see he gets Christian burial. Adepts, we may now resume our journey."

We rode off along the trail. I expected to be questioned about the spell I had used on Vernon, but I wasn't. Nobody said anything at all for several miles. Amé and Guiscard, I assumed, had been shocked into reverent silence by my divine deliverance. And so had I.

I knew that *J'écrase vos testicules* enchantment. I had found it in one of the grimoires I had been given as payment for my services in Barton two years ago. I had judged it to be a curse, definitely black magic, but I had copied it out in a more modern, easily read script, because it was so beautifully composed, a minor masterpiece of the enchanter's art.

I could remember finding my copy of it when I was going through my collection of Release spells while waiting for the king's messenger to arrive at Helmdon on that epochal Monday morning. Had I known that I would be going off to battle treason and Satanism, then I would very likely have chanted it as a handy weapon. I had not done so! I was certain of that. I had no idea how I could have invoked a Release spell that I had never chanted, and I still don't.

At the first church we came to, I called for a break so I could go in and say a prayer of thanksgiving, and my companions went with me. I also left a generous donation from the money Queen Eleanor had given me to fund prayers for Sir Vernon's soul.

I have never again risked my life by way of wager of battle.

chapter 31

After Northampton, my first stop had to be Pipewell, to greet the mother and brothers I had not seen in eight years. It was a long ride, and the encounter with Sir Vernon had delayed us, so we arrived very near to sunset. It was likely that my family had all fallen into bed to rest after hard days' labor in the fields, so we rode straight to the abbey gates in search of hospitality. There I was blessed yet again with good fortune, because the brother on duty was one I could recall from my youth. He did not recognize me until I gave him my name and he saw my limp, but then his face lit up like a welcoming beacon.

I did not mention knighthood or enchantments, and I introduced my companions as healers, not adepts. So I remained "You-remember-Durwin-son-of-Durwin?" and there was no mention of devil worship. Yes, Reverend Paul was still abbot, and of course we were welcome . . . When His Reverence straightly asked me whom I served now, I had to admit that I was sworn to the king himself, and they were all hugely impressed.

The beds were hard and the fare simple, but a long day on horseback can overcome any memories, even memories of murder, and I slept the sleep of the innocent. All three of us attended morning prayers in the minster, and I know that at least one of us said prayers for the soul of Sir Vernon Cheadle.

The morning saw epochal excitement in the hamlet of Pipewell itself, because there I revealed my knighthood and my high office as advisor to the king. As was required of her, my mother wept with joy on seeing me. In eight years she had changed much less than I had expected. I learned that the stepfather I had never met had wandered away a couple of years after the wedding—and good riddance, I gathered.

Elis, my eldest brother, was in Brittany, fighting in the king's army as one small part of the monastery's feudal service. Hamon was apprenticed to a higgler, traveling around the country with a horse and cart, buying, selling, and carting. He was not home that day. Wilky was still a child but hoped to enter the monastery school and become a monk, or even a priest. I told him I needed someone like him praying for me.

I explained that I could not stay because I must see Amé and Guiscard safely delivered to Lincoln—although they would have been quite capable of finding it for themselves. I assured everyone that I would be coming again very soon, when I brought my bride south. I also assured my mother that she would see much more of me in future, because my duties for the king would require me to do a lot of traveling. That turned out to be the truest prophecy I ever made.

So we set out northward again: Pipewell to Nottingham to Newark to Lincoln. I could have made much better time on my own then, riding the king's horses, posting from castle to castle, but I enjoyed the company and the leisurely journey.

It was close to evensong when we arrived at the town gates—dusty, weary, and stinking of horse. I was in no condition to go wooing, and duty required that I call first on Lord Richard and Lady Nicholaa, who joyfully made us all welcome. My letter had told them no more than that I had managed to foil the Satanists' plot and now stood high in royal favor. I had to swear them to secrecy before I could give them any of the details. They had already obtained a new sage for the castle. He was happy to welcome Guiscard and Amé, promising to see them established in the town.

When Lars opened his father's front door the next morning to admit the half dozen patients waiting outside, I was with them, robed in my new splendid best. He greeted me with a joyful shout and a rib-crushing embrace. Of course the spectators insisted that I precede them, but no sooner had I stepped over the threshold than my way was blocked by a scowling Harald Larson. Lovise came running down the stairs, and halted behind him, her face shadowed by dismay.

"You again?" the healer snapped, but he had noticed my garb, which was much grander than he had seen on me before. "You brought enough trouble with you the last time. I was hoping we'd seen the last of you."

What he was really hoping, I suspected, was that he was not going to lose his fabulous, gorgeous daughter. Perhaps the prospect had brought him to realize just how precious she was.

"No such luck, sir. I promised your daughter that I would return, and I am a man of my word."

He grunted, making no effort to move out of the way, although Lovise was right behind him, staring dolefully at me over her father's shoulder.

"If you're still dreaming of marrying her, you'll first have to convince me that you can support her and whatever brats she drops for you."

"Set your mind at rest, sir. His Grace the king has appointed me to high office, and granted me a noble residence in the grounds of his palace of Beaumont. Her Grace Queen Eleanor is very anxious to meet Lovise."

Lars, behind me, let our a whoop of joy. Lovise made no sound, but her beaming smile said everything necessary. The patients were murmuring like bees.

"However," I continued, "although I had previously asked her to become Goodwife Lovise, I must confess that this will no longer be possible."

Her face fell. Her father smiled. "Remembered a previous wife, have you?"

"No, sir." I held up my hand with the signet ring. "Now I intend to make her Lady Lovise, wife of Sir Durwin of Pipewell, Enchanter General of England."

At which point Harald Larson was hurled aside by the future Lady Lovise as she rushed into the arms of her betrothed.

And that was that.

I had brought a letter written by one of the sages and signed by Father Osric—the only words he could write—to certify that I had no other wives hidden away in Helmdon. Lady Nicholaa brought pressure to bear to speed up the normal procedure, and we were married on Monday, exactly three weeks after Sir Neil d'Airelle rode into Helmdon. The ceremony was held in in St. Paul's within the town, not the cathedral. We had decided not to embarrass the bishop by asking him to admit an enchanter.

I won't go into details. You have all heard of happy marriages, and ours has been as happy as any ever could be. I cannot say we lived happily ever after, but the first half-century has gone well.

We proceeded south by way of Pipewell and Bicester, where we discovered that Eadig had settled his affairs to everyone's satisfaction. His mother was indeed legally married to John Thatcher, who had no children of his own, so there could be no future inheritance squabble. Eadig was free to continue his studies as he wanted, and his mother was happy, because Beaumont was an easy hour's ride away. She could see him often, and he could keep an eye on John Thatcher, to make sure that he stayed honest and worthy.

By November I had adepts and sages hunting all over England for grimoires, copying out any incantations we did not have, especially those in the old tongue, and bringing them back to Beaumont, where our sages could check them for trip wires. I intended to build up the finest library of magic in Europe, and eventually did.

On the Feast of Stephen, the day after Christmas, Queen Eleanor gave birth to her fifth son, who proved to be her last child. He was baptized John. Two years earlier, when she commissioned me to draw up a horoscope for Prince Richard, who had also been born in Beaumont, I had promised to be completely honest. This time she trusted me enough that she did not lay that restriction on me, for which I was truly glad.

I did draw up Lord John's horoscope for her, but I left out all the bad bits, which shortened it considerably. Although he had three older brothers, I could see that he was destined to inherit the throne and be at least as bad a ruler as King Stephen, probably worse. But that horrible prospect lay far in the future.

afterword

i have tried to keep my imagination within historical bounds, but it did slip out in one place: there is no record of Henry II returning to England in 1166. [He ordered that to be kept secret, remember?] He was fully occupied in Brittany and he had no reason that I know of to send Hugh de Cressy to Glastonbury that year, because the monks' claim to have discovered Arthur's grave came some twenty-five years later, after Henry's death. However, he was always a generous supporter of Glastonbury Abbey, because of its association with the Arthurian legends and the political leverage this gave him in his struggles with the Welsh. In those days the tales were all believed to be true, and medieval English kings used Arthur as a precedent to claim the thrones of both France and Scotland.

Queen Eleanor was one of the most remarkable women in history— duchess of Aquitaine in her own right, married (successively) to the kings of both France and England, mother of ten children, two of whom became kings. When young she went to the Holy Land on crusade and, in her old age, ruled England as regent. She famously described herself (in a letter to the pope!) as "Eleanor, by the wrath of God, queen of England."

The officials I have named in Lincoln—constable, sheriff, bishop—were all historical persons. The most interesting by far was the constable's daughter, Nicholaa de la Haye, who comes a close second to the queen in the formidability stakes. She did succeed her father as constable of the castle. She outlived two husbands, and was still constable fifty years after the date of my story, when King John visited Lincoln in 1216. Lady Nicholaa came out to greet him at the gate and begged him to let her retire, on account of her age. He refused to accept her resignation and later that year she defended the castle against attack by the invading French army. (If you did not know that the French had an army in the middle of England back then, that is probably because the English still do not like to talk about it.) Nicholaa died in 1230, aged about eighty.

Both Richard the Lionheart and the ill-omened John were born in Beaumont Palace, which no longer exists. Oxford University, the oldest in England and one of the oldest in Europe, had its beginnings just about this time, in a number of religious schools set up in the town.

about the author

Dave Duncan is a prolific writer of fantasy and science fiction, best known for his fantasy series, especially The Seventh Sword, A Man of His Word, and The King's Blades. He is both a founding and an honorary lifetime member of SF Canada, and an inductee of the Canadian Science Fiction and Fantasy Hall of Fame. His books have been translated into fifteen languages.

Dave and his wife, Janet, his in-house editor and partner for fifty-seven years (so far), live in Victoria, British Columbia. They have three children and four grandchildren.

acknowledgments

Covering roughly six acres, Lincoln Castle is still an impressive place to visit. It would have been much more so in the twelfth century, when its walls and towers were higher than they are now. For its geography I drew extensively on *Lincoln Castle, the Medieval Story* by Sheila Sancha (Lincoln County Council, 1985) and *The Knight Who Saved England* by Richard Brooks (Osprey Publishing, 2014). I also used my imagination and the requirements of my story.

I relied heavily on *Henry II* by W. L. Warren, University of California Press, 1973. I am also indebted to two excellent books by Alison Weir: *Eleanor of Aquitaine* and *Britain's Royal Families;* also Desmond Seward's *The Demon's Brood, a History of the Plantagenet Dynasty.*

All the towns and villages mentioned in this book were genuine and still exist, except for Pipewell, which is now nothing but a name on map (pronounced *Pip-well* by the locals). Pipewell Abbey Church is of Victorian age.